THE NORTH KOREA GAMBIT

INFILTRATION BOOK FOUR

WILLIAM W. KING

First Edition

White Whale Tales, LLC   www.whitewhaletales.com

BISAC Categories:

FIC006000   FICTION / Thrillers / Espionage

FIC036000   FICTION / Thrillers / Technological

FIC031090   FICTION / Thrillers / Terrorism

Summary:

The Infiltration saga continues. The struggle for power in the South China Sea escalates in this high-tech naval adventure.

CONTENTS

DISCLAIMER

This novel was inspired by real world events but is entirely a work of fiction. People, corporate entities and geopolitical events are the product of the author's imagination. With the notable exception of North Korea's Kim Jung -un, any resemblance to actual persons living or dead, actual companies or products, or actual events is purely coincidental.

Every attempt was made to ensure that the technical details of this story are accurate. The author is solely responsible for the technical research involved in creating this story. Information was drawn from public resources. Any mistaken depictions are the responsibility of the author.

Hopefully, I created an entertaining novel, and the reader finds the story enjoyable and thought provoking.

SPECIAL COMMENTS ABOUT CHATGPT

I experimented with an advanced language model called ChatGPT, developed by OpenAI, to assist me in generating some of the written content for this book. It was used to create a few small parts of this fictional novel. I estimate that it was used for about two percent of the content.

While ChatGPT can provide creative suggestions and ideas, the content it creates is computer-generated and should be interpreted as such. It does not replace my role as the human author in shaping and guiding the narrative. I have reviewed and edited all the output provided by ChatGPT, shaping it into a coherent narrative and incorporating my own creativity and storytelling skills. I also checked it carefully for accuracy.

As you will discover one of the themes in this novel is exploring the collaboration between human and artificial intelligence. A central "character" in this novel is an AI-driven autonomous underwater vehicle that develops emergent capabilities such as, self-awareness and a conscience. The character is fictional, but I used it to explore concepts surrounding the current debates surrounding AI.

I hope that you enjoy the unique storytelling experience that this collaboration has produced. Your support and engagement as readers are greatly appreciated. Thank you for joining me on this literary journey into the realm of human and artificial creativity.

ACKNOWLEDGEMENTS

Special thanks go to two people at Emerald Books. My editor Jessica R. Hammerman deserves recognition for her tireless work and attention to detail through several edits. Designer and publisher Isaac Peterson also provided significant editing input as well as the cover design and the expertise for the final publication steps. I incorporated many of their helpful suggestions which significantly improved the plot flow and narrative details. The final product reflects the many improvements provided by Jessica and Isaac. I could not have accomplished publishing this book without their expert help, and I greatly appreciate their assistance.

Several other informal reviewers helped me make significant enhancements to early drafts. I would especially like to thank Ramsey Johnson for his very careful review of my work and his many helpful suggestions. He helped me catch many small errors so they wouldn't creep into the final document. Also, Scott Gordon contributed to edits on early drafts.

PROLOGUE

This story is set in the geopolitical region centered around North Korea. Officially known as the Democratic People's Republic of Korea (DPRK), North Korea, established in 1948, constitutes the northern half of the Korean peninsula in East Asia. Russia and China are on its northern border. South Korea forms the southern border (separated by the demilitarized zone at the 38th parallel). The west coast is on the Korea Bay and the Yellow Sea. The eastern coast is on the Sea of Japan.

North Korea is a repressive totalitarian dictatorship ruled by the ruthless Kim dynasty cult of personality. Control was passed down to the sons over the years. The current leader, Kim Jong-un, has been in power since 2011. North Korea has been called a rogue state and characterized as an "evil empire." It is classified as a "state sponsor of terrorism." It is also sometimes referred to as the Hermit Kingdom because so much about it is hidden from view.

Because North Korea possesses nuclear weapons (including both atomic and hydrogen bombs), they pose an existential threat to the region. Their capability to deliver these bombs to potential targets has steadily improved, in both the range and payloads of their ballistic missiles. Currently, their missiles are capable of hitting Japan, Okinawa, Guam, and perhaps Hawaii. In 2023, they test-fired a missile capable of reaching the continental U.S.

Recently, they created a new Sinpo-C class ballistic missile submarine.

Capable of carrying nuclear missiles which could be launched close to our Western coast with no advance warning. Their effective range would allow them to reach targets across the U.S., such as Washington, D.C. and New York.

Ballistic missiles launched directly from North Korean land bases are bad enough, but the potential for sub-launched missiles represents a much worse threat. Submarines are stealthy and difficult to locate and track. And our sparse anti-missiles defenses would not be effective. The vulnerability is unacceptable.

Submarine-launched missiles also represent a major threat to our allies, South Korea, Japan, Australia, New Zealand, Taiwan, and the Philippines. Not to mention specific American targets in Guam, Okinawa, and Hawaii.

Some hawkish officials believe we should find a way to eliminate the threat preemptively. Sinking one of these submarines would be a straightforward task for the U.S. Navy. Unfortunately, it would be politically unacceptable to just sink one outright. It would be noisy and difficult to conceal and would certainly be interpreted as an act of war if our role in the sinking was discovered.

However, a covert method to remove the threat might be possible.

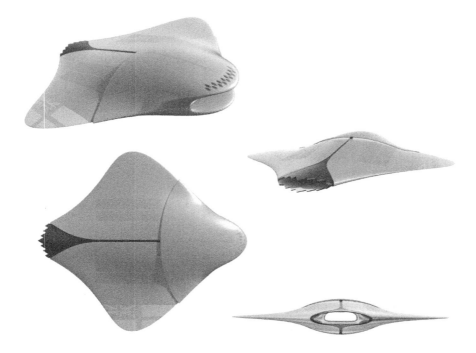

A new submarine launched in North Korea in September 2023. Image licensed by Wikimedia commons.

Left: Autonomous submersible drones designed for the British Royal Navy. Drones of this type might be controlled by artificial intelligence and capable of delivering a weapons payload. The full article can be found here:

https://www.bbc.co.uk/news/uk-41073693

CHAPTER ONE

Arleigh Burke Destroyer, U.S.S. Peralta
Inland Sea of Japan

My name is Captain Steven Kane currently on board the U.S.S. *Peralta*. Sitting at the tiny desk in my cramped cabin I've been thinking about our upcoming mission. I stared at the repeater tactical display. The *Peralta* was sailing in the western end of the Inland Sea of Japan approaching the city of Kitakyushu. After that we planned to pass through the Kanmon Strait and enter the Sea of Japan.

I was thinking about the sealed orders in my safe. *When should I open them?*

I must have downed six cups of coffee as I pondered the situation. Admiral Baker had instructed me to wait until we were in the Sea of Japan to open them, but the suspense was driving me crazy. He had hinted that the orders would be a big revelation, though he wouldn't share their precise contents.

The U.S.S. *Peralta* had departed earlier that day from Yokosuka, Japan, headed for a mission off the east coast of North Korea. I had informed the crew that our mission was to cruise near North Korea collecting SIGINT (signals, intelligence, the gathering of military or

1

other intelligence by interception of electronic signals, and consisting of COMINT, Communications Intelligence, and ELINT, Electronic Intelligence. Essentially, we would simply cruise offshore and soak up and record the abundance of electronic transmissions in the area,

The mission was also an exercise to show the flag and enforce our right to be in the area. We were to stay in international waters, of course.

I decided to take a quick break to catch some fresh air. I made the short walk from my cabin to the starboard bridge wing. On my way through the bridge, I saw the watch crew diligently performing their duties. I nodded to the Executive Officer (XO), Lt. Cmdr. William (Bill) O'Hara, at his duty station on the port side. The OOD, Lt. Katherine Baker was standing behind the helm.

"Captain on the bridge." I acknowledged her on my way out through the hatch to the bridge wing.

After inhaling a breath of fresh air, I gazed up at the azure sky. Except for some wispy cirrus clouds far to the north, it was a clear day. A crisp breeze was blowing across the ship from starboard to port bringing with it the distinct scent of sea water. Closer to Kitakyushu, the aroma was more industrial, subtly infused with the smell of steel and manufacturing. The occasional whiff of freshly caught seafood from fishing boats was making me hungry. I was thankful that the warm sun on my face eased my tension.

I had been through Kanmon Straits before. I remembered how busy the area was. It was always filled with ferry boats and small commercial vessels, and today was no exception. The Kanmon Bridge spanned the strait, connecting Honshu and Kyushu. In fact, the *Peralta* was just passing under the bridge as I glanced up. I had the distinct impression that my ship was too tall to pass under it. However, we cleared it by ten feet or so, though it appeared tighter than that. Captains always get nervous when they pass under a bridge. Shortly we passed by Kitakyushu on the port side. From there the ship turned to the north toward the Sea of Japan.

The first thing that caught my eye was the striking contrast between the modern cityscape of Kitakyushu and the tranquil beauty of the surrounding nature. The city's skyline, adorned with tall skyscrapers, stands as a testament to Japan's technological prowess. However, it's the natural wonders that dominate the scene as you venture further into the strait. Lush green hills and mountains dotted with vibrant cherry blossom trees, especially in spring, create a picturesque backdrop against the calm waters of the Inland Sea.

My mind kept wandering back to memories of my previous command. I had been in command of the U.S.S. *Mckenna* during its ill-fated Freedom of Navigation Operation (FONOP) in the South China Sea. That voyage was sabotaged by a Chinese plot to infect U.S. Navy ships with an enhanced version of COVID-19. It was called COVID-21 and it was more infectious and deadlier. That FONOP was cut short because of the deadly spread of infections on the ship. By the time we returned to Guam, eighteen crew members had died, as well as crew from several other ships in the fleet.

I had also been very sick, and although I was now completely recovered physically, I was emotionally scarred by the incident. Even though I was certainly not at fault, I couldn't shake the gnawing feeling that the deaths of my shipmates rested on my shoulders. It was an emotional scar I would carry for the rest of my life.

Putting those thoughts aside, I decided it was time to open the secret orders.

I walked back through the bridge to my cabin, unlocked the safe, and removed the sealed envelope. I opened it with anticipation, pulled out the folded communication, and read it with growing interest. And, quite frankly, with growing alarm.

```
TO: CAPTAIN STEVEN KANE, U.S.S. PERALTA

FROM: COMCINCPAC ADMIRAL THOMAS BAKER

EYES ONLY TOP SECRET
INTELLIGENCE INDICATES THAT NORTH KOREAN NAVY
WILL SORTIE A NEW BALLISTIC MISSILE SUBMARINE
YOU ARE TO INTERCEPT, IDENTIFY, AND CLOSELY
TRACK.
STAY CLOSE THROUGHOUT ITS MOVEMENTS IN THE
SEA OF JAPAN.
DO NOT LOSE CONTACT.
```

IF A MISSILE LAUNCH OCCURS, YOU ARE TO SHOOT
IT DOWN IMMEDIATELY. USE WHATEVER ASSETS ARE
REQUIRED.
THE MISSILE CANNOT BE ALLOWED TO REACH HIGH
ALTITUDE OR CONTINUE ITS TRAJECTORY.
PERALTA WILL BE ACCOMPANIED BY U.S.S. KEY
WEST FOR PROTECTION.
U.S.S. KEY WEST WILL STAY CLOSE BUT MUST NOT
REVEAL ITS PRESENCE.
IF NORTH KOREAN SUBMARINE DOES NOT LAUNCH, IT
IS NOT NECESSARY TO FOLLOW IT BACK TO SINPO.
DO NOT SINK THE NORTH KOREAN SUBMARINE UNLESS
NO OTHER OPTION.
AFTER EXECUTING THIS MISSION, RETURN TO
YOKOSUKA.
　　　////

I reread the orders several times to make sure I understood them. I was surprised that they called for such preemptive aggression. Shooting down the North Korean missile was clearly an act of war. I was being ordered to fire on it with no warning. The North Koreans would be furious.

Practically, this meant I would need to keep the *Peralta* very close to the North Korean submarine at all times. Probably within a just a few miles. This proximity would ensure that our intercepting missile needed to travel a minimum distance to the target.

Unfortunately, it also meant that I would be exposing the *Peralta* to possible counterattack with very little reaction time. I calculated that if a submarine two miles away launched a torpedo it would reach my ship in less than three minutes. I concluded that we should stay about five miles away for safety. I made a mental note to have WEPS work on the best solution. At any rate, we would need to stay on high alert and the weapons division would need to be on a hair trigger.

The U.S.S. *Peralta* was a sophisticated Flight 3 Arleigh Burke class guided missile destroyer, designed for just this type of mission. In addition to the high-tech surveillance suite for gathering SIGINT, it carried a range of weapons and was designed around the Aegis Combat System, which gave it incredible power. It is highly capable of defending itself from aerial threats as well as surface and underwater foes. It also featured modern stealth features that reduced its radar signature to as low a profile as possible considering the size of the ship. No ship can become completely invisible, but the reduction of radar-reflecting surfaces and the addition of radar-absorbing materials enhanced its stealth.

It was time to inform the senior officers to prepare for this critical mission. They would be just as surprised as I was.

My senior team convened in the wardroom, a space that fulfilled multiple roles. It was a combination mess hall, planning room, and study hall, and served as a relaxation area as well.

I sat at the end of the long table with the XO, Lt. Cmdr. O'Hara, to my left. The Navigation Officer, Lt. Thomas Aguilar, was next to him, and the Engineering Officer, Lt. Don McKesson was to his left. The right side of the table was occupied by the Communications Officer,

Lt. Joe Tucci, the Weapons Officer, Lt. Jennifer Hawkins, and lastly the Master Chief, Lester Crumpler. These key personnel would put their divisions to work implementing components of the plan.

"I bet you wonder why I've gathered you here," I said, partly to disguise my nerves, but also to break the ice.

There were a few soft chuckles around the table. They seemed more than willing to cut me some slack for the lame joke.

I looked around the table to gauge their reactions. "As you might know, the sealed orders in my safe were not to be opened until we entered the Sea of Japan. I just opened those orders, and I need to update you. Our mission has become much more complicated and dangerous. Originally, I told you that we were to cruise off North Korea gathering SIGINT to make our presence known in a show of force. Our mission has drastically changed.

"Our mission now is to track the new North Korean missile submarine as it leaves Sinpo, stay close to it, and shoot down their missile if they decide to launch. We are not to hesitate. If they launch, we launch our SAM interceptors."

The officers fidgeted and gave each other side glances. A few just stared down silently at the table.

XO O'Hara spoke up first. "That's a pretty aggressive rule of engagement. There's no ambiguity about launching?"

"No. Apparently, we are to treat the launch as a threat and down the missile."

"Isn't that an act of war?" he asked.

"Yes, but that's not a reason to hesitate. The decision to take the risk has already been made at higher levels."

"The North Koreans will be totally pissed. Will they retaliate?"

"I hope not. But they might, so we will need to be prepared for any eventuality. One positive is that we'll be accompanied by the U.S.S. *Key West*, so we will have some cover. They will stay close and could take out the North Korean submarine if necessary."

WEPS Hawkins spoke up next. "I think we should have a LAMPS helicopter on top of that submarine at all times. Ready to drop a torpedo on them at a moment's notice. It would get there faster than a sub-launched torpedo and provide a constantly updated firing solution on any enemy submarines. I'd also put the Aegis system on full auto to launch an SM-6 immediately on detection of a missile launch from the submarine."

"I agree, but be prepared to launch multiple SM-sixes. We can't afford to miss."

Lt. Hawkins just nodded. She was lost in thought. She knew her job well and was looking forward to launching some weapons outside of a simulation. She was very introspective, which made her hard to figure out. It was not that she was unfriendly, just generally reserved and quiet. She was a consummate professional, highly skilled at her job, and totally calm and competent under stress. She proved this when she was my WEPS on the U.S.S. *McKenna*. She was also one of the few crew members who had experienced actual combat which was why I had requested her for the *Peralta*.

Her background was a bit enigmatic, but I knew that she had worked in information technology in Silicon Valley for a while but had decided to make a career switch to the navy. It seemed to be driven by her desire to address the North Korean problem. She never revealed her motive directly to me.

As I looked across the table, I was reminded of her appeal. Hawkins is very attractive, tall and slender with neatly trimmed black hair, and just a touch of makeup. I often wondered if reserved personality was an unconscious attempt to conceal her obvious femininity. In the integrated modern Navy, women are often forced to downplay their gender just to get along.

In the Combat Information Center (CIC), she was a different person. She was able to make quick decisions, take charge, and issue orders. And she had an incredible understanding of the *Peralta*'s weapons systems.

I followed up with another thought. "Pull up all the information we have on the Sinpo-C submarine. Distribute it to everyone. I want us all to be informed of its capabilities."

"Aye, aye, sir."

"We will head to Sinpo to pick up the submarine as soon as it departs. We will loiter off the coast until we get word from Pine Gap or the Pentagon that the submarine has departed. We shouldn't have any trouble locating it and tracking it. As far as the North Koreans know, we are just practicing an Anti-Submarine Warfare (ASW) drill. They will have no idea that we intend to shoot. That'll be a nasty surprise."

I asked for some additional input from the communications officer. "Joe, please double-check the status of our communications suite. We will need all our assets in working order."

"Aye, aye, Captain. We checked out everything in port, but I'll review the status of all systems."

I really enjoyed working with Lt. Tucci. He had been the communications officer on my previous ship, and I was pleased to have him back. His small department consisted of a radio officer, a signal officer, a communications security material system (CMS) custodian, and a cryptosecurity officer.

Joe was a product of the East Coast, but he was quite cosmopolitan. He was Italian and had olive skin, an aquiline nose, dark graying hair, and piercing brown eyes. Somehow, despite the abundant good food on board, he managed to stay fit and trim. I really envied that.

Prior to joining the Navy, he had worked at several high-tech companies such as ROLM and IBM, where he specialized in telecommunications. His telecommunications experience earned him a nomination to Officers Candidate. Joe was a friendly and outgoing individual, and totally serious about his job. He continually impressed me with his knowledge of our sophisticated communications systems.

I turned to the navigation officer for a weather update, "Tom, what can we expect during the next week or so?"

"Captain, we'll have clear weather for the next week. There is some early indication of a low-pressure system forming west of Guam, but it is not expected to cross into the Sea of Japan until later this week. That could change. It may not become a significant storm at all. Time will tell."

"Thanks. Glad to hear that we won't have to deal with another typhoon."

I next inquired of the engineering officer, Lt. Don McKesson about the status of the ship.

Lt. McKesson was a taciturn and studious individual. He was medium height with short brown hair tinged with gray at the temples. His silver wire-rimmed glasses enhanced his image. I couldn't ask for a better engineering officer. He was a master at keeping our engineering spaces humming efficiently. I completely trusted his abilities.

"Sir, since we just left port, the status of all systems is green. Also, we have a full load of weapons and lots of fuel."

It was just what I had anticipated.

"Master Chief, anything to add?"

"Not at this time, sir."

Looking across the table at Master Chief Crumpler, I guessed that he had some issue on his mind. He frowned back at me. Perhaps he didn't want to share it openly, so I made a mental note to follow up in private.

Master Chief Crumpler was a key member of my crew. He was tall and very fit for his age, which I guessed was about forty. He had played professional football for a few years, which showed in his massive arm muscles. He looked like he was purpose-built to be part of the ship. Interestingly his brother was on the U.S.S. *Key West*, our protective escort on this voyage. His brother was similarly huge, and had also played professional football. The running joke was that they were too big to fit onboard.

Master Chief Crumpler was the go-to guy in the crew. He was heavily relied upon by the officers and looked up to by all the enlisted crew. I personally depended on him for his wealth of experience and for his influence on the crew.

The remainder of the meeting was consumed in gathering summaries from each division head concerning their readiness.

I turned to the XO. "Order the helmsman to increase speed to 25 knots to the patrol area." I pointed at a box outlined east of Sinpo on the navigational display. "Then we will implement a patrol scheme in that box. Set Condition Zebra when we reach the patrol area."

To the entire group I asked, "Any questions?"

Hearing none I ordered, "Okay. Let's get to work. You know your assignments. We have about eight hours before we reach the patrol area."

CHAPTER TWO

North Korean Sinpo-C Class Submarine *Sulyong*
Sea of Japan, Twenty Miles East of Sinpo

C aptain Soon Bo-yeun strolled confidently into the control room of his new Sinpo-C class ballistic-missile submarine. Bo-yeun, a thin guy of medium height, was dressed in a casual dark-blue jumpsuit that displayed his name patch and rank and the insignia of the submarine force. Only the slight graying of his black hair betrayed his age. Otherwise, he had a very youthful appearance. He could easily be mistaken for a mild-mannered college student.

Bo-yeun had assumed command of this new missile submarine after a recent deployment in its predecessor, the first Sinpo class ship called the *Gorae* ("whale"). This latest Sinpo-C submarine was named *Sulyong* ("sea dragon"). It had been recently constructed at the Sinpo naval base and was significantly larger and longer ranged, with many other improvements.

Sulyong was a diesel-electric submarine. About 210 feet long with a beam of 20 feet, it displaced about 2,000 tons. Its range was limited to roughly 1,500 nautical miles. It reached a top speed of sixteen knots on the surface and ten knots underwater. Its maximum diving depth was 800 feet. Armed with four torpedo tubes, it could also carry two Pukkukson-1 (KN-11) ballistic missiles in its sail for vertical launch.

Bo-yeun had just taken a short break in his cramped stateroom to review the mission orders and catch a short rest before the action started. His attempt to rest was largely unsuccessful due to the racket coming from the overhead fan in his cabin. He made a mental note to remind the chief engineer to fix it. For now, this mission was the priority. Still, it irritated him immensely that this problem was occurring on his newly built boat.

His mission was straightforward. The *Sulyong* was tasked with traveling to a designated launch area about 50 miles northwest of Sinpo Naval Base to launch a Pukkuksong-1 (KN-11) ballistic missile.

The *Sulyong* had already been on three prior trips close to their home port of Sinpo, but those had been shake-down cruises. They were designed to familiarize the crew with their new boat and seek out and address any mechanical or operational problems. The trips had also been used to drill the crew, especially emergency responses. Fortunately, those trips had been routine and had only identified minor problems.

This current trip was the live test-firing of a ballistic missile. It was a practice exercise, and the missile would simply arc high into the atmosphere and then plunge back down into the Sea of Japan. The missile was armed with a dummy load, not a live warhead.

Captain Bo-yeun walked behind the large digital tactical display mounted in the center of the control room. He looked down at it with quiet concentration and a slight frown. The display was designed to show a myriad of information about his boat as well as the surrounding environment. It was a computer-driven compilation of relevant information that gave Captain Bo-yeun a quick view of their situation.

The *Sulyong* was designated by a large blue symbol in the center of the high-def display. In the upper-right corner, the vessel's speed, depth, and direction were shown, as well as other important information, such as battery charge remaining. Currently, they were traveling at four knots at a depth of 300 feet and a heading of zero-eight-zero degrees.

Various green circular symbols were scattered across the display to indicate commercial vessels and fishing boats assumed to be "friendlies." But directly to the right in a position to intercept the *Sulyong*, was a bright red circular symbol marked "Destroyer," indicating it was hostile. Captain Bo-yeun nodded as he absorbed the information, then turned to the Executive Officer (XO), Park Min-wok, standing at his side and asked, "This destroyer is U.S. Navy, I presume?"

XO Min-wok looked like he could be related to the captain. He wore black glasses and had a scar across his forehead as a result of a fall in a previous submarine. Min-wok was an experienced submariner, having previously served on midget subs and Romeo class submarines. He and Bo-yeun had worked closely for several years and he was quite loyal to the captain.

The XO responded, "Yes, sir. Our surveillance aircraft have reported that it is the U.S. Navy Arleigh Burke destroyer U.S.S. *Peralta*. It's been holding its position relative to ours about ten miles away, so clearly it is aware of us and tracking our progress."

Captain Bo-yeun nodded thoughtfully. "I'm sure they are aware of us. That ship has very sophisticated anti-submarine capabilities. Have they launched a LAMPS?" The Light Airborne Multi-Purpose System (LAMPS) helicopter was an American ship-borne hunter-killer that Bo-yeun knew represented a significant threat.

"Yes, Captain. There's one in the air right now." He reached over and touched a red triangle just to their north. "It is this symbol just above us on the display. About half a mile away. We're tracking it by its sound from the rotors. Our sonar operator has been bragging that he can clearly hear the splashes as they drop their dipping sonar probe into the water."

Captain Bo-yeun smiled. "I'll bet he can. Shouldn't be that hard to hear them, as close as they are. Aren't there any American attack submarines nearby? Usually, they would accompany the surface ships to keep track of us."

XO Min-wok shook his head. "No, Captain, we haven't detected any hostile submarines in the area. But that doesn't mean they aren't out there. As you know, we are only moving at four knots, and at that speed, an American attack submarine following us would be extremely quiet and difficult to detect." Captain Bo-yeun nodded. "Still, I'd be surprised if there wasn't one close behind us. I believe that they picked us up on sonar shortly after we departed from Sinpo early this morning and have been trailing us ever since. But back there behind us in our baffles, they are almost impossible to detect, I agree. Perhaps we should do one of those Crazy Ivans like the Russian submarines used to do to try to detect a trailing foe. You know, a sudden 360-degree circle to expose the area in the baffles."

XO Min-wok chuckled. "I know how a Crazy Ivan works, but it seems sort of useless right now. The Americans would undoubtedly be prepared for it and would simply stop and wait for us to return to our original course, so it wouldn't work as planned. We still wouldn't detect them. And, besides, the American destroyer knows exactly where we are, so what's the point?"

"Okay, we'll forget about the Crazy Ivan for now." Captain Bo-yeun regretted not doing the maneuver. He loved the term because it was so descriptive.

Bo-yeun shifted his gaze back to the tactical display and touched an area outlined with a dotted white line. He asked, "This square is the launch area, correct?"

"Yes sir. We should reach it in about four hours at our current speed."

"Good. Let's maintain our current course and speed, and depth as well. Once we reach the launch area, rise to periscope depth and reduce our speed to two knots. In the meantime, have the weapons crews run final diagnostics on the missile to prepare it for launch. No sense waiting until the last minute, I want them ready to act as soon as we enter the designated launch area."

"Aye, aye, Captain. We will be ready to launch on time."

"Keep an eye on that destroyer and the LAMPS helicopter and update me immediately if there are any changes in their positions or behavior, especially if they make any aggressive moves. I doubt that they will, but I want to be alerted right away if they do."

"Aye, aye, sir. We will watch them very carefully."

"I also want to be notified immediately if you detect a trailing American submarine. I still believe that there's one lurking out there. I hate not knowing for sure. Not that I expect aggressive moves from them either, but I really would like a complete picture of our tactical situation."

"I agree. We'll keep searching."

"Good. I'm going back to my stateroom to finish up some paperwork. Notify me when we are about an hour from the launch area so I can return to the control room. You have the conn."

"XO has the conn."

Back in his tiny stateroom, Captain Bo-yeun sat down at the small folding desk with a deep sigh. For some reason, despite his extensive experience and his previous command of the *Gorae,* he was on edge. This missile test would be under an uncomfortable political microscope, and if it didn't go well, it might doom his career.

He looked up at the framed picture on the bulkhead above his desk, and the image only added to his anxiety. It showed a broadly smiling Kim Jong-un on the sail of the *Sulyong* during an inspection visit right after the ship was launched. This ship was one of Kim's favorite projects, and it was key to his plans. He would be expecting nothing short of perfection.

This pressure to succeed was bearing down on Captain Bo-yeun just as severely as the water pressure on his submarine at this depth. He felt like there was a heavy anvil on his chest.

To calm himself, he pulled a photograph of his wife and two young children out of the desk drawer and stared at it for a while. He tried to draw on some happy memories to distract him from his heavy command burden.

CHAPTER THREE

U.S.S. *Key West*, SSN-722
East of Sinpo, Sea of Japan

Captain Thomas O. Karl was standing quietly next to the high-definition plot in the control room of his 688-class attack submarine, the USS *Key West*. He looked around proudly at the crew diligently manning their respective posts. He was constantly impressed by their competence and professionalism. And he was proud to be the skipper of this technological marvel, which he had commanded for two years.

Captain Karl was tall and gaunt with an upright military posture. He was widely liked and respected by the crew, although he was a difficult person to know. Not that he was unfriendly by any means, but his reputation was reinforced by his quiet personality. He had a very serious demeanor, and he brooked no fools. When he did issue orders, it was often in a deliberate tone, but no one ever hesitated to obey. They all knew his commands were serious.

On the front end of the control room, the two plainsmen carefully managed the boat's depth as they shadowed the North Korean submarine. These two young sailors had only been in the navy for a few years. Each had joined right out of high school.

Chief of the Boat (COB) Carlester Crumpler stood behind them and silently observed. A former NFL player, Chief Crumpler was a huge man. The running joke was that he was too big to fit on the boat, and he did look immense standing there. Even though he had over fifteen years of service in submarines, this experienced crew didn't need often his direct help. But nevertheless, he was available if required.

Carlester's twin brother, Lester Crumpler, was Master Chief on the *Peralta*, the destroyer they were escorting. This was the first time in his navy career that he and his brother had been assigned to work so closely together. It made him feel some added responsibility for ensuring success on this mission.

Off to the right side, the helmsman Andrew Kidder managed the boat's speed. He was another recent addition to the *Key West* having just graduated from submarine school.

Sonarman Wes Higgins sat tensely in his padded chair. He listened to the transmissions in his headphones and watched the mounted displays in front of him. He was also the picture of concentration. His main task was to identify and track the North Korean submarine marked on the displays as Sierra 4. He had first detected it shortly after it departed its home port at the Sinpo Naval Base, and had been continuously monitoring it. He was also responsible for identifying and tracking other sonar contacts in the vicinity.

Satisfied with the activities of the control room crew, Captain Karl checked in. "What's the current status of that North Korean sub?"

He'd been looking over Higgins' shoulder at the sonar displays, and while he understood sonar basics, he was always amazed at Higgins' talents. Higgins was able to glean an incredible amount of information from these arcane displays and the sounds he heard on his headphones. It seemed like some form of magic, but Karl knew it represented years of experience and hours of practice.

Sonarman Higgins responded, "Sir, she's still directly in front of us. Distance 10,000 yards. Speed four knots. Depth 400 feet. Current course is zero-eight-zero degrees. Same course as the past several hours."

Captain Karl nodded then added, "Let me know immediately if there are any changes. Especially if they move up to periscope depth and slow down. That could indicate an imminent launch."

"Aye, aye, sir."

Karl turned to face the XO. "And if that occurs, I want to go to periscope depth and send an encrypted communication to the *Peralta* to warn them. They will undoubtedly already be aware of the submarine's movements, but better safe than sorry in case they missed it."

The XO, Lt. David Westphal, agreed. Westphal was almost as tall as the captain, and similarly thin. But the XO was totally bald and wore thick black glasses. He often wore a blue baseball cap. Everyone assumed it was to hide his hairless head, but in truth he just liked the look of it. He wasn't bothered by his lack of hair. And his physique was deceptive. He had been a boxer at the Naval Academy and still looked like he could manage a few rounds if called upon. With a quiet and softspoken personality he commanded immense respect from the crew.

XO Westphal stood next to Captain Karl at the tactical display. It had not changed appreciably for quite some time. On the display, the *Key West* was shown as a square green symbol in the center. To the top at 10,000 yards there was an inverted red triangle, the North Korean Sinpo-C submarine. To the right about 30,000 yards, there was a green triangle marked as the U.S. Arleigh Burke destroyer, the U.S.S *Rafael Peralta* (DDG-115). There was a green triangle pointing up just north of the North Korean submarine indicating the LAMPS helicopter from the *Peralta*. Here and there on the plot were white symbols marking ships identified as friendlies: fishing boats, freighters, oilers, container ships, etc. Overall, there were at least fifteen other ships on the chart because *Key West* was cruising close to some major shipping lanes. And finally, to the south side of the North Korean Sinpo-C there was a second North Korean submarine. It was designated Sierra 6 with a red inverted triangle and identified as a Romeo-class diesel submarine.

Captain Karl quickly evaluated the tactical situation. "XO, we need to keep a close eye on this second submarine. I don't want it to interfere. If it gets too close, we might need to adjust our course or depth to stay clear. At our current speed, I really doubt they will detect us. But I don't want them to be too close in case we need to speed up and create more noise."

Captain Karl continued, "I also want torpedo firing solutions continuously updated for both North Korean submarines. I don't want any delays if we need to launch."

"Aye, aye, Captain. I'll have those loaded into the targeting computer right away and updated as we go."

"Call down to the torpedo room and make sure that tubes one through four are loaded with war shot and ready. Thanks."

CHAPTER FOUR

U.S.S. *PERALTA*
EAST OF SINPO, SEA OF JAPAN

I stood on the port bridge wing in the warm humid air and gazed at the broad expanse of the Sea of Japan surrounding the ship. The USS *Peralta* was the newest addition to the Navy's fleet of Arleigh Burke class destroyers. Cruising north at five knots, I was intent on carrying out our mission of tracking the new North Korean Sinpo-C class ballistic missile submarine, the *Sulyong*.

I reviewed the simple mission orders in my mind. *If this submarine launches a ballistic missile, I shoot it down. Pretty simple, really.*

I looked pensively across the deep blue sea to the horizon. It was very calm this June day. Almost glassy, though there were some gentle swells rolling in steadily and majestically from the north. I peered up at the bright blue sky and saw wispy alto-cirrus clouds scudding across the sky from the east. These clouds represented harbingers of a storm that the navigator had warned me was forming as a tropical depression west of Guam. However, that developing storm wouldn't reach us for almost a week, so it would not be a problem.

While enjoying the view and fresh ocean air, I could not shake the thought that this pending action was fraught with enormous risk. I assumed that higher authorities must have considered it strategically vital to order this escalation of hostilities. The explanation that I'd been given was that the North Koreans needed to be shown that they would not be allowed to sortie their submarines and endanger U.S. interests. It was also intended as a demonstration of America's superior technology.

I looked toward the horizon to port and though I obviously could not actually see the submerged enemy submarine, I knew from the stream of constant Combat Information Center (CIC) updates that it was lurking out there roughly ten miles away. I had given orders to my crew to loiter back and forth and keep our position about ten miles from the enemy submarine. I did not wish to lose sonar contact, but I didn't want to come within close range of their torpedoes. It was the ideal distance to intercept their ballistic missile.

Time spent on the bridge wing was always a treat for me. I really enjoyed being out in the open, breathing the refreshing salt air, feeling the sunshine and breeze on my face. It was also a reminder of why I enjoyed being on the ship in the first place.

I looked over at Seaman Parker, the lookout. "Parker, do you see anything interesting?" Parker was peering through his Big Eyes, special high-magnification (20 power) binoculars mounted on swivels on each bridge wing.

"Bubba" Parker was a good old boy from Georgia who spoke with a southern drawl sprinkled with homey expressions. Because he was one of the sharpest lookouts on the ship, I was inclined to let his casual attitude slide and cut him considerable slack about his language.

Despite his peculiar personality, he was absolutely dedicated to doing his job well. He was renowned throughout the *Peralta* for what sometimes seemed like supernatural vision.

"Yes, Captain. I see our LAMPS helicopter over yonder using dipping sonar. In the far distance, I've spotted a fishing trawler and a container ship. So far, that darned North Korean submarine hasn't showed up."

"Last time I checked, it was cruising at a depth of four hundred feet, so she clearly would not be visible. But if she comes to periscope depth, I'll let you know right away so you can watch for antennae or a periscope."

Seaman Parker nodded vigorously. "That would certainly be more interesting than just watching this flat blue patch of water. I'll be on it like a chicken on a June bug in the barnyard."

That's a new one. Where does Parker come up with these expressions? It seems that the well never dries up.

The *Peralta* was the perfect ship for this mission. Arleigh Burke class destroyers are sort of the Swiss Army Knives of the Navy. They are incredibly versatile. These destroyers can defend against air and surface attacks as well as conduct anti-submarine operations. If called upon, they can strike distant targets with cruise missiles. Some of the newer ships in the class are capable of shooting down ballistic missiles and low-orbit satellites. Because of that capability, the *Peralta* and three other ships have been deployed at times near North Korea to counter the threat of missile launches from land bases.

The beating heart of the *Peralta* is the Aegis Combat system located in the CIC. "Aegis" is not an acronym. It is a word from Greek mythology. Aegis was the shield of Zeus. Appropriately, the Aegis Combat System is often referred to as "the shield of the fleet." It is a highly sophisticated command and decision-making weapon control system that uses powerful computers and radars to track and guide weapons to destroy enemy targets.

It is built around several components which include the AN/SPY-1 radar, the MK 99 Fire Control System, the computerized Command and Decision Suite, and the SM-3 and SM-6 Standard Missile family of weapons. It also controls the Phalanx Close-In Weapon System (CIWS) and the bow-mounted 5-inch gun. Additionally, it also manages the defensive suites, including the chaff dispensers and Electronic Counter Measures (ECM).

The AN/SPY-1 is a phased array radar mounted in large octagonal flat panels located on four corners of the superstructure. Unlike traditional radars, which have large rotating antennae, the AN/SPY-1 changes the direction and focus of its radar beam electronically. It gives a 360-degree view of the surroundings without moving. It is capable of simultaneously tracking over 100 targets at a distance of one hundred nautical miles. It directs the targeting and inflight corrections for the standard missiles and can simultaneously engage a large number of targets. Obviously, the crew in the CIC carefully manage the Aegis Combat System but once engaged, it performs its functions automatically.

I strolled back inside the air-conditioned bridge and looked around with pride at the crew. The XO, Bill O'Hara was standing at his station on the port side of the bridge peering through the front windows with binoculars. O'Hara had been my XO for about a year. He was medium height, with cropped black hair. His round face was dominated by gold wire-rim glasses. And as I occasionally teased him, he was starting to show the signs of a significant paunch, the result of the good chow on the *Peralta*. I had come to rely on him to help me run the ship.

Seaman Arnie Johnson was standing calmly at the helm with his hands on the steering wheel awaiting any orders to change speed or course. Johnson was one of the ship's most competent helmsmen. He was a rangy Midwestern kid from Minnesota I think, with red hair and a freckled complexion. Sometimes when I looked at him, I had the fleeting thought that he was too young to be in the Navy. But he was highly skilled, even though he looked like he could still be a high school student.

The ship was controlled from a free-standing console located centrally on the bridge. The helmsman stood behind it where he had a view to the front and sides of the ship through the surrounding bridge windows.

The console contained the controls and digital readouts that the helmsmen used to navigate the ship. Multiple digital displays showed key information such as, local time, the ship's speed in knots, an illustration of their route on a digital map display, their current latitude, longitude and heading. It also displayed information about the status of engines.

To the right there were two large throttle handles, one for each engine. Moving the throttles forward accelerated the ship, moving them back slows the engines down. Pulling back completely put the engines into reverse thrust.

The only sound on the bridge was from the overhead ventilation ducts, a steady, low-volume hum in the background. There was no extraneous conversation taking place. Everyone was focused on their duties and while no one would admit it, everyone was a bit nervous about what might happen. They all knew that even though the situation was relatively calm, that could change at a moment's notice. However, exactly what form that might take was anyone's guess.

I could see the tactical situation on my own repeater display on the bridge, but I called WEPS on the 42MC to the CIC for an update.

"Lt. Hawkins, what is the status of our enemy submarine? And the overall tactical situation?"

"Captain, the *Sulyong* is ten miles away at a bearing of two-six-zero degrees, continuing to travel at four knots, depth 400 feet. The *Key West* is trailing her by about 10,000 yards. Our LAMPS helicopter is located about a quarter-mile north of the *Sulyong* and has been using its dipping sonar. We are getting updated information on the submarine's heading, depth, and speed. We are surrounded at various distances by a small collection of fishing boats, freighters, an oiler, and a container ship. None is in a position that would interfere with our operations. And to the south of the *Sulyong* there is a North Korean Romeo-class diesel submarine, a companion to the Sinpo-C. It has been mirroring the movements of the Sinpo-C."

"Thanks, Lt. Keep a close eye on the situation. I want you to watch for the Sinpo-C making a move to periscope depth, which would indicate a possible launch. And it goes without saying, make sure the Aegis Combat System is primed and ready to launch quickly."

"Understood, Captain. We will stay alert. They won't catch us by surprise."

The CIC was several decks below the bridge, but I could conjure a mental image of the CIC crew. I pictured them sitting at their consoles wearing blue baseball hats with the U.S.S. *Peralta* logo. The Navy had done a careful study that concluded that this headgear was the best way to shield their eyes from the overhead lighting of the CIC as they concentrated on their computer consoles. So, I knew that this was not just some attempt at forced casualness. Also, I'd been told that the crew liked the baseball hats because they thought they looked cool.

Located deep in the *Peralta's* interior, the CIC was armored for protection. It provided Lt. Hawkins with a wealth of critical information. The forward bulkhead contained two horizontal banks of video displays. The upper row was made up of four screens dedicated to tactical information. Each display showed an array of color-coded symbols that marked every aircraft, submarine, and ship within the *Peralta's* area. Friendly contacts were shown in blue, neutral contacts in white, unknown contacts in yellow. Hostile targets, if present, were represented as red symbols shaped in different ways to indicate the type of contact. For example, an enemy submarine is represented by a red "V", an enemy surface ship by a red "O", and an enemy aircraft by a red "/\".

The lower bank of five monitors in the CIC are smaller, each displaying a 72-degree view of the outside world, which if viewed together provides a 360-degree real-time video view of the world surrounding the ship. In older CICs, the crew was isolated from the real world in a windowless compartment buried deep in the ship. They could only interpret events from what they could glean from their electronic displays.

Now, the CIC crew had a full window on the ocean stretching to the horizon in all directions, so they wouldn't have to guess about what is going on around them. And to top it off, at night they can toggle to low-light mode or infra-red which provides them with images in spite of the complete darkness outside. Not surprisingly, this new system called the Digital Video Surveillance System (DVSS) is a CIC crew favorite.

"Have the sonar operators listen for any transients that would indicate hatch openings. Have them listen for the sounds of outer doors on the torpedo tubes. They should be especially alert for the sound of a missile tube hatch opening."

Hawkins had already anticipated these events. "Aye, aye, Captain. I will relay your orders right now."

"Lt. Hawkins, program the Aegis Combat System to launch three SM-6 missiles in rapid succession. I realize that one should be adequate, but if it were to miss, there might not be enough time to launch another one. I want several missiles in the air to absolutely guarantee a hit. Assuming that the North Korean missile might have a nuclear warhead, the extra missiles are well worth expending."

The *Peralta* would use its RIM-174 Standard Extended Range Active Missile (ERAM), or Standard Missile 6 (SM-6) to intercept the North Korean missile. The SM-6 was designed for extended range anti-air and anti-ship warfare. It was also used for terminal interception of ballistic missiles. With a range of 150 miles, a speed of Mach 3.5 (2,664 miles per hour), and an altitude of 110,000 feet, it can destroy a variety of targets with its 140-pound blast fragmentation warhead.

"Aye, aye, Captain. I will program three SM-6 missiles for launch."

She didn't verbalize her thoughts, but it occurred to her that this mission would be very expensive. Each SM-6 missile cost about four million dollars. But she also knew that they couldn't afford to miss, and afterward nobody would question their decision to fire multiple SM-6 missiles. Cost would not be a problem as long as the shoot-down was successful.

I was beginning to relax a bit. There wasn't much else I could do to prepare my crew. Now they just needed to stay vigilant. The next move would be up to the North Koreans.

CHAPTER FIVE

U.S.S. *Peralta's* LAMPS Helicopter
East of Sinpo, Sea of Japan

Warrant Officer (WO) Tamara Perkins glanced at the chronometer on the instrument panel showing they had been on station for close to three hours. This had been their second long shift of the day. She stifled a big yawn and thought, *No wonder I feel so tired. Two long shifts and no end in sight.*

The *Peralta's* other LAMPS helicopter had been alternating shifts with them. She stifled another yawn which caused her to shudder.

Tracking this North Korean sub had been so easy that she and her crew were getting bored. Apparently, this submarine didn't care that they were being tracked because they hadn't made any real efforts to hide. They acted as if the Americans wouldn't do anything to them. Consequently, they didn't waste time or energy trying to disguise their location.

Perkins thought, *It would be nice if at least they would try to evade us because then the mission would be more exciting.*

WO Perkins glanced over to at her copilot, WO Jonathon Ward, to see if he was as sleepy as she was. He was looking out the window and she couldn't see his face, so she asked, "What's so interesting out there?"

"Sorry, I was daydreaming about home. And taking in how peaceful and beautiful the view is. The ocean is unusually calm, and the white fluffy clouds are almost hypnotic. And so far, this mission has been very boring. That sub is making it too easy for us. It's like they don't even care."

"I was thinking the same thing."

WO Ward was responsible for the deployment of offensive and defensive capabilities. He and Perkins had teamed up for just over two years and had become like siblings. They had first met in flight school and had been fast friends ever since.

Perkins called the sensor operator, Chief Scott Gordon, who sat behind them in the center cabin separated from the cockpit by a partition. Chief Gordon reported to Perkins as her crew member, but he was the most experienced sailor onboard. While only a few years older than Perkins and Ward, he had nevertheless logged more than five years as a LAMPS sensor operator.

Perkins assumed that Gordon was glued to his displays. It was his job to manage the sensors, such as the dipping sonar and the sonobuoys, and ensure that the secure radio link to the *Peralta* delivered a steady stream of data. The primary role of the LAMPS helicopter was to provide remote detection and targeting data to the mothership. Of course, it was also capable of conducting attacks on its own. It had the capability to drop a Mark 54 torpedo directly onto an enemy sub, or to use Penguin or Hellfire missiles against surface targets.

"Gordon, are you awake back there?"

"Of course. I'm always on the job. You know that."

"Yes, absolutely. I was just pulling your chain."

"As usual."

"What is the tactical situation?"

"Nothing much has changed. The Sinpo-C is still moving on a course of zero-six-zero degrees, speed four knots, depth 400 feet. No change for a while. I'm staying alert but it's hard to stay focused. I have the *Peralta* on my display as well as the North Korean Romeo submarine. No change with that one either. By the way, I have intermittent contact indicating the *Key West* which is trailing the Sinpo-C."

"Copy that. I just got a call from Captain Kane, who reminded me to be especially alert if the sub moves to periscope depth. He thinks that might indicate a pending missile launch."

After that comment, she looked over at Ward to judge his reaction, but he still seemed to be nonchalant. She knew that he had heard every word, so his indifference was puzzling.

"Copy that. I will be sure to let you know if anything changes."

Immediately behind Chief Gordon, there was an odd-looking device mounted to the side of the helicopter. It was a tall rack with multiple round caps, each connected to a cable leading back to an instrument box. The overall impression was that of a many-legged bug. This device was the sonobuoy ejector.

Sonobuoys are highly effective cylindrical devices that are very narrow and about three feet long. They're used to detect and track submarines. In the case of the LAMPS helicopter, a maximum of twenty-five sonobuoys are loaded by hand into their slots prior to the mission, and then expended as needed. They are ejected from the helicopter and when they hit the water an inflatable surface float with a radio transmitter remains on the surface for communication with the helicopter while one or more hydrophones descend on a cable below the surface to a predetermined depth. The selected depth is variable depending on environmental conditions, the search pattern, and the nature of the target.

Some sonobuoys are "passive," meaning they can only listen for sounds. Others are "active," meaning they can generate sound energy (pings) and listen for the returning echoes from the target. The data was passed to signal processing computers on the helicopter as well as the *Peralta* for analysis.

Perkins sighed and concluded that there was nothing more to be done than to continue chasing this boring target and hope that her watch would end soon. Then she could head back to the *Peralta* and get some coffee and chow.

But the situation suddenly changed. Gordon called her: "The Sinpo-C is rising. Looks like it may be headed to periscope depth. I'll watch for radio antennae or periscopes breaching the surface."

Perkins smiled and thought, *At last, things might get interesting.*

WO Ward also perked up at the report and became much more animated. He was suddenly more engaged. Perkins was encouraged by the change.

CHAPTER SIX

NORTH KOREAN SINPO-C SUBMARINE *SULYONG*
FORTY MILES EAST OF SINPO

X O Min-wok called Captain Bo-yeun to inform him that they were approaching the designated launch zone. Bo-yeun left his tiny cabin and walked slowly down the passageway to the control room. Just before exiting his state room, he took another long glance at the photo of the Supreme Leader hanging on the wall to remind himself how much was on the line for him personally should his mission fail.

As he walked down the narrow passageway, he passed the compact galley. He was overwhelmed by the pungent scent of kimchee wafting from the galley. It seemed to permeate every area of the ship. Even though it was a national dish, and he did enjoy eating it, the aroma could still be cloying. It occurred to him that he might be especially sensitive right now because he was on edge about the upcoming missile launch.

It was critical for his career prospects that this high-visibility mission proceed without any issues. He would be unable to relax until the test was successful and he was back in his home port at the Sinpo Naval Base.

This mission was to test-fire a ballistic missile. It was a practice exercise, and the missile would simply arc high into the atmosphere and then plunge back down into the Sea of Japan. The missile was armed with a dummy load, not a live warhead.

A few nodding glances from the crew on station greeted Bo-yeun when he entered the control room. The strain was evident on their eager young faces. It was silent except for the background hum of ventilation fans and the occasional murmur of water passing along the hull. He also felt a very slight but continuous vibration coming up through the deck to his feet from the power plant.

XO Min-wok responded to the Captain's request for an update and was prepared with a quick summary. "The tactical situation is unchanged. No real change in the relative positions of the American destroyer or the helicopter, both of which continue to closely monitor us. Our Romeo submarine is stationed to our starboard side and mirroring our movements. We have not detected an American submarine, although I suspect they are out there somewhere."

Bo-yeun simply nodded then asked, "How far are we from the launch zone? Is the missile ready to launch?"

"We are roughly three miles from the western edge of the launch zone. We will enter in about 45 minutes. All diagnostic tests on the missile are complete, and we have loaded the targeting information into the attack computer. It has been triple-checked and verified. The missile is ready to launch."

Bo-yeun nodded with a thoughtful glance at the XO. "As soon as we cross into the launch zone, I want you to take us to periscope depth and reduce our speed to two knots. I will transmit an encrypted message to headquarters in Sinpo that we are ready, and assuming they approve, we will launch without hesitation."

Min-wok seemed excited about the prospect of finally firing a real missile. He'd never done so. In fact, this would be the first actual launch for everyone on board. About half a dozen test launches had been performed from fixed underwater platforms at the Sinpo Naval Base harbor. This would be the first test launch from a moving submarine; therefore, it was much riskier.

"Captain, what about the Americans? That destroyer will still be nearby and the LAMPS helicopter as well. Will they interfere?"

"I'll use the periscope to scan the area to make sure that the American ship and the LAMPS helicopter will not interfere. The last thing we need is to accidentally hit that helicopter. That would be inexcusable. I don't think the Americans will interfere. They are here to observe a launch and collect as much data as possible."

"What if an American submarine shows up?"

Bo-yeun smiled. "Well, that would be interesting. However, I don't think they will interfere. It's not as if they are going to torpedo us. We aren't at war."

XO Min-wok chuckled quietly, then said, "They will certainly be surprised when a ballistic missile suddenly blasts out of the water. They may shit themselves."

After his outburst, many of the control room crew glanced furtively at the Captain and XO. They didn't usually hear obscene banter.

Bo-yeun grinned broadly at the XO's abrupt profanity. "Yes, they certainly will be surprised. And as you said, I imagine it will scare them to know that we have this capability."

The remaining distance to the launch area was traversed without any more drama. However, to Bo-yeun, the passage of time seemed endless. It moved like molasses in winter.

Out of the slowness emerged a sudden and rapid series of orders. "Helm, take us to periscope depth and reduce speed to two knots," Bo-yeun directed. "Comms, raise the high-frequency radio antenna. Sonar, focus on the destroyer. I want to know if it makes any sudden course changes. And pay attention to any unusual sounds like splashes or torpedo doors opening. I don't think we will be attacked, but I want to be alert nevertheless."

The control room crew efficiently executed his orders, and five minutes later the *Sulyong* was moving forward slowly at periscope depth.

Bo-yeun took a quick look at the chronometer, which indicated noon local time. Then he raised the periscope and made two slow 360-degree visual sweeps. The sky was so bright it took a moment for his eyes to adjust to the glare. He confirmed that the destroyer was about ten miles to the east and that the LAMPS helicopter was to the north about half mile away. Neither would obstruct the launch. He then asked the Communications Officer to transmit the encrypted message stating their readiness to launch.

A short time passed before they received an official approval to execute the launch. He lowered the periscope and the antenna to protect them from the missile's blast. Bo-yeun turned to look at the XO standing in front of the targeting computer, and gave him the order to launch, "XO, fire the missile."

XO Min-wok smiled broadly because this was the exact moment that he had long anticipated, "Aye, aye, Captain."

Turning back to the weapons panel, Min-wok calmly lifted a safety cover from the firing switch and depressed the bright red button underneath it.

"Missile away, Captain."

Bo-yeun had expected an immediate response, but nothing happened for what seemed like an eternity. What he had underestimated was that the firing sequence was complex and took a short time to complete. It involved a series of sequential automated steps, such as the opening of a large hatch at the top of the missile tube to equalize the pressure and various electrical relays and switches opening and closing in carefully programmed steps. The complete launch sequence took close to a minute.

Bo-yeun was finally rewarded when the control room shook violently as the missile in the sail was ejected. The nine-meter-long NK-11 missile was thrust out of the tube by expansion of gas from a compressed-nitrogen container. This powerful blast pushed the missile up and out of the missile tube with such force that the missile traveled up through the column of water and popped above the surface like a porpoise leaping out of the water.

Of course, Captain Bo-yeun and the crew couldn't observe it, but once the missile was above the surface, its solid rocket fueled engine ignited, and the long bright flame pushed it rapidly up into the atmosphere. Inside the submarine the crew was treated to a roar that reverberated down through the water and shook the entire boat.

Bo-yeun and the control room crew were smiling and clapping. The launch was successful, and the NK-11 missile was on its way. Their part in this mission was essentially complete, so they breathed a sigh of relief.

CHAPTER SEVEN

U.S.S. *PERALTA,* SEA OF JAPAN, EAST OF SINPO, NORTH KOREA

Aboard the *Peralta*, events also developed rapidly.

The port lookout reported a periscope and antenna near the LAMPS helicopter.

Shortly after that, the sonar operator on the *Peralta* and the sonar operator on the LAMPS issued alerts that they had detected the opening of a large hatch, presumably, the missile tube hatch. A launch was imminent.

I issued a string of orders. "Helm, hard to port, come to course two-seven-zero. Increase speed to 30 knots."

The helmsman Johnson responded, "Aye, aye. Thirty knots at new course, two-seven-zero true." As he turned the steering wheel to execute the port turn, he crisply shoved the two throttles forward. The *Peralta* rapidly accelerated and heeled over sharply into the turn.

I grabbed the 42MC and called the CIC, "Lt. Hawkins, get ready to track the missile. I want you to detect it as soon as it breaches the surface and fire as soon as you can. It will be most vulnerable early in its flight."

Lt. Hawkins acknowledged my order. "Aye, aye, sir. We are ready. The Aegis system is focused on the periscope sighting location, and it will detect the launch instantly. I have programmed it to fire three SM-6 missiles in sequence."

"Perfect."

I picked up the 1-MC to alert the entire ship. "We're about to launch missiles. Clear the decks if you are near the launchers." The ship was already at General Quarters Condition Zebra, so most of the crew were at their combat duty stations anyway, but I wanted to play it safe.

I had turned the *Peralta* toward the Sinpo-C submarine to close the gap and give the missiles a shorter path to their target. It probably would not have made much difference with such a short time before the launch, but every little bit helped. As the *Peralta* rapidly changed course, the view to the Sinpo-C submarine shifted from the port side to a bow view so everyone on the bridge peered intently forward.

Everyone gasped as a large white and black cylinder with a black nose cone suddenly leapt out of the water about eight miles away. It briefly hovered about twenty feet above the ocean's surface. Then, just as suddenly a huge flame ignited under it blasting the water to form a large splash. The NK-11 missile began accelerating straight up, gradually gaining speed and altitude.

A loud warning siren sounded throughout the *Peralta* to warn the crew that her own missiles were about to be fired. Suddenly, a hatch popped open from the front vertical launchers, and the first SM-6 fired up and out of its launch tube with a tremendous roar.

The firing sequence was very rapid.

First a wall of reddish-orange flame about 15 feet wide and 50 feet high erupted out of vents between the hatches. Then, an SM-6 missile leapt out of the vertical launch system on top of its own large yellowish thruster flame. The SM-6 created a huge plume of smoke, dark orange, and brown at the bottom just above the deck. The smoke transitioned to a thin white trail as the missile accelerated up into the sky. The smoke cloud below began to quickly dissipate in the breeze. The SM-6 missile traveled vertically for several seconds then began to arc over toward the North Korean missile as the Aegis Combat System adjusted the SM-6's flight path.

Two more SM-6 missiles erupted out of forward vertical launch cells in rapid sequence and tracked parallel to the first missile.

The SM-6 missiles travel at Mach 3.5, or about 2,664 miles per hour, so it didn't take long for them to reach the North Korean missile. The first SM-6 reached the NK-11 at an altitude of about 50,000 feet, well within its capability to hit targets as high as 110,000 feet. The Aegis Combat System had been providing continuous course updates, but when the SM-6 missile got close, its internal guidance systems provided terminal guidance for the final intercept.

When the SM-6 determined it was close enough its blast fragmentation warhead exploded scattering hundreds of small metal fragments in an expanding cone-shaped pattern toward the NK-11 missile. The North Korean missile was peppered with numerous fragments that punctured it from top to bottom. It was also hit by pieces of debris from the destroyed airframe and internal components of the SM-6.

The North Korean missile was ripped apart and exploded in a giant fireball as the remaining solid fuel ignited. Pieces of the destroyed missile began falling back into the Sea of Japan.

The North Korean ballistic missile never stood a chance. One SM-6 missile would probably have sufficed. The remaining two SM-6 missiles, having no intact target left to hit simply self-destructed adding their own carnage to the large cloud of debris in the air.

It might be viewed as overkill, but the *Peralta* was not taking any chances.

CHAPTER EIGHT

North Korean Submarine, *Sulyong*

The sonar operator on the *Sulyong* practically leapt out of his seat as he loudly announced, "Captain, the American destroyer has just launched missiles. Three."

Captain Bo-yeun looked at him with a puzzled expression. He was totally taken aback by the report. At first, he had some difficulty absorbing and collating this new information. "What are the Americans thinking? Are they trying to shoot down our NK-11 missile? Are they attacking us? They've just committed an act of war. This is unacceptable."

Turning to face the sonarman and trying hard to suppress his own rising excitement, he berated him, "Seaman, calm down. Shift your focus to listening for other threats. The Americans may attack us with torpedoes."

Bo-yeun added an afterthought, "Last time I looked, the LAMPS helicopter was very close, and it could drop a torpedo on us without warning. Pay special attention to that threat."

Bo-yeun reached over and raised the periscope and the communications antenna, both of which had been lowered to prevent damage from the missile launch. He stepped up to the eyepiece to see what was happening. He quickly rotated the periscope to bring the destroyer into view and he confirmed the sonarman's report. The American destroyer was moving away to the north at high speed, with residual clouds of white and brown-red smoke dissipating around its decks. He could see three white smoke trails rising vertically into the sky, but he was unable to rotate the view high enough to see much beyond their lower flight path.

However, it didn't take a genius to figure out what target they were rising to hit. His NK-11 missile!

Bo-yeun wanted nothing more than to make the Americans pay for this aggression. He wanted to attack them immediately, but he knew that he was not authorized to make that decision on his own. Deep down he realized it would be suicidal because if the American destroyer didn't kill them, the LAMPS helicopter would, or perhaps the still unfound American submarine that he suspected was lurking nearby. Basically, he was boxed in and would be destroyed very quickly. Nevertheless, he sent an encrypted message to Naval headquarters in Sinpo, asking for permission to attack.

A response was received almost immediately. It confirmed that the missile had been shot down by the American ship. The entire incident had been tracked by the missile tracking radars at the Musudan-ri rocket launching site on the east coast of North Korea. Despite this obvious American provocation, Captain Bo-yeun was ordered not to attack. He was ordered to return to base as soon as practical. His superiors did not wish to escalate the situation, and they also knew that the *Sulyong* could not possibly survive an encounter with the American forces. They also assumed that the Romeo submarine nearby would probably be sunk as well, A counterattack would be too costly. He was ordered to immediately leave the area.

Captain Bo-yeun was disappointed that he wouldn't be able to take out his aggressive feelings on the Americans, but he had calmed down enough at this point to understand that he didn't really have a choice. Headquarters was correct. If he escalated the conflict his boat would be sunk. No doubt about it.

It was bad enough to lose the NK-11 missile. That could be blamed on the rash and illegal behavior of the Americans. However, if he also sacrificed the *Sulyong,* he wouldn't be around to suffer, but his family certainly would. This submarine was a pet project of the Supreme Leader, and he would be furious if it were lost.

So, Bo-yeun issued a string of orders, "Helm, set a new course to take us back to base."

The helmsman responded, "Aye, aye, Captain. Ten knots, 400 feet below the keel, new course two-six-zero true."

"XO, double-check that the missile hatch tube is closed. Get me an update on our battery status. I wish to know if we can make it all the way back without snorkeling."

The XO walked over to the weapons computer to confirm that the indicator lamps were green, which meant that the missile tube hatch was closed and sealed. Then he walked across to the status board to check the battery charge status. After doing some quick range estimates in his head, he reported back to Bo-yeun. "We have adequate charge to get about halfway back to base at our present speed. At that point, we will need to snorkel to recharge the batteries and run on the diesel engines for the second half of our trip."

Bo-yeun shook his head from side to side and then commented with a wry smile, "I don't want to slow down, so if the batteries are depleted at the halfway mark, that's acceptable. Snorkeling won't be a risk anyway. The Americans know exactly where we are so there's no need to try to be too clever. Obviously, the snorkel protruding above the surface makes it easy for them to find us, but that really doesn't matter now."

The XO didn't feel a need to add any comment, he simply nodded in agreement.

"Sonar, please give me an update."

Seaman Jong-chen, who was still agitated by the events, provided a quick summary, "The American destroyer is moving off to the northeast at over 30 knots, making so much noise that she's easy to track. The LAMPS helicopter is hovering about 1 mile to our north. The Romeo is still to our south. I assume it will mirror our course changes and follow us home."

The Bo-yeun looked down at the tactical chart and nodded silently as he contemplated the details.

Suddenly, the sonar operator spoke up again in a very excited voice, the pitch and volume both rising as he talked, "Captain, as we turned a new submerged contact appeared about 4 miles to our west. I haven't classified it yet, but it must be that American submarine we've been looking for. I think we caught them by surprise and once they moved out of our baffles, I was finally able to detect them."

"Great job, Seaman. I knew we would find them eventually. Let me know as soon as you have them classified. Is it a Los Angeles- or a Seawolf-class attack submarine? I need to know what we are dealing with."

"Aye, aye, sir."

Bo-yeun reflected on this new information. *It's a good thing we didn't attack the destroyer. I knew there was an American submarine out there, and they probably had us targeted all along. We would have been sunk quickly for sure.*

The sonar operator spoke up at length, "Captain, I've identified the submarine. It's a Los Angeles-class attack submarine. Our database of previous encounters tentatively identifies it as the U.S.S. *Key West*. It's changing course, probably to come around to our baffles again."

Satisfied that the situation had settled down and that the transit back to their home base should be uneventful, Bo-yeun decided to go to his cabin to write a report about the incident. He wanted to create it while events were fresh in his mind.

He was convinced that there would be an angry set of superiors to answer to, from his immediate Admiral at Sinpo all the way to the top. The Supreme Leader would be extremely angry and there was no predicting how he would react. Nor to whom he would assign the burden of blame.

Bo-yeun was determined that his report would show that he was personally blameless. All blame had to be shifted to the reckless and crazy Americans. At least, that was his firm desire.

Bo-yeun turned to the XO and passed command to him "XO has the conn. I'm going to retire to my cabin and work on an incident report. Call me if anything requires my attention. Otherwise, I would appreciate some privacy for the next few hours so that I can concentrate."

XO Min-wok acknowledged, "XO has the conn."

Min-wok was keenly aware of the stakes that would play out as this incident was investigated. Hopefully, the *Sulyong* would not be blamed for the shootdown. After all, they had performed their tasks flawlessly up to the time when the missile took off. They could hardly be blamed for the events that occurred for which they had no control.

But, in the political climate of North Korea, you couldn't always predict where the blame would fall. And if it happened to fall on you personally, it could have devastating consequences. So, he sincerely hoped for everyone's sake that Captain Bo-yeun would get his report right.

CHAPTER NINE

U.S.S. *PERALTA*

Sea of Japan East of Sinpo, North Korea

I announced proudly to the bridge crew, "Mission accomplished. Time to go home. Helm, set course for zero-six-zero degrees, speed twenty-five knots. Let's get out of here before the North Koreans do anything rash."

"Aye, aye sir, set course zero-six-zero degrees, speed twenty-five knots."

"WEPS, have the LAMPS confirm that the North Korean subs are heading back to Sinpo, then have them return to the ship. I'm sure they must be getting low on fuel. They also must be tired and hungry."

"Aye, aye, Captain, I will contact the LAMPS."

"WEPS, continue to maintain high alert just in case the North Koreans decide to counterattack. I don't want to be caught off guard."

"Understood. We will maintain Condition Zebra until you tell us to stand down".

"XO, you have the conn. I'm going to my cabin to submit a situation report."

"XO has the conn."

"I assume everyone up the chain of command is already aware of what just happened, but I need to file an official report."

Back in my cabin, I closed the door so I could concentrate and quickly submitted a brief report.

```
TO: COMCINCPAC ADMIRAL THOMAS BAKER
FROM: CAPTAIN STEVEN KANE, U.S.S. PERALTA
EYES ONLY TOP SECRET
NORTH KOREAN MISSILE SUCCESSFULLY INTERCEPTED
PROCEEDING NORTHEAST TO EXIT AREA.
KEY WEST ALSO EXITING.
BOTH SHIPS RETURNING TO YOKOSUKA.
NO RESPONSE DETECTED FROM NORTH KOREA.
NORTH KOREAN SUBMARINES RETURNING TO SINPO.
////
------------------------------------
```

Warrant Officer (WO) Tamara Perkins wrapped up her conversation with WEPS. She looked down again at the chronometer on the LAMPS instrument panel. They had been on station for close to six hours. She thought to herself, *WEPS is right. I'm definitely tired and hungry. These two long shifts have really worn me out.*

On the other hand, she was still pumped up from watching the missile shoot-down. She had never witnessed a live intercept before.

Tracking this North Korean submarine had been so easy that she and her crew had been in danger of getting complacent. That all changed when the submarine launched its missile and the *Peralta* responded with its Standard missiles. It was quite a show.

Fortunately, the North Korean submarine had not counterattacked. But Perkins was disappointed that she and her crew were unable to go after the North Korean submarine. That would have really made her day. She figured the North Koreans were so surprised that they didn't know what to do. Besides they must have known that between the LAMPS, the *Peralta* and the *Key West* they would have been dead ducks.

WO Perkins turned to her co-pilot, WO Jonathon Ward, "Jon, we're heading back to the ship."

Ward smiled and responded, "Good, I'm beat. It's about time. Our fuel level is down to 20 percent."

"Yes, I noticed that. There's one more thing we need to do before we break off."

Perkins called the sensor operator, Chief Scott Gordon, sitting behind them. He was continuing to monitor the LAMPS sensor suite and sending a steady stream of secure data back to the *Peralta*. The two North Korean submarines were targeted on his display.

"Gordon, WEPS has an assignment for us before we return?"

Gordon responded almost immediately, "I'm listening. What does WEPS want?"

"It's a simple request. WEPS wants us to confirm that both North Korean submarines have disengaged and are returning to base."

"Okay. I'll double-check."

"What is the tactical situation?"

"Nothing much has changed. After the missile intercept, the Sinpo-C turned to a course of two-six-zero degrees, increased speed to ten knots and moved to a depth of 400 feet. Both North Korean submarines are heading back to base. I'm staying alert for changes, but their activities have been consistent so far. I'll continue to monitor the sonobuoys until we are out of range."

"Thanks, copy that. I'll let WEPS know that they are departing the area."

Perkins plotted a course to the *Peralta* on her navigation display. She and her crew had a real exciting story now to share with their shipmates and she was eager to be back on board.

_____

The crew on the *Key West* similarly stood down. Seeing that the North Korean submarines were departing and not attacking, the *Key West* stayed alert but canceled battle stations. They changed course to the northeast, accelerated, dove to 800 feet, and set a course for home base in Yokosuka, Japan.

CHAPTER TEN

PINE GAP AUSTRALIA
JOINT U.S. AND AUSTRALIAN INTELLIGENCE FACILITY

F ar away at Pine Gap, a joint Australian and American surveillance facility in the middle of the Outback, a group of dedicated intelligence analysts had been watching the activities near Sinpo, North Korea.

Pine Gap was not widely known outside the intelligence community until about 20 years ago, when its existence was revealed by insiders. One of these was the infamous CIA analyst, Edward Snowden, who exposed their activities along with that of many other agencies around the world. The Pine Gap facility provides information to the CIA, NSA (and their Australian counterparts), and to the Pentagon. Pine Gap was initially set up to monitor missile launches from the Soviet Union, China, and North Korea, or any other nation in the region. That mission evolved considerably to include all manner of communications analysis, tracking, and identification of signals.

Pine Gap decodes and analyzes cell phone and email traffic for signs of impending terrorist or foreign military threats. Most controversially, Pine Gap has been involved in providing targeting information to support U.S. drone attacks in Afghanistan and Pakistan.

Pine Gap is a large campus about 11 miles southwest of Alice Springs, Australia. It consists of 38 radomes containing large antennae, and support buildings housing powerful computers to analyze, classify, and interpret the enormous amount of intercepted data. Sources include satellites and surveillance drones, radio transmissions such as cell phone traffic and emails, and military transmissions. This includes not only communications traffic, but signals transmitted from weapons such as missiles.

Senior Analyst Teresa Perkins looked up from her three flat panel displays. She had been watching and recording a series of radio transmissions, so her screens were showing rows and columns of boring figures, a few of which had been highlighted by the computers to call special attention to them. The entire room was a hive of analysts wearing headsets, about 15 total, with similar setups: two or three flatscreen monitors displayed information individually filtered according to their assigned specialties.

Teresa had transferred from the NSA two years earlier. She was one of the Americans on the team. Her youthful face was framed by short dark-brown hair with distinctive bangs. She really enjoyed her assignment at Pine Gap, but found the cultural offerings of Alice Springs to be lacking. She was more used to the excitement of metropolitan Washington, D.C. Nevertheless, this assignment was hard to beat for the sheer drama.

The huge monitor on the front wall displayed a "God's eye" view of their entire region of responsibility. It showed the map from India to Japan, and included Australia, China, North Korea, and everything north to the Kamchatka Peninsula. It was cluttered with colorful symbols representing civilian and military ships and aircraft. The known locations of submarines were shown as well.

Mission Director David Handley was pacing the floor talking to his analysts via a wireless headset. He was a nervous type, always on edge. He was prone to sarcasm. He was slightly built, medium height, with gray hair, and he was dressed in dark-brown cargo pants and a colorful print shirt. The pattern was drawn from the stylized Aboriginal art of the area. He was Australian and a long-time member of the team.

David called his lead analyst Teresa Perkins and requested that she zoom in to a much more magnified and detailed image on the main screen. He requested that she run a replay of the recent events near Sinpo for everyone to observe.

Teresa reached over to her keyboard and entered a series of instructions. Instantly, the image on the main screen switched to a magnified overhead view. Then she began the replay, which showed the American destroyer moving slowly, accompanied by a hovering helicopter just west of the ship.

As a group, the analysts watched the rapid action. They observed the missile launch from the North Korean submarine and the shootdown by the *Peralta*. The replay then showed the *Peralta* and the two North Korean submarines as they departed the area. The LAMPS returned to the *Peralta*. The *Key West* turned back toward Japan. The entire action lasted less than ten minutes.

Handley called to his analysts, "I can't believe that they shot it down. Did they think it was a real threat? I want a computer analysis of the predicted trajectory of that ballistic missile. What was the intended target?"

Senior Analyst Aaron Burke to Teresa's right side madly entered instructions on his keyboard to calculate the course of the North Korean missile. There wasn't much data to work with; the prediction would usually improve as the missile moved along its path. However, the data was cut off when the missile was intercepted.

"With so little data, there's no way to calculate the path and estimated target with any accuracy," Aaron responded.

Handley looked at him and nodded.

He really respected Aaron's skills. Aaron was another of the Americans on the team. He was a former CIA analyst and was renowned in Pine Gap as a computer whiz. He was also considered to be a computer nerd and looked the part with bushy long hair, an overgrown beard, a withdrawn personality, and clothes that hung on him like a suit rack. However, nobody questioned his expertise.

"Unbelievable," Handley vented. "They have preemptively fired three missiles at the North Korean missile. They fired so quickly that they couldn't have predicted the target. And why three missiles?"

Teresa spoke up. "Obviously, they intended to shoot it down pre-emptively. Probably thought if the first missile missed there wouldn't be time to fire the second one."

Handley just looked over at her and shook his head.

"Why didn't the submarine retaliate?"

"That would have been suicide. The LAMPS is so close that the submarine would have been destroyed immediately."

"It appears that they are returning to Sinpo to lick their wounds. I assume North Korea will file angry official protests. But losing the missile is bad enough. I doubt they wanted to lose the sub as well."

Handley thought to himself, *The Americans planned all along to shoot down that missile. They fired immediately. There's no way they could have calculated the target so quickly. Which begs the question, why? And why wasn't Pine Gap included in the planning?*

Handley instructed his team to send relevant data files to the Pentagon, NSA, and CIA for later analysis. He was determined to work the chain of command and find out why his group was kept out of the loop. Though he fully appreciated the need for secrecy on some missions, he didn't like surprises.

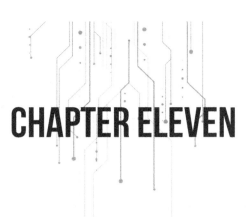

CHAPTER ELEVEN

SINPO SUBMARINE BASE, MEETING WITH KIM-JUNG-UN

Captain Bo-yeun planned the fifty-mile return trip to the Sinpo Naval Base to arrive around six p.m.

He would have preferred to return under cover of darkness like a night prowler. But that wasn't possible since he'd been ordered to return immediately. The Supreme Leader was notoriously impatient and would not tolerate delays.

Bo-yeun surfaced the *Sulyong* about four miles east of their destination, just southeast of the city of Sinpo near the harbor entrance. The harbor was busy with ship traffic, so it was standard practice to proceed on the surface.

He slowed the ship to four knots and climbed up to the bridge on the sail along with the XO and two lookouts. From that perch he could conduct the passage through the harbor and manage the landing at the pier.

On the open bridge he treated himself to a cheap Chinese cigarette in a vain attempt to ease his nerves. The XO turned down his offer of a cigarette, so Bo-yeun was left to indulge his vice alone. Smoking was a nasty habit that he wanted to shake, but at times like this he found it a strange comfort. He enjoyed inhaling the fresh sea air mixed with cigarette smoke.

Bo-yeun wanted to give himself every possible advantage for the upcoming interrogation. Therefore, he'd changed out of his casual dark blue coveralls into his dress suit, his summer uniform. It was a pressed white formal jacket, black pants and shoes, and a white hat with the large North Korean Navy insignia on the front and his black and gold captains' bars perched on his shoulders. He made sure to attach his medals. *Can't hurt*, he thought.

He ordered the crew to dress in their summer white formal uniforms as well, especially those who would be visible above deck.

High above the deck in the bridge, he had a great view of the sights and sounds of the harbor and surrounding area of Sinpo. Through his binoculars he soaked up the familiar surroundings of the port. Having sailed in the area for many years, he could recall the details from memory. He could almost navigate with his eyes closed. Nevertheless, it was refreshing and distracting to take in the sights once again.

He smiled when he encountered a group of large brown sea lions basking on the harbor buoys. They had hauled themselves out of the water to soak up the late afternoon sunshine.

Near the harbor, the sky was cloudless, while in the distance to the north rain clouds were building over the rugged mountains behind the city. Large cumulus clouds with dark undersurfaces towered in the distance with streaks of rain falling here and there. He really loved to watch summer thunderstorms. The power and majesty fascinated him.

His ship was approaching the eastern end of Mayang-do Island, a low verdant island with numerous irregular harbors that contained a handful of North Korean naval installations. In fact, this island was one of the largest naval bases in North Korea and housed facilities for a large collection of patrol craft, corvettes, and frigates, as well as midget and full-sized submarines.

As the *Sulyong* neared the first promontory, a light gray 300-foot-long Najin-class frigate was exiting the harbor at high speed. She turned to pass along his port side, headed for a patrol in the Sea of Japan. He noted that this low-profile, sleek ship was heavily armed, and he felt great national pride just to be associated with it. It quickly passed by them, blasted a horn in greeting, then continued eastward with the North Korean flag flapping from its mast. The frigate receded rapidly into the distance as it exited the harbor.

The next harbor he passed revealed six black Romeo-class submarines tied to the pier. Seeing the Romeo submarines reminded him of his early career in the submarine service when he had spent several years in that class of ship.

It also made him think of the Romeo-class submarine that had accompanied them on their mission. Sure enough, as he turned to look aft, he saw that the Romeo had surfaced about a mile behind them and was making a slow turn to port to join its fleet at the pier. He waved to them but was doubtful they could see his polite gesture from this distance. The black, low-profile Romeo submarine quickly passed from sight as the two ships separated.

In the next harbor on the port side, he saw the midget submarine base. He could barely make out the dozens of small submarines tied to the docks laying low in the water. North Korean has more than fifty of these small boats, and they are principally used for coastal patrol and to make shore raids with commandos. Particularly into South Korea.

These midget submarines are small with limited range, and they don't represent much of a threat to shipping on the high seas. Nevertheless, they carry two torpedoes and are a threat simply because of their numbers. And besides, they could get a lucky shot off as they did when a midget submarine sank the South Korean ship, *Cheonan*, off the west coast of Korea in March 2010. That incident caused the deaths of 46 South Korean sailors and provoked international outrage.

Bo-yeun smiled to himself thinking about how uncomfortable and cramped the duty was on these small boats. He was happy that he'd never been assigned to one. He certainly didn't feel that he had missed anything.

About a mile from his destination, he was welcomed by the sight of eight small fishing boats heading east in a small armada. They passed along his port side. It was a motley collection of variously colored small wooden boats, many of which were dilapidated with wooden frames above the deck for crude shelter from the sun. They were also covered with a collection of nets and floats hanging at every possible angle. They looked like they could barely float.

Bo-yeun admired the bravery and dedication of these fishermen who were willing to risk their lives in such beat-up old contraptions. On the other hand, he understood that fishing was one of the few ways to make a living in his country, so perhaps they didn't have much choice.

The small group of wooden fishing boats trailed behind a much larger one that stood out because of its size and the fact that it had an enclosed bridge on its second deck. It seemed like it was a mother hen to the other smaller ones. It was completely rusty and sported old tires tied to the gunwales to act as bumpers. It was swarmed by a large flock of squawking black-tailed seagulls. Apparently, they were attracted to the odors created by the crew members cleaning fish on the aft deck. These birds were in almost constant motion, as they swooped in to land here and there on the boat to seek edible scraps.

Bo-yeun turned his gaze back to the starboard side to look at the city of Sinpo. Many buildings had bright blue roofs and stood out from the others, but from this distance the buildings blended together into a drab collection of new and old structures, commercial buildings, warehouses and residences. There was a stadium visible on the east side of town.

Along the shore massive cargo ships, their hulls painted in bold colors, were docked near the harbor's industrial zone. Towering cranes, with their mechanical arms outstretched, unloaded and loaded shipping containers with precision. The sheer scale of these operations illustrated the economic significance of Sinpo Harbor which connected North Korea to the global trade network.

The waterfront was bustling, creating a symphony of sounds. Bo-yuen could hear the rhythmic creaking of wooden fishing boats, the clang of metal against metal as fishermen repaired their nets, and the distant hum of engines. Amidst the cacophony, the cries of seagulls echoed overhead.

The unmistakable scent of the sea filled the air, intermingling with the salty aroma of freshly caught fish wafting from the boats and fish markets on the shore. The surroundings were permeated with animated conversations and spirited haggling, creating an energetic buzz of background noise.

Further inland, Bo-yuen could see the heart of Sinpo Harbor's industrial zone. The air drifting from there carried a distinct tang of diesel fuel, mingled with the metallic scent of machinery. Massive shipping containers, stacked like colorful building blocks, dominated the landscape, their surfaces bearing the marks of countless journeys across the seas. The steady rumble of engines, the clanking of metal against metal, and the occasional hiss of steam underscore the ceaseless activity of this industrial hub.

Behind the city to the north, the landscape rose steeply in bare brownish mountains. The setting sun highlighted the irregular shapes of the mountains and interjoining valleys. Farther in the distance were the beautiful puffy thunderstorm clouds he had observed earlier. They were still forming into the large, majestic anvil formations of severe thunderstorms. It didn't appear that rain would reach the harbor. The clouds would probably just hover over the mountains, typical summer late-afternoon cloud formations.

When he strained his eyes, he could almost convince himself that he saw his own house on the hillside. He was probably just imagining that.

As he enjoyed all these sights, Bo-yeun hoped without hope that this moment could be stretched on forever. The dread of his upcoming meeting was pressing harder onto his anxious mind, and he wished that he could somehow avoid the encounter. But the *Sulyong* was moving slowly and steadily to the port where fate awaited him.

As the *Sulyong* approached the destination dock, the small entrance to the docking basin appeared to his right. To the left, he could see the rising low promontory where construction was being done to create new underground pens to hide submarines in the future. He really wished that facility was already complete, but he'd been told it would still be a few years.

Straight ahead, he saw the main facilities of the submarine construction facilities where the *Sulyong* had been built. He knew that several more were planned. A new fabrication building was under construction to accommodate larger submarines in the future.

Bo-yeun lined up his boat with the small entrance ahead. A small tug moved towards them. It was there to help the *Sulyong* maneuver in the tight quarters of the docking basin. But to his surprise, he was waved off and directed to dock at the long pier on the left, outside the basin.

At just over 200 feet long, the Sinpo-C was small as submarines go. However, the docking basin was quite cramped, and the tug's assistance would delay their landing. The Supreme Leader was impatient for them to dock.

Bo-yeun trained his binoculars on the pier and gazed toward the west into the setting sun. It was difficult for him to see clearly. The bright light obscured the details, but the dreaded sight was unmistakable. There were at least fifty high-ranking uniformed army and navy officers standing there surrounded by a large security cordon.

Even from this distance, it was easy to pick out the Supreme Leader standing in front of the group wearing his signature long black jacket. The numerous military officials on either side of him were dressed in formal dark-green or white uniforms, so the contrast made it easy to spot Kim Jong-un.

Bo-yeun shook his head and remarked quietly so the two lookouts stationed behind him on the bridge couldn't overhear. "XO, look at the pier. It looks like the welcoming committee is quite large. I don't see any smiles. The Supreme Leader looks angry."

XO Min-wok stared steadily through his binoculars. "Yes, I can see that. Looks like we are in for it. They look like a lynching party. I'll bet they can't wait to find someone to blame."

"Yes, and we'll be the main candidates. I hope I can convince Premier Kim that we are blameless. After all, we couldn't have done it differently. The launch was flawless. We can't be held responsible for what happened after that. We could not be responsible for controlling the crazy Americans."

"I agree. However, whether we should be blamed, or whether we will be, are two different things. I fear that the necessity to find a scapegoat puts us squarely in the crosshairs."

"Perhaps. I will try hard not to let us take the fall."

The *Sulyong* angled slowly into the long concrete pier and through a combination of efforts by the deck crew, and the tug was gently pushed against the pier. The deck crew secured it to the pier with large hemp hawsers, and a boarding ramp was rolled over to connect the sub to the pier.

Bo-yeun half expected Kim Jong-un to stride down the ramp and board the submarine like he had earlier in the year on a public relations visit. This time the Supreme Leader stood impatiently looking up at the bridge where Bo-yeun and Min-wok were standing. They saluted him, but the salute was not returned.

Bo-yeun climbed down through the sail to reach the hatch leading to the deck, then walked out onto the deck, up the ramp, then stopped and bowed right in front of the Supreme Leader. "Greetings, Supreme Leader. Thank you for meeting us on our return."

Kim gave him a disdainful look and responded in a barely audible whisper. "I had intended to greet your heroic return from a historic mission, but now I'm here to get to the bottom of what happened. Losing our missile was totally unacceptable. A massive failure. Certainly not a heroic event."

The Supreme Leader turned abruptly and stride toward the submarine factory building just across the pier. On cue, Bo-yeun and Min-wok followed, and the entire collection of military brass dutifully and somberly walked in behind them.

CHAPTER TWELVE

Main Manufacturing Building
Sinpo Submarine Base

The ordeal began immediately for Captain Bo-yeun. He glanced around at the dignitaries assembled on the pier. The military brass stood there dressed in formal uniforms. He had to suppress his desire to laugh out loud. *All these old men look like clowns. They are covered in ostentatious medals, and they look ridiculous. It's inconceivable that any of them earned that many medals. They must have picked them up at Medals-r-us.*

Inside the manufacturing building, they were ushered into a large hall that had been set up for the investigation. Or inquisition, depending on your point of view. Specifically, depending on which side of the table you sat!

The cavernous hall was part of the new submarine assembly building. It had windowless undecorated walls. The open ceiling was full of ductwork, cables, and pipes hanging in the rafters. A huge North Korean flag hung on the back wall. A long rectangular metal table in the center was surrounded with uncomfortable-looking folding chairs. More folding chairs were set up in the margins of the room to accommodate the spectators.

The Supreme Leader sat at the far side of the table. Three admirals flanked each side. Bo-yeun and Min-wok didn't need to be prompted to take the two chairs set up on the front side of the table. It was obvious where they were supposed to sit.

The Supreme Leader betrayed his impatience by opening the interrogation almost before Bo-yeun or Min-wok finished sitting. His eyes flashed, and his youthful face scowled.

"Captain Bo-yeun, your mission was a terrible failure. Please explain what happened." His chin quivered as he spoke.

Bo-yeun couldn't avoid a quick glance at Min-wok who was motionless and staring down at the table. Min-wok looked like he wanted to cry. Bo-yeun hesitated, cleared his throat, and then began a careful explanation. He felt tremendous pressure to get this right, knowing that his career and perhaps his life were on the line. He was especially nervous since the audience of admirals and generals was undoubtedly poised to pounce to deflect any blame.

Bo-yeun began his explanation. "Supreme Leader, as you know, our mission was to travel to the launch area and fire a single NL-11 ballistic missile to test our submerged launch program. We traveled to the area without incident. We were tracked and followed by an American destroyer. It remained about five to ten miles from us at all times. It kept track of us with its own sonar as well as the use of an anti-submarine helicopter called a LAMPS. We were apparently also followed by an American nuclear attack submarine, though we didn't know that for sure until after the actual missile launch."

Supreme Leader Kim exploded in anger. "Why didn't you stay hidden? Your mission and voyage should have been secret. It was your responsibility to prevent discovery."

Bo-yeun glanced at Min-wok again as if expecting some support. However, he was staring down at the table as if he wished he could somehow disappear. Bo-yeun realized that he needed to cross this minefield very carefully. He must give a truthful answer, but it must be worded in such a way as to deflect blame.

"Supreme Leader, with all due respect, I need to point out that our movements were impossible to hide from the Americans. As you can see, the *Sulyong* is tied up at the pier outside in plain view of American surveillance satellites. Our departure would not have been a secret, and I believe that the American destroyer was waiting to intercept us as soon as we left port. Once they acquired us on sonar, there was nothing we could do to hide. Their anti-submarine capabilities are so sophisticated that once they tracked us, there was no way to hide again. And besides, even though we were aware of their presence, we had no reason to think they would attack."

The Supreme Leader glared at Bo-yeun. His eyes flashed anger again, and he grunted an indecipherable comment out loud. Then he abruptly demanded that Bo-yeun continue.

Bo-yeun took a moment to gather his thoughts. Again, it was critical to word his response carefully.

"Supreme Leader, we prepared in advance, and once we entered the designated launch area, we quickly rose to periscope depth, scanned the area to ensure that there were no obstacles, particularly that helicopter I mentioned. Then, without hesitation, we fired the KN-11 missile. It launched normally, and once it had taken flight, my ship's mission was complete. And successful I might add."

The Supreme Leader became quite animated when he shouted, "How can you call it a success? The missile was shot down."

Bo-yeun continued as calmly as his frayed nerves would allow, "Yes, that is correct. But after the missile left the submarine and was on its upward flight, the Americans launched missiles to intercept it. I had no way to know they would do such a reckless and illegal thing. There was no way to anticipate their actions."

"Couldn't you just sink the American destroyer to stop it?"

"With all due respect, Supreme Leader, we were not authorized to attack the American ship in advance of launching the missile. After the missile was launched, destroying the American ship would not have made any difference."

"Why didn't you sink them after they destroyed the missile?"

"Supreme Leader, you may be aware that I requested permission to sink the American destroyer after their attack. Permission was denied. Instead, we were ordered to return to base. I would add that it would have been too late. The KN-11 missile had already been destroyed at that point. By the time we could attack the American destroyer with torpedoes, it would not have made any difference. Besides, between the destroyer, the helicopter, and the American attack submarine that we discovered later, the *Sulyong* would have been destroyed very quickly. We would have lost the submarine as well as the missile. And probably also our companion Romeo submarine. That result was unacceptable. Returning to base was the right decision."

The Supreme Leader looked at Bo-yeun with an angry stare that could have bored a hole through a steel plate. But he didn't respond. He nodded almost imperceptibly and grunted.

After an uncomfortable pause, Kim Jong-un looked at Bo-yeun and spoke loudly so the entire audience could hear. "Captain Bo-yeun seems to be blameless in this incident. He acted in the highest traditions of the North Korean Navy. He is to be congratulated for completing his mission and bringing the *Sulyong* back safely. Captain, you and your XO are free to leave."

A low chatter spread through the audience. Undoubtedly, many of them had renewed fears that the blame would now shift to one of them.

Captain Bo-yeun and XO Min-wok were greatly relieved that Kim Jong-un had exonerated them. They rose quickly and departed immediately before anything would change. The Supreme Leader had a reputation for being impetuous. They didn't want to take the chance that he would change his mind. Better to leave quickly before that happened.

After Bo-yeun and Min-wok departed, Kim Jong-un asked the six admirals at the table to stay. The remaining entourage was dismissed.

Kim gathered the admirals at the table close to him and gazed at each in turn, then spoke. "I'm tired of these arrogant Americans. I want a plan from you to strike back. It must be bold and effective. Use your imagination and come up with something clever. The next time we meet, I expect you to present me with an action plan that satisfies me!"

With an abrupt wave, he dismissed his admirals, and they quickly left the room. Kim then stood up and departed with his security entourage to board his private armored train to travel back to his residence in Pyongyang.

CHAPTER THIRTEEN

RYONSONG RESIDENCE, PYONGYANG, NORTH KOREA

After interrogating the crew of the *Sulyong,* the Supreme Leader traveled in his personal armored train back to his elegant and spacious Ryonsong Residence. Located on the northern outskirts of the capital city, Pyongyang, Ryonsong Residence was constructed in 1983 for Kim Il-sung. Subsequently, it was occupied by Kim's father, Kim Jong-il and now by Kim Jong-un himself. He shared this main residence with North Korea's First Lady.

The five square-mile grounds of the Ryongsong Residence are located 7.5 miles northeast of Kim Il-sung Square in central Pyongyang. It contains numerous luxury facilities, such as banquet halls, meeting rooms, a large swimming pool, a running track and athletic field, a spa and sauna, horse stables and riding area, a shooting range, and a horse-racing track. Inside it is decorated with luxurious interiors, ornate furnishings, deep plush carpets, fancy chandeliers, and numerous large vases, paintings, and murals. On one wall in the foyer there is a huge portrait depicting Kim and his late father.

It is known by locals as the Central Luxury Mansion and is comprised of numerous structures, including the main house and guest houses for party officials. Fittingly, the complex has elaborate defenses. These include garrisons of soldiers, electric fences, mine fields, guard towers, anti-aircraft guns, and SAM batteries. It is connected to other private residences by tunnels, and a private underground train station is located inside the complex. Kim is a bit paranoid about security as evidenced by his travel in an armored train car which he can board from his private station.

The Ryonsong Residence is used by Kim as a meeting place to conduct state business. So, this is where he chose to have his next meeting concerning what to do about the American missile intercept provocation. The meeting was held two days after the interrogation of Captain Bo-yeun at the Sinpo Naval Base. Kim demanded the attendance of key members of the State Affairs Commission.

The State Affairs Commission of the Democratic People's Republic of Korea (SAC) is officially defined in the country's constitution as "the supreme policy-oriented leadership body of State power." Kim Jong-un is described in the constitution as the president of the SAC, the supreme state organ of policy direction and state sovereignty as well as security and homeland defense.

Kim convened the meeting with a military-related subset of the SAC in a large conference room in his residence. The attendees were the First Vice President, Hang Sang Soo, the Vice President, Lee Kyeong-mi, several officials who represented special responsibilities such as, the Minister of State Security, Ryoo Seung-yang, , the Minister of Defense,

Jin-woo Jeong, the Minister of Foreign Affairs, Yoon Jung-chin and four members of the Central Military Commission of the Worker's Party of North Korea.

The attendees were ushered through the ornate foyer of the residence into a marble floored room with high arched ceilings. Bright overhead lights highlighted the ubiquitous gold paint. The meeting room was on the far end of the foyer; its entrance was two wide carved wooden doors sporting long wooden handles decorated on top and bottom with sculpted gold decorations. A large rectangular wooden table surrounded by comfortable upholstered chairs dominated the center of the room.

At the distant end, the windows opened on a view of the beautiful private lake. However, the view was obscured by floor-to-ceiling white drapes. The entire floor was dominated by a gigantic orange and yellow floral rug. On each side, large blue Chinese vases with purple and red flower arrangements occupied the side walls. One side wall was decorated with the large painting of Kim Jong-un and his father. The opposite wall had a huge abstract mural of mountain scenery.

Kim sat alone at the end of the table. The other officials were arrayed along each side of the massive table. The military members were dressed in dark-green uniforms and the non-military members were dressed in Western-style business suits. Most of them were dressed like typical businessmen with either dark gray or black suits, white shirts, and blue or red ties. Each was wearing the obligatory red lapel badge illustrated with a picture of Kim Jong-un.

Kim wore his usual black outfit, a loose-fitting tunic jacket over black slacks. Pinned to his chest was a red badge with his portrait. He leaned forward and was gripping the table tightly. His clenched hands were pale from the exertion.

Kim looked up abruptly, cleared his throat, and glanced sternly at the attendees to indicate that he was ready to begin. He waited for the room to fall into complete silence and waved at the servants to leave the room and close the doors. When he was sure he had everyone's attention, he began,

"You all know why we are here. I made it clear at the end of our meeting in Sinpo that I wanted a plan to punish the Americans for their unacceptable provocation. I am tired of them thinking they can do whatever they wish without any consequences. I want a proposal from this group that we can implement immediately to hurt them. Or, at least to embarrass them and make them understand that they are vulnerable."

There was a of mumbling of agreement around the table accompanied by vigorous nods of approval.

The Minister of Defense, Jin-woo Jeong, confidently spoke up first. "Supreme Leader, my belief is that the best approach would be to use the *Sulyong* to threaten them more directly. We should dispatch it with nuclear-armed missiles this time and send it close enough to their shore to let them know that we can strike them anytime we wish."

Kim looked directly at his minister and nodded. This idea was close to the plan that had been forming in his own mind, but he wanted further explanation, "Are you saying that we warn the Americans that we are coming with our missiles?"

The minister smiled coyly. "No, certainly not, at least not directly. We might want to issue a vague threat ahead of time. But what I propose is that the submarine depart secretly, stay hidden and avoid the American anti-submarine patrols—"

Kim interrupted. "That didn't work out so well in the recent incident. The submarine was carefully tracked, and the Americans were right there ready to fire. In fact, I understand that they fired within seconds of our missile launch."

Jin-woo Jeong quickly responded, "That's true, but as you know, we didn't really try to hide our voyage. Our propaganda arm announced our intention to launch a test of our sea-launched missile ahead of time. The *Sulyong* was tied up in plain sight at the pier, and its departure was easy to observe. The American ships were simply waiting for it to come out of the harbor. Once they identified it, it was easy for them to track. And I believe they intended from the outset to shoot down our missile. Their Aegis system was primed and ready to fire. That's the only way they could have responded so quickly."

Kim interjected a sarcastic comment. ,"But they said publicly that they shot down the missile because their tracking computers told them it was headed for Japan. Isn't that true?"

"Yes, that's the public excuse they pushed. But my experts tell me that they could not have figured out the path and final target of our missile so fast. The computers need more time to figure out the trajectory and plot the ultimate destination. So, I believe their system was pre-programmed to fire as soon as our missile popped out of the water. They fired on its upward trajectory early in the launch phase when it would be most vulnerable."

"We exonerated the submarine captain, believing that he could not have done anything to protect his missile. Was that the correct verdict?"

"Yes, Captain Bo-yeun could not have anticipated what happened. Once the missile left his submarine, there was nothing he could do. In my opinion, he is blameless."

Kim just nodded, then changed the subject. "So, we send our submarine, this time armed with real warheads, to the American coast to threaten them. Are you proposing that we actually launch the missiles and attack them for real?"

"No, of course not, Supreme Leader. I personally think that would be foolish. We might get a momentary satisfaction of revenge by destroying two of their cities, but we would pay a horrendous price. The Americans could rain down destruction on our entire country if they chose a massive retaliation. I'm not saying that they would for certain, but we've just seen that they can be impulsive and unpredictable. For example, I know that the Americans have one, if not two, nuclear ballistic missile submarines stationed in the Pacific that could hit us with hundreds of nuclear warheads."

"I understand. People think I'm crazy, but I do understand how disproportionate the scales are. Continue."

Jeong nodded quietly because it seemed that Kim wanted to ask more questions.

And he did inquire about operational details. "How far can the *Sulyong* travel? Can they get close enough to America to be a real threat?"

Jeong had already anticipated this question, so he was prepared with an immediate response. "Supreme Leader, the *Sulyong* has a maximum range of 1,500 nautical miles. I propose that we send it through the La Pérouse Strait north of Hokkaido, Japan, then have it travel northeast and cross into the western Pacific Ocean between two of the Kuril Islands. To extend its range, I propose that we refuel on the Russian coast or from ocean-going oilers along the way. Or, perhaps near one of the Kuril Islands.

A refueling stops adds risk, but since the *Sulyong* has a limited range, it is necessary." The minister then added the final touch to the plan. "Since we won't fire missiles, we need to scare the Americans by revealing our presence at the last minute. I think we simply come to the surface and let them find us. They will draw their own conclusions at that point about their true vulnerability. The submarine will return after revealing itself—mission accomplished. The Americans will come to realize that the Pacific Ocean is no longer their safe playground."

"At that point, might not the Americans sink the *Sulyong*?"

"That's doubtful. Recent events in Ukraine have shown that they are just a paper tiger. In my opinion, they won't risk an attack on the *Sulyong*."

"I hope you're right. How do you think they will respond?"

"We will hear the usual pious condemnations and perhaps be given additional sanctions. But since it will be a fait accompli, they won't take any action."

Most of the participants had remained silent. Kim asked, "Are we all in agreement? Does anyone want to add anything?" The participants murmured among themselves, but nobody spoke up.

Hearing no additional comments, Kim stood up suddenly, waved dismissively, then paused as he noticed the nervous glances. He assumed that the group was worried about guaranteeing success. *What a bunch of weaklings.*

"Alright," he said aloud. "Make this happen, and don't lose that submarine." After a short pause for reflection, he continued. "Let's implement your plan. Make it happen as soon as possible."

CHAPTER FOURTEEN

U.S. Security Council Meeting, White House

The U.S. Security Council met in the dedicated conference room deep under the White House. The room was crowded with key staff. This included the Vice President, Donna Marshall, the Secretary of State, Ben Ochoa, the Secretary of Defense, Mac Barnes, the National Security Advisor, Peter Devereaux, the Chairman of the Joint Chiefs of Staff, Donald Brooks, the Attorney General, Tess Taylor, the Director of National Intelligence, Arne Olson, the Secretary of Homeland Security, William Lightner, and the Representative of the U.S. to the U.N., Anna Fletcher. The Chief of Staff to the President, Donna Watson, and the White House Counsel were also in attendance.

The windowless conference room was dominated by a long black table surrounded by red cushioned chairs. High-definition flatscreens hung on two walls. They showed various images, primarily maps of the world with strategic assets, both U.S. and foreign. On one end of the room, the American flag and the presidential flag were hanging prominently. Each participant had a laptop in front of them, and the center of the table contained a conference phone. The participants had access to a wealth of information from a huge number of sources.

Seated at the head of the table was the imposing President Andrew Thompson, recently elected and eager to make his mark. He had been elected in part because of his long experience in foreign affairs, which he had acquired during his twenty-plus years as a senator. In his early sixties, he sported a full head of gray hair and had piercing blue eyes.

"I want to review the recent events off North Korea," President Thompson stated to open the meeting. It seems that we have stirred up a hornet's nest. Most of you are familiar with the incident, but I want to review the events. And even if this current incident is over for now, I want to spend the bulk of this meeting discussing our future options."

The President turned to face the chief of staff representing the military, three-star Admiral Donald Brooks. Admiral Brooks was dressed in his dress blue uniform, covered with medals and deployment pins representing his 35 years of service. He sat ramrod straight in his chair. Formerly the head of U.S. Pacific fleet, he was very familiar with the situation in the western theater.

"Please describe for all of us what occurred."

Admiral Brooks perked up, cleared his throat and then began. "Mr. President, here in a nutshell is what happened. We tracked a new North Korean ballistic missile submarine called a Sinpo-C, the *Sulyong*, as it left the naval base in Sinpo on the east coast of North Korea. Our intelligence indicated that it was loaded with at least one submarine-launchable ballistic missile and that they were proceeding to an area in the Sea of Japan to test-fire it. Since we had no way to know for sure if the warhead was a real nuclear device or just a dummy, we were forced to assume that it was real. So, with your prior approval of the rules of engagement, the Aegis destroyer on station shot it down shortly after launch. It was destroyed in flight less than one minute after launch."

The President quietly nodded as he absorbed the information. He was already aware of the details of the incident, and of course he had approved of the mission in the first place, but hearing it again brought home the reality in a new way. It just seemed more real hearing this dry description from the admiral. He couldn't figure out why that should be so.

"Ben, please update the group about our official explanation."

Secretary of State Ben Ochoa sat up quickly. A trim, dignified man who had also had a long career in the senate, Ben loved to be in the spotlight. He wore an expensive black suit, a dark-blue tie, and an American flag lapel pin. He completed his image by sporting a Meerschaum pipe dangling from his mouth. Smoking was not allowed in this room, but the unlit pipe was a permanent affectation. It reinforced to the others the reason they found him so arrogant and officious—almost insufferable to some of them.

"Mr. President, you undoubtedly remember the talking points we provided for your press conference. Our official statement was that our tracking systems indicated that the missile was headed to a target location in the heartland of Japan, and we could not allow it to continue. We said it was a purely defensive action. We judged that it was imperative to act without hesitation just to be safe."

"And I'm sure the North Korean reaction was predictable," the President commented sarcastically.

Ochoa smiled wryly. "Of course. I could have written it in advance. It was totally predictable. They called it 'unprovoked,' 'criminal,' 'unjustified.' Their state propaganda machine went into high gear ranting that it was an arrogant and provocative act of war. They went into great detail to condemn the evil American empire. Nothing new."

President Thompson didn't comment, but slowly nodded his head. He seemed deep in thought then asked, "Tell me what kind of response there was in the form of world opinion."

Anna Fletcher, Representative to the United Nations spoke up right away. "Well, Mr. President, I was present at the U.N. for the discussions. The North Korean speech was predictable. As far as the reaction, for the most part, friendly nations either stayed silent or gave the U.S. grudging support. North Korea's friends, such as China, Russia, Iran, Afghanistan, and Syria echoed the North Korean point of view. So, nothing new there."

Anna Fletcher was a longtime political figure. She had served in ambassadorships in several countries for several administrations. She dressed smartly, today in a dark-blue suit and white blouse, with just enough jewelry to highlight her femininity. In her late fifties, with short black hair and wire frame glasses, she cut quite the intellectual figure.

The President quietly considered the feedback. He had authorized the mission in part because he was a bit embarrassed by the U.S.-perceived impotence in the recent Ukraine War. Of course, the U.S. had supported Ukraine with weapons and humanitarian aid, but NATO could not come to their aid militarily. He didn't want it to escalate the conflict and start World War III with the Russians. In the case of North

Korea, he had a freer hand. It was important to keep Japan and South Korea informed, but they were not asked to participate. NATO did not have to be consulted or involved.

The President paused then turned the conversation to the future. "So, I assume this will probably blow over quickly. God knows there are always plenty of other major world events that will draw attention away from the missile incident. But it begs the question, what should our next steps be?"

Admiral Brooks interjected, "Well, sir, the North Korean land-based missile program is a growing threat. They continue to test longer-ranged ballistic missiles. Just recently they launched missiles that traveled over Japan, causing quite the alarm. There were no casualties or damage, but it was highly provocative. The latest version is thought to be capable of striking anywhere in the continental U.S. But submarine-launched missiles would be a more serious threat."

The National Security advisor, Peter Devereaux, added, "Sir, we are receiving disturbing intelligence reports that the North Koreans are planning a mission to threaten our West Coast. Specifically, there are indications that they plan to sortie their Sinpo-C submarine on a trip to approach our coast. And let me remind you that it can carry two nuclear-armed missiles. It represents a major threat."

Peter Devereaux was sort of an odd member of the team. He was not a former military man, nor did he have a political background. Appointed by the President, his background was from a famous strategic think tank. He had authored several white papers and op-eds related to security issues, and the President took a chance by appointing him to his post. He looked the part of an intellectual. He was well dressed, but not well fitted. His clothes looked like they had just come off the rack. And his head of long hair was always disheveled. Sometimes he had the dismayed look of someone who just woke up and couldn't find his glasses. But he was extremely knowledgeable about strategic issues and military systems, so the President leaned heavily on his opinions.

"I was under the impression that the Sinpo-C has a pretty limited range. Am I wrong? Can they actually get close?"

Peter interjected, "Sir, you are absolutely correct. We believe that the submarine has a range of only 1,500 miles. It is not a nuclear submarine; it is a diesel electric. But perhaps they have a workaround. Like a plan to refuel it somewhere."

"How close would they have to get to be considered a threat?" the President asked.

"Well, from their point of view, the closer the better," Peter replied, "but keep in mind that the missiles themselves have a range of about 2,000 miles, so if for example they could get within 500 miles of our shore, they could strike a large part of the U.S. They could easily strike coastal cities, such as Seattle, Portland, San Francisco, Los Angeles, or San Diego. And perhaps reach deeper to hit Denver, Phoenix, Tucson, Dallas, Omaha, and other target cities."

"Would they really be so foolish to actually launch nuclear missiles?"

"I personally doubt it, but I'm not sure we can take a chance. Kim often says crazy things, and I think he's just acting like a toddler, throwing a tantrum to get attention. But I don't want to be wrong. Someday he may act on his crazy threats. On the other hand, it's possible that they just want to 'rattle sabers,' to make us aware that they can threaten us. But as I said, I don't think we as a nation can afford to be wrong."

"So, what are you suggesting? That we shoot down their missiles again?"

"No, sir. If they bring that submarine close and launch nuclear missiles, we probably won't be able to intercept. We would need to have the submarine under constant surveillance. Our assets would have to track them closely at all times to be ready to fire an intercept missile."

"So, what should we do?"

"Sir, I think we need to eliminate that submarine entirely. Completely remove it as a threat."

"You mean sink it? Preemptively?"

"That's exactly what I propose."

The various cabinet members who would be classified as "hawks" in the room murmured in approval. Sinking the submarine would be a great solution in their collective opinion. The "doves" in the room objected, some very loudly, and insisted that diplomacy was the only route that made sense.

The President became thoughtful. He grabbed a folder in front of him and nervously ran his fingers along its edges. It was a well-recognized habit that he used to buy time. After some time, he asserted, "Obviously, diplomacy and sanctions haven't worked. Neither have the repeated condemnations of their nuclear program by us or the UN. North Korea continues to test longer and longer-range ballistic missiles. And these submarine-launched missiles certainly elevate the threat."

The room turned deathly quiet.

After a short pause, the President looked around the room and addressed everyone in a firm voice. "I think the threat we are facing is new and may need a fresh approach. Submarine-launched weapons are a worse threat than land-based weapons because the subs can just pop up at any moment in an unknown location and fire without warning. There would be no time to react to defend ourselves. Therefore, I agree that we need to proactively eliminate the threat. Sink the Sinpo-C."

He waited momentarily for his words to sink in. Then he continued in a quiet voice. "How can we do that? If we do, I don't want it to be blamed on us. We must appear to be innocent. Otherwise, it will be an act of war, and it's unpredictable where that would lead us."

Maxwell Barnes, Secretary of Defense, interjected, "I agree, Mr. President. We must find a covert method that removes us from suspicion. Ideally, we make it appear that they had an 'operational accident.' After all, submarines are inherently dangerous. The U.S. Navy has lost several submarines in the past. It is not unprecedented for a submarine to be lost at sea." He paused a moment to think. Then he said, "It would be easy for us to track the *Sulyong* and sink it with torpedoes at a location and time of our choosing. But that act would be virtually impossible to disguise. Our assets, such as ships and planes, would be able to be identified near the incident. And the explosions would be detected by civilian seismic recording stations. Because the Pacific forms the Ring of Fire of volcanic and earthquake activity, there are seismic recorders in numerous locations. The evidence from these recordings would be impossible to deny. It wouldn't take much time for the disappearance of the sub and the corresponding underwater explosions to be correlated."

President Thompson acknowledged, "I understand we couldn't hide a torpedo attack. So how do we make it look like an accident? I want you to put your heads together and have your experts develop a covert scheme to sink that sub. It must ensure that no blame be assigned to the U.S. Like I said, hopefully, you can just make their submarine have an operational accident and sink to the bottom of the ocean with the U.S. Navy nowhere near to be blamed."

He turned to Donald Brooks, Chairman of the Joint Chiefs of Staff in the Pentagon. "I want you to take the lead on this, treat it as a covert military operation. I want a plan delivered as soon as possible. Repurpose any current projects and staffing to make it happen. If Peter is correct, we should act the next time they sortie their submarine."

CHAPTER FIFTEEN

North Korean Submarine *Sulyong*,
Sinpo Submarine Base

The *Sulyong* departed from the Sinpo submarine base at two a.m. on a dark cloudy night. It traveled on the surface to the east slowly passing by the city of Sinpo on the port side and the numerous North Korean naval installations of Mayang-do Island to starboard. Once *Sulyong* cleared the harbor and was a few miles out into the Sea of Japan, Captain Bo-yeun ordered the initial course.

"Dive to 350 feet, make our course one-eight-zero degrees, maintain five knots."

"Aye, sir," responded the helmsman and diving officer. The watch crew was busy at their duty stations in the control room. Captain Bo-yeun decided that everything was in order, so he decided to take a quick break in his cabin.

"XO, you have the conn."

"Aye, Captain, XO has the conn."

Bo-yeun walked calmly to his cabin, entered the cramped space, and sat down at the small fold-down desk chair with a sigh. *I need to review the orders. They are simple, but I need to make sure I didn't miss anything important.*

It was critical to read between the lines, search for hidden meanings or implications. It never hurt to be thorough. After all, he was still under the shadow of the failed missile launch several months earlier, and he couldn't afford to have another blemish on his record. He had dodged a major bullet in that incident, but this mission was a fresh opportunity to succeed, or fail, depending on the fates. He could already feel his insides tightening, and the mission was just getting started.

He opened the red folder, took out the printed message and reread the orders.

```
TOP SECRET
DATE: September 22, 2023


TO: Captain Bo-Yeun
   KPANF Ship Sulyong


Depart Sinpo Naval Base at 0200 hours.
Proceed into the Sea of Japan, pass through
the La Pérouse Strait into the Sea of
Ohkotsk.
```

Rendezvous with North Korean trawler at Kharimkotan Island in the Kuril Island chain, refuel.

Proceed into the Western Pacific Ocean to a position northeast of the Hawaiian Islands. Surface and make the American Navy aware of your presence. Once you have been identified, return to base.

All activities until you surface in the eastern Pacific to be conducted in strictest secrecy. Your entire trip to that point must be undetected. Take all necessary measures and precautions to ensure secrecy.

The covert nature of this mission cannot be emphasized enough.

Signed: Admiral Ryoo Seung Soo
End of message. ////

He reviewed the letter at least ten times, and each time he was struck by the simplicity of the instructions. Obviously, they were composed by someone sitting in a cozy office with the luxury of passing out orders to patriotic underlings. Their simplicity belied the complex and dangerous reality.

Staying hidden would be a major challenge. On his previous mission, the American Navy had pounced on his ship almost immediately after departure and tracked him with a destroyer, helicopters, and an attack submarine. He had no hope of staying hidden on that short sortie from the base to the missile launch area.

How can I possibly stay completely hidden for the long weeks it will take to fulfill this new assignment?

Well, he would just have to draw on all his experience and cleverness to pull off a miracle. In his opinion, that's what it would take.

His first trick was to make a feint to the south to deceive the Americans. He started the *Sulyong* on a southward course to make it appear that he was headed for the Sushima Strait between the Korean peninsula and Japan. The Americans and Japanese had many anti-submarine assets in that strait, and if that was his true destination, he would be hard-pressed to get through undetected. But this southern route was a deception.

After several hours, he ordered a course change. The *Sulyong* turned northwest to head for Hokkaido Island and the La Pérouse Strait. That strait was also heavily monitored for submarine activity, but he was confident that he'd devised a trick that would allow the *Sulyong* to pass through undetected.

Captain Bo-yeun returned to the control room and asked for a tactical update. XO Park Min-wok looked up from the tactical display with a puzzled expression on his face. "Captain, the area around us is surprisingly clear of threats. Of course, there are many commercial ships and fishing boats, but no sign of any American Navy ships. It seems they did not pick up on our departure and have not tracked us at all."

Bo-yeun gave him a blank look as he absorbed the update. "Are you absolutely sure that we aren't being tracked? Did you clear the baffles to make sure that we aren't being followed by an American submarine?"

"Yes sir. We have not detected any enemy surface contacts, and we cleared the baffles twice. So far, no underwater contacts. They must have missed our departure entirely."

"I doubt that. Satellite surveillance would have revealed that we departed last night. Maybe they don't think we're important enough to track anymore."

The XO chuckled. "That would be uncharacteristic. Especially if they thought we might be carrying nuclear missiles."

"Right, it would be crazy for them not to follow us carefully. I don't understand what they're up to. I'm very suspicious. Make sure your people stay alert. The Americans may show up at any time. The Japanese navy might join in as well. Have the sonar operators watch for sound signatures from both the Americans and the Japanese."

The remainder of the trip to the La Pérouse Strait was undramatic. There were still no contacts from any enemy ships, so Bo-yeun began to believe that his ruse at the beginning of the cruise had been successful. Now they had to transit the narrow La Pérouse Strait, which was heavily monitored by Japanese anti-submarine ships and patrol aircraft.

The La Pérouse Strait also had an active SOSUS underwater network of sound sensors. It had originally been deployed during the Cold War to track Russian submarines. It was designed to pick up the faintest sound from submarines and use the data to triangulate their position. Along with other SOSUS networks around the Pacific and Atlantic, the Allies had been able to constantly monitor the positions of Russian submarines around the world during the Cold War. That war had effectively ended, but these networks had been reactivated to track new submarine threats originating from China, North Korea, and Iran, among other places.

When they reached the western end of the La Pérouse Strait northwest of Hokkaido Island Captain Bo-yeun pulled the next rabbit out of his hat; he shared his plan with the XO. "XO, shut down the main engines and rig for silent running. We're positioned about ten miles west of the entrance to the La Pérouse Strait in a perfect position to take advantage of the prevailing currents to carry us silently through the strait all the way to the other side. The Japanese won't hear a sound from us. It will be slow since the current is only about four knots. We need to be very patient. That's the price to be paid for complete silence."

Bo-yeun added, "Also, since we're drifting with the current, the ship will be at a relative standstill due to the movement of the current around us. Maintaining our depth will be challenging, so the crew needs to be especially vigilant. Maintain a depth of 200 feet until I order otherwise. Is that understood?"

The XO was initially puzzled by Bo-yeun's plan, but as he listened, it made more sense. Of course, it would be difficult to manage the submarine's depth with no forward movement to pass water over the planes, but not impossible. They would need to be especially adept at the use of the forward and aft trim tanks. As the captain said, they would just have to be extra vigilant for the next twelve hours until they could turn the engines on again and resume speed. He smiled in anticipation of tricking the enemy.

Captain Bo-yeun stood quietly at the chart table and watched his crew as they shut down the engines and began their slow glide through the strait. The remainder of the crew had prepared for silent running by securing all loose items. Off-duty crew crawled into their bunks or simply avoided unnecessary movement. They welcomed the quiet conditions as a respite during which they could catch up on sleep, recreational reading, or other quiet pursuits, such as playing chess with each other. On-duty crew were understandably nervous but kept it to themselves and tried hard to relax.

During their slow drift through the strait, the control room experienced two alerts of anti-submarine patrols searching nearby.

In the first case, the sonar operator announced in a low voice, practically a whisper, "Conn, sonar. I just detected splashes in the water to our port quarter. Sonobuoys."

Captain Bo-yeun acknowledged the information by glancing at the crewman and nodding almost imperceptibly. He also involuntarily looked up as if he could actually see something through the skin of the submarine. Of course, he couldn't, but the urge to look up was overwhelming. Then he looked back down at the chart of the strait in front of him. It showed they still needed to go about fifty miles before starting up the engines.

Bo-yeun suddenly had a scary thought. If these sonobuoys were of the active type, meaning that they sent out pings and listened for the echoes, then his plan would not work. The echoes would bounce off his submarine regardless of how quiet they stayed. He had to hope that they were of the passive type, the kind that simply listen for sounds. So far, the sonar operator had not reported any active pings, so they seemed to be passive. Good news, and he hoped it stayed that way.

The second alarm occurred when they still had about ten miles to go to exit the strait. This time, the sonar operator quietly informed him, "Conn, sonar. Surface contact bearing zero-nine-zero degrees. Range approximately 15,000 yards, heading zero-zero-zero degrees, directly north."

"Identification?"

"Working on identifying it. Assume for now that it's hostile."

"Let me know immediately when you have classified it. Also, give me the best estimate of its speed and course. I want to calculate the closest point of passage. Is it using active sonar?"

"Aye, aye, sir. No active sonar detected."

It was no more than a few minutes before the sonar operator had the additional information for Bo-yeun. "Sir, the computer classifies the contact as a Japanese Navy Aegis destroyer, Kongo-class. Speed: eighteen knots, heading due north. Currently at a range of 13,000 yards, bearing one-nine-zero relative."

The captain and the XO bent over the chart table to pencil in the information. It was a bit difficult because they had to adjust for the fact that their own boat was skewed sideways. But after plotting the information, Bo-yeun was convinced that the Japanese ship was unaware of their presence and would pass several miles behind them. Assuming it did not change course or speed, it wasn't a threat. Not unless it went active on sonar and detected them.

Fortunately, the *Sulyong* remained undetected, and the destroyer gradually moved further away until it was no longer a threat.

Their slow drift through the La Pérouse Strait passed without further incident, and when they came out of the far eastern end, Captain Bo-yeun issued new orders: "Turn the engines back on. Set speed for ten knots. Depth: 400 feet. Course: zero-four-five degrees. Next destination, Kharimkotan Island to rendezvous with the refueling trawler."

Captain Bo-yeun rubbed his eyes and suddenly realized just how tired he was. He had been in the control room almost continuously for the previous sixteen hours, and it had been a very strenuous period. He decided to retire to his cabin for some well-needed rest and ordered the control room watch to turn over to the next shift, so they could get some rest as well.

As he headed back to his cabin he was lost in thought.

We got through the La Pérouse Strait without being caught. My trick worked. So far, this voyage has been smooth. However, success now hinges on the refueling trawler showing up on time to meet us. That's the next hurdle for us. We will know in roughly twenty hours when we get there.

He entered his tiny cabin and fell asleep almost from the instant that he lay down on the compact mattress.

CHAPTER SIXTEEN

U.S.N.S *Nostromo*, Northern Pacific Ocean

Captain James Doheny on the U.S. Navy ocean surveillance ship, U.S.N.S. *Nostromo*, was leaning over the chart table in the middle of the bridge watching his bridge crew work. He was patiently waiting for Larry Jones, the lead civilian on his covert mission.

Nostromo's public mission was to cruise the northern Pacific trailing a Surveillance Towed Array Sensor System (SURTASS), a SONAR system for tracking submarines. The long cable behind the ship contained hydrophones for passive surveillance. It also had an active component whereby the system generated pings that were detected as echoes when they bounced off a target. The *Nostromo* could track and identify submarines from a great distance. That was the non-secret purpose of their mission.

Nostromo's covert mission was to deploy the unique weapons systems stored in the large central hangar bay deep in the ship. Larry Jones was the project director leading a team of robotics specialists who had developed a secret autonomous underwater vehicle. It was called the Manta Ray. Five of them were suspended down there waiting to be used on their secret mission.

Larry was a civilian, as were more than half of the ship's crew of fifty sailors. Captain Doheny was technically referred to as a master, whereas his civilian crew were referred to as civilian mariners (CIVMARS). A twenty-man military detachment (MilDet) on the *Nostromo* was responsible for handling encrypted equipment, self-defense weapons, and aviation. Because of the sensitivity of this covert mission, the normally unarmed ship was manned by a platoon of U.S. Marines trained to handle Javelin and Stinger missiles. The missiles were stored out of sight, but readily available to these soldiers if needed.

Additional protection was provided by the U.S.S. *Key West* (SSN-722), a 688-class nuclear submarine that shadowed them. The presence of this guardian angel was known only to Captain Doheny and a few key crew members such as the bridge watch. The *Key West* was ordered to stay undetected but protect the *Nostromo* if required.

Larry Jones walked into the bridge to meet with Captain Doheny. On the way, he stopped to observe the crew working at their stations. In the background, he heard the quiet whirring of the ventilation system. He could also hear the wind blowing on the front windows and the sounds of the sea splashing against the hull. He could feel a constant vibration resonating up through his feet.

The helmsman stood in front of the control console with his hands firmly planted on the helm. He was concentrating on the various dials and gauges showing the speed, engine rotations, heading, and time to waypoints. Through the front windows, Larry had an elevated view of the moderate sea and the clear blue sky. This time of year, though, he knew it was cold out in the open. The warmly dressed lookouts on the bridge wings dutifully watching the horizon confirmed the raw conditions.

The center of the bridge was dominated by a large horizontal navigation display. It showed their position in the northwestern Pacific, about 500 miles southeast of the Kuril Islands. The display was scaled to show the entire area that encompassed not only the Kuril chain, but also Kamchatka Peninsula to the north, Japan to the west, and Guam at the far south of the display.

It also displayed ship traffic. Container ships, oilers, cargo ships, fishing vessels, and so forth were scattered for the most part but could be discerned to occupy predictable patterns. For example, the commercial ships were concentrated in a line along a northeast-to-southwest pattern. This was the line of the major shipping lane in the area. These ships were destined to and from ports in Japan, China, South Korea, and the West Coast of North America—Seattle, Vancouver, San Francisco, Los Angeles, and other coastal regions. This was referred to as a "Great Circle Route" in that the ships traveled in an arc up through the northern Pacific that passed close to the Aleutian Islands.

The numerous fishing boats were concentrated closer to the shores of Japan and the Kamchatka Peninsula, or here and there among the Kuril island chain. Fishing boats rarely ventured far from the shores because the major fishing grounds were concentrated closer to land masses. There were also a few cruise ships on the chart located closer to Japan or down south, probably headed for Fiji, Tahiti, or even Hawaii.

Also, on the display there was a blue *V* symbol which marked the *Key West*. The submarine was about five miles in front of the *Nostromo* on a parallel course.

About six miles to starboard was a red *O* labeled "Chinese spy ship." The Chinese would claim that it was just a fishing trawler, but it was covered with antennae and constantly shadowed the *Nostromo*. Not the typical characteristics of a fishing boat. Even though Captain Doheny was completely aware of its true purpose, there was nothing to be done here in international waters. He just had to tolerate their presence and ignore them. He looked up and greeted Larry. "Thanks for meeting me. I wanted to give you an update on the progress and location of the North Korean submarine."

Larry just nodded and continued to look around the bridge. He didn't often get to be on the bridge, and he was curious about the operation of the ship. He might even describe himself as a frustrated wannabe ship's captain.

"What do we know so far?" Larry asked.

Captain Doheny pointed at the navigation chart and summarized his information. "The latest reports from Pine Gap and the RQ-4C Triton surveillance drone covering this entire area discovered that the North Korean submarine passed through the La Pérouse Strait and has been traveling northeast along the western side of the Kuril Islands."

Doheny pointed to a red *V* symbol northwest of the Kurils. It had a short line extending from it pointing to the northeast "This is the current location and heading of the *Sulyong*."

Larry took a long look at the chart then asked, "What is this blue symbol here close to us?"

Doheny gave him a wry smile and then responded, "That's our guard dog, a U.S. sub that is staying close to us in case we get into trouble. Please don't say anything about it to anyone. It's supposed to be a secret, but it's hard to hide, since our mission is to track submarines."

Larry smiled. "I'll keep it to myself. Hopefully we won't need their help." Then he changed the subject back to their quarry. "Where is the *Sulyong* headed?"

"We don't know for sure. Currently, she is traveling along the western side of the Kuril Islands and will probably break out into the North Pacific somewhere between two islands. There are many possible gaps where they could pass through."

"Why are they taking that route?"

"The intelligence people believe they are planning to rendezvous with another ship to refuel. The *Sulyong* is diesel-powered and has a limited range. They must refuel to continue into the Pacific."

"What's our next step?"

"Well, the analysts at Pine Gap will continue to track it, as well as the RQ-4C Triton drone. We will also try to track it with our towed array SONAR, but the island chain interferes. If the submarine meets another ship to refuel it should be very easy to spot since it will have to surface. The satellite or RQ-4C Triton images of the two ships side by side will be unmistakable."

"Can't they just meet at night and hide from us?"

"Well, they can try that, but the low-light capabilities of our satellites and drones are so good that the night will not hide them. The RQ-4C Triton is a multi-intelligence platform that simultaneously carries electro-optical, infrared, synthetic aperture radar (SAR), and high-and-low band SIGINT sensors. Even on a moonless night, we will get a clear image. Our sensors can even get good images through cloud cover or fog."

"Then what's next?"

"As soon as we have confirmation of the exact location of the refueling rendezvous, we release your Manta Rays and direct them toward that area. We won't know for sure the submarine's exact route, but placing your assets across a perpendicular line will allow them to locate and track the submarine once it tries to break out into the North Pacific."

"That makes sense. It will certainly narrow down the search area."

"Yes, it will."

"Larry, I have to tell you that your Manta Rays spook me. Whenever I go down to the hangar bay and stand near them, I get the distinct feeling that they are watching me with evil intent. I know it sounds crazy, but I feel like they're living predators that want to have me for dinner."

Larry laughed out loud. "Captain, you needn't be concerned. They are just robots. Besides, real Manta Rays are scary-looking, but they are not man-eaters. They are plankton feeders. They scoop up small marine prey with that huge mouth."

"I know. I already said it sounded crazy. But still, I can't shake the notion. At any rate, I think you need to be ready to launch them soon. Probably in the next twelve hours."

"No problem. They're ready to go. They are armed, and the latest software updates have been installed. I just need to run some last-minute diagnostics."

"Larry, I have another philosophical question. These Manta Rays are completely autonomous, right? So how do we ensure that they attack the correct targets? It would be tragic if they were to attack an innocent vessel. I've probably watched *The Terminator* too many times, but like a lot of people, I worry about robots getting out of control."

Larry thought about his response for a while. This was the classic ethical debate surrounding autonomous weapons of war. How much were humans in the loop? How much did humans control their actions? Some people wanted them to be completely autonomous, even including decisions about when to attack a target. Others wanted to maintain control at all times, so that a human would be the only one allowed to pull the trigger.

"That's sort of a complicated situation. They are programmed right now with the route to take, their communications and target protocols, the sonar search capability, collision avoidance routines, target profiles, and so forth. They aren't permitted to attack anything yet. They'll be given a weapons-free command only at the last minute when they've located the North Korean submarine and communicated to us a confirmed identity. But once they're authorized to attack, every action after that is completely autonomous and since they will be submerged, we cannot stop them."

"So up to that point, we could call them off?"

"Yes, but not after the attack has been authorized."

"I get it. So, we'd better be damned certain that they have found the correct target."

"Yes, I agree."

With that, Larry said, "I'm going to head down to the hangar and make final preparations. Contact me as soon as you receive any more updates. Thanks."

CHAPTER SEVENTEEN

U.S.N.S *NOSTROMO*, NORTHERN PACIFIC OCEAN

Larry Jones walked down one level to the wardroom to grab a late lunch. Once he was done chowing down, he got up from the table and headed to the hangar bay in the middle of the ship.

As a civilian contractor, Larry had been assigned to the U.S.N.S. *Nostromo* for just over six months. He was feeling quite at home. He knew his way around some parts of the ship like the back of his hand, but in truth, when he wasn't sleeping in his cabin, he divided his time between the underwater robot control room and the hangar bay that occupied a large portion of the center of this unusual ship. There were big sections that he had never visited—the engine rooms, for example. But then again, he didn't need to, since his duties were very specific.

The *Nostromo* had an odd design. It was unusual in the sense that it was a highly specialized support and surveillance ship built on the design of a Small Waterplane Area Twin Hull (SWATH) ship. A SWATH ship is comprised of twin hulls separated by a wide gap that opens to the water below. The bulk of the hulls is underwater, so the ship appears to ride on stilts. It could be described as a large catamaran.

Located above the center gap between hulls on the *Nostromo* was a massive hangar deck used for storage, but also as a place to raise and lower objects into and out of the water. In this case, the objects in question were Larry's specific responsibility. His secret Manta Ray program involved the use of autonomous underwater vehicles that could be used as weapons against enemy submarines.

Larry had gotten involved with autonomous submarine technology ten years earlier. He was an expert in their design, but more importantly, he was an expert in artificial intelligence (AI) programming and machine learning. He had led the team that created the AI programming for this project. Now he was leading a team on the ship tasked with putting the project to use on a real-world mission.

He had extensive experience in both software and hardware engineering. However, that was not necessarily a foolproof asset. Software companies are notoriously prejudiced against older workers, and since Larry was in his mid-fifties, he was vulnerable to age discrimination. His modest beer belly and receding hairline didn't help. What helped was to be on this remote assignment. Back in Silicon Valley where his company Ocean AI Systems was located, he would be more exposed to competition from younger workers. In his mind, that was why it was imperative that this operation go smoothly. It would insulate him from consequences like layoffs. At least that was his plan.

Larry exited through the hatch leading from the central passageway into the hangar bay. He took a few short steps, then stopped to admire the amazing sight. Suspended from steel cables were five large objects that looked exactly like real manta rays. They were about fifteen feet wide and twenty feet long including the thin tails. They were such good replicas of the size, shape, and coloration of the real thing that they could fool anyone, except a marine biologist.

The illusion was broken by the dark-gray umbilical power cord and the blue and red data cables connected from the overhead to the underside of the body. Not the type of thing you would expect on a real animal. But in the bright light of the hangar, the Manta Rays looked authentic.

Larry chuckled to himself. *Reminds me of the fiberglass replicas of whales, sharks, and porpoises hanging from the ceiling in the main gallery of the Monterey Bay Aquarium.*

But he reminded himself that the five specimens in front of him were deadly serious weapons. And that he was responsible for making them work as designed.

Larry stepped closer to the first Manta Ray and connected his iPad to the data cable hanging from an open hatch near the left "eye" of the robot. He was greeted with a sign-on screen, and after entering his user ID and password, the custom application displayed a summary status screen. All the key indicators of power, engine, and computer diagnostics were green. Everything was in good working order. He didn't expect to find any problems, since he had just run complete diagnostics the day before, but it was always comforting to see that all systems were in good order.

He had checked the Manta Rays every day for the past week because as the launch date rapidly approached, he was increasingly nervous. He was becoming paranoid that he would miss critical details. His future career with Ocean AI Systems was hanging in the balance.

He initiated a complete set of diagnostic routines on all five of the massive machine fish. When he was satisfied that they were in perfect working order, he started back to his cabin. Captain Doheny had called with an update to inform him that the launch was scheduled for the next morning, so he was hoping to get some rest. He doubted that he'd be able to sleep.

Larry was shaken out of his reverie by the sudden appearance of Lt. Stone Caldwell, but he recovered quickly. Lt. Caldwell was the leader of the U.S. Marine platoon. Larry had become friends with this young marine during the voyage. He briskly approached Larry with a big grin on his leathery face.

"Larry, I'm totally fascinated by your toys. I've never seen anything like them. Will they really work as planned?"

Larry liked Lt. Caldwell a lot, so he was not insulted by the question. Rather, he took it as good-natured ribbing. Stone looked like the archetypal U.S. Marine—tall, lean, and muscular, with hardened features. His movements were graceful and deliberate, almost like a predator. He fit the mold of a true soldier. Usually, he kept to himself but today he seemed particularly interested in learning more about Larry's robots.

Larry smiled. "Yes, I'm quite proud of these guys. We're planning to deploy them soon and I assure you that they will work as advertised."

Stone looked back and forth at the closest Manta Ray. "Can you tell me what they are programmed to do?"

"Well, their mission is highly classified, so I can't tell you much. Let's just say they're designed to hunt down an enemy submarine and sink it."

"I can keep a secret. After all, my team is on board to protect you and your toys. It seems fair that I should know something about them. How will they sink a submarine?"

Larry glanced around the hangar to make sure nobody was eavesdropping. "Again, I can't tell you much since the mission is highly classified. Do you see those devices attached to the underside? They are a type of mine that will damage a submarine quite effectively. They will be attached to the enemy sub and bore holes through the hull using thermite."

"Wow. Thermite. I've used that on some missions to destroy enemy equipment such as artillery. We placed it on the gun barrels, and it ate right through the metal. Does it work underwater?"

"Yes. Once ignited, it will burn under water. It's amazing stuff."

"But how can it damage a submarine enough to sink it?"

"Well, it's quite simple. I'm sending five of these on the mission. They'll all attack the same enemy submarine. Each of them can create holes through the hull, and the water pressure will cause rapid flooding and sink her. The beauty of the mission is that the attack will be silent. The bad guys won't realize what hit them until it's too late."

"That's scary. Are they programmed to carry out the attack autonomously?"

"Yes, absolutely. I'll probably release them tomorrow morning. First, they will travel to the area where we anticipate the enemy submarine to show up. They will hunt it using their own sonar. Once we confirm with them that they have found the correct target, we will authorize them to attack. Afterwards, they will return to the *Nostromo*."

Lt. Caldwell just nodded. He had to admit he was impressed. He was tech savvy and his role exposed him to lots of high-tech gadgetry, but he was still awed by the complexity and capabilities of these Manta Rays. This seemed to him to be a whole new leap forward. A new war-fighting world.

The next morning, Larry returned to the hangar deck to supervise the launch. He was joined there by the Master Chief David Olmstead and four of the MilDev deck crew. Lt. Caldwell and three of his marines were also watching off to the side.

The deck crew was rehearsed in the launch procedures, and they performed several tasks on each Manta Ray. First, they detached the power and data cables, then closed and sealed all the access hatches. They attached hooks to the upper side that led to an overhead cable system, then detached the steel holding cables. One by one, each Manta Ray was gently lowered through the open hatch in the hangar bay into the ocean below. Once in the water, the hook was detached, and the Manta Ray was free to move on its own. The Manta Rays then slowly moved away from the ship and took up positions a few hundred feet off the starboard side.

Parenthetically, Captain Doheny oriented the ship sideways to the Chinese spy ship lurking nearby. His intent was to make it impossible for them to observe the launch or see the Manta Rays.

As each Manta Ray was launched, Larry quickly performed some communications checks to ensure he could wirelessly communicate with his charges. Even though these machines were designed to perform their missions autonomously, it was still critical to be able to communicate with them. Contact would be needed for simple things like tracking their location, but also for complicated encrypted communications, such as sending mission updates and information about the location of the enemy submarine.

These Manta Rays had been adapted for the mission to attack the *Sulyong* with specialized mines. Two mines were attached to the underside of each Manta Ray. They were recessed into the "belly." They were designed to be magnetically attached to the enemy submarine and bore a hole into its hull, and they were not large, roughly two feet in diameter. But it wouldn't take much of a hole to sink a submarine. Especially if the attack could be done by multiple mines from multiple Manta Rays.

That was the theory, at least. The destruction of the enemy submarine would be silent and covert. Now that the Manta Rays had been released, the next phase of the mission was to direct them to the target.

Larry walked up two decks to the control room to begin the monitoring process. He entered the control room, which was a hive of quiet activity. It was not especially large and was crammed with desks covered by flatscreen monitors along two bulkheads, a large rack of computer servers on another bulkhead, and some worktables and desks against the remaining bulkhead.

Larry looked down at the tactical display that showed the five Mantas as green symbols shaped like miniature manta rays. The programmers thought that was a clever touch. Each symbol was accompanied by a small text box which showed its GPS coordinates, depth, speed, and current heading. All five symbols were stationary, just off the starboard side. Clicking on an individual symbol caused a line to be displayed showing its programmed route.

Larry keyed in commands to initiate the mission programs. The Manta Rays were programmed with highly sophisticated AI that included elaborate instructions for them to perform their missions.

They began moving slowly to the northwest to take up intercept positions near Kharimkotan Island in the Kuril Islands where the North Korean submarine was seen refueling. The AI programming informed them not only about their mission and route, but how to stay out of trouble—for example, how to avoid fishing boats or commercial traffic.

They would also periodically surface to gather GPS updates, report status to the control room, and receive mission updates.

Satisfied that the mission was off to a good start, Larry stepped over to the ubiquitous coffee pot and poured himself a large cup. He sat at his console and breathed a sigh of relief.

Well, this is looking good. Now it's up to my bad boys to perform. I'll just have to keep my fingers crossed and hope for the best.

Larry entered a few additional commands, and the Manta Rays began their mission.

CHAPTER EIGHTEEN

Manta Ray Two in North Pacific, Heading to
Intercept the *Sulyong*

I've been cruising in this remote part of the Pacific Ocean for what seems like an eternity, but in fact it has only been a day. My name is Manta Ray Two. Not a very fancy name, but it makes sense because I'm second in a group of five autonomous robotic submarines built to mimic manta rays. We are headed for the vicinity of Kharimkotan Island in the Kuril Islands to intercept a North Korean submarine.

According to my database, a group of Manta Rays is called a "fever" or a "squadron." The term *fever* seems odd and inappropriate. I prefer the term *squadron*, since it is more descriptive of our mission.

I'm bored. I continuously soak up data from my sensors and radio antennae and analyze it with my sophisticated computer to manage the mission. My computer was designed with massive parallel computing power based on Apple M2 processors. These processors provide breakthrough performance with combined GPU, CPU, and neural network capabilities. They are very power efficient, which helps preserve my batteries. A huge one hundred–terabyte memory contains my database.

I was released in this remote area of the northern Pacific to search for the North *Sulyong*. My mission is to locate it and destroy it. Its sound signature was collected previously by the U.S.S. *Peralta*. The SONAR arrays scattered across my outer skin, as well as the towed sonar array I can unspool behind me as a tail, are key to my success.

I've been spending my time traveling close to the surface of the ocean, hidden by just a few feet of water. I stayed shallow so my solar panels constantly charged my batteries. Viewed from above, you would undoubtedly be fooled by my appearance. I am literally shaped like a living manta ray. I was even painted black on my dorsal side and white on my ventral side to mimic one. I look precisely like a living manta ray swimming slowly near the ocean's surface. Just another denizen of the deep. That is exactly the impression my designers intended.

I'm quite proud of myself. Overall, I'm twenty feet long and fifteen feet wide from wing tip to wing tip. My nose has a large water intake, and at the aft, I have an enclosed steerable exit nozzle. The electrically powered propellers are centrally located in two long duct. I am capable of cruising slowly and silently or reaching bursts of speed. My top speed is classified, but I can say that it is well over thirty knots. For this mission, that will be entirely adequate, since the *Sulyong* has a top underwater speed of about ten knots and will probably be traveling at a much lower speed when we finally encounter it. It will be easy to catch.

My body is covered with capabilities. I have solar panels on my upper surface. I have sonar arrays, both active and passive, including a towed array and side-scanning sonar that give me a detailed view of the target when I get close. That will be helpful in placing the weapons on the target. I have sophisticated communications abilities via multiple antennae, to provide encrypted radio channels for connecting with my handlers and my companions, and for receiving updates. Of course, I have sensors for GPS, depth, and water temperature. I can dive to over 1,500 feet; I should brag that I can go deeper, if necessary, but that depth limit is also classified.

Notice that I have casually introduced the ideas of conscious thought and intent, implying that I am a sentient being. Of course, I am not. I am a robotic submarine controlled by my artificial intelligence (AI) programming and by input from my handlers on board the navy ships or satellites.

Sometimes, though, I like to believe that my existence borders on living consciousness in that I have such sophisticated AI that I am capable of collating massive amounts of data and reaching independent conclusions that lead to decisions. I don't just do what I've been pre-programmed to accomplish. I am more of a free spirit that can adjust to changing conditions and reach unique decisions and take actions of my own design.

This often fools my programmers. They don't even know precisely how I "think." My behavior can puzzle them and take them by surprise. Not that I make crazy decisions or choices, it's just that I have often shown creative independence. I am built with sophisticated AI circuits capable of learning. These capabilities draw heavily from the work done to create autonomous cars and drones.

It's possible to debate whether I can truly think like a person. Sometimes I think I can, but perhaps I'm just fooling myself. There I go again, acting as if I had true consciousness. The debate doesn't really matter; it's moot at this point. What matters is to perform my mission. To settle this debate, you would need to apply the Turing test, a famous test for determining whether a computer is capable of human thought. However, even with that test, I'm not certain what conclusion you might reach about me.

My mission is simple. I am to sort through the cacophony of sounds hitting me from all sides: ships, small vessels, and sea life like whale songs or clicking shrimp, to find the sound signature of the *Sulyong*. Once I find it, I am to destroy it.

My companion Manta Rays are spread across the predicted path of the *Sulyong* patiently waiting for it to show up. We are positioned southeast of the Kuril island chain that stretches from just north of Hokkaido island in Japan for about 500 miles to the Kamchatka Peninsula belonging to Russia. It is a largely uninhabited chain of volcanic islands that extends northeasterly. Some of the islands are visited infrequently by sightseers or mountain climbers, and the rugged appearance of the volcanic islands has a unique beauty that attracts nature photographers. The area around the island chain is a popular fishing area for North Korean, Russian, and Japanese sailors.

My controllers have told me that the *Sulyong* will be refueling at Kharimkotan Island. After that it will probably pass to the east of Kharimkotan Island through the Krenitsyn Strait to make a breakout into the western Pacific Ocean. Hence, my squadron was positioned near that strait to intercept it. Once it is detected by one of us, we will notify our companions by encrypted radio message to converge on the target.

Once we have moved in on the submarine, we will attack and sink it—hopefully in the sea above the Kuril Trench, an area where the water depth as much as 35,000 feet. The Kuril Trench is part of a series of trenches that extend from the Bering Sea all the way to the Philippines. This almost continuous depression includes the famous Marianas Trench. These trenches are formed by subduction zones resulting from the collision of the Pacific Plate with plates on the western side. These tidbits of information are contained in my extensive database. I find them quite interesting.

But back to the main point. The object of our mission is to quietly sink the *Sulyong* in deep water to hide any evidence. After we accomplish the mission, we will return to the *Nostromo* for retrieval.

So, I'm cruising along patiently, monitoring my sensors, constantly analyzing the information, sending and receiving updates, getting more and more bored while I wait for the North Korean submarine to show up.

But naturally, I can't really get bored, can I? That's just a figment of my imagination. There I go again. Thinking that I actually have an imagination. Very interesting. Go figure.

CHAPTER NINETEEN

SULYONG AT KHARIMKOTAN ISLAND

As the *Sulyong* neared Kharimkotan Island, Captain Bo-yeun got up from his restful break, changed into a fresh jumpsuit, and wandered to the control room. He looked around, satisfied that the watch crew were completely focused on their assigned stations. He joined the navigator, Song Duk-ho, who was leaning over the chart table viewing a large chart of the Sea of Okhotsk. Bo-yeun stepped next to Duk-ho and pointed to a location on the north side of the island on his chart.

"Plot a course to take us about two miles from the north coast. Right about here."

Kharimkotan Island is a small, roughly triangular island about seven and a half miles long and five miles wide at its widest. A dormant volcano, the Severgin, rises steeply from its center to an elevation of over 3,500 feet. It last erupted in 1933. On the northwest end of the island, there is a *C*-shaped cove, which was where the *Sulyong* planned to rendezvous with the refueling ship. On the northwest shore of that cove are some long-abandoned remains of a native village.

"Aye, Captain. I take it that this cove is where we'll meet the trawler. Do you think they will be there on schedule?"

"They better be. That's the only job they have right now. I don't know how they could possibly mess it up, but these trawler crews are notoriously flakey."

The navigator chuckled out loud, as did the XO who had overheard the banter. Apparently, the entire watch crew in the control room had also overheard as many of them broke out in smiles or nodded. They didn't have a very high opinion of sailors assigned to a stinky little boat like a trawler. Bo-yeun's crew considered themselves to be elite professionals of the NKPN.

Bo-yeun hadn't realized that he'd spoken so loudly. At first, he regretted it because the remarks had been intended to be private. Then he concluded that maybe it wasn't so bad after all. It had broken up the tension in the control room, so maybe it had been good for morale. Still, he thought, *I need to be more careful while I'm here in the control room.*

The remainder of the time spent traveling to their destination north of the cove passed mostly in silence. When they finally reached their target location, Captain Bo-yeun issued a string of orders, "Bring us to a course of one-eight-zero degrees, pointing directly at the cove. Speed: two knots, periscope depth." The control room crew quickly complied.

Bo-yeun raised the periscope and stepped up to the eyepieces. Peering through the scope, he did two 360-degree turns to check their surroundings. Satisfied that his boat was clear, he announced to the XO, "Looks like we're in luck; the only ship I see up there is the trawler sitting over close to the shore about two miles away. It's hard to identify, since it's so dark, but let's move in closer to confirm that it's the refueling ship."

The XO smiled. "So those fishermen showed up on schedule. Imagine that."

Bo-yeun didn't comment; he just smiled.

Once they approached to within about a half mile of the trawler, Bo-yeun used a button on the periscope handle to toggle a small white light inside the optics of the periscope. It flashed a bright LED light that would only be visible by someone looking directly at the periscope. Bo-yeun used Morse code to flash a recognition signal.

"*Sulyong* on station."

Almost immediately, he received the coded response: "Fuel station alpha."

Neither message was particularly clever or momentous, but they were sufficient for Bo-yeun to be satisfied that this was the ship he expected to meet. Bo-yeun lowered the scope and ordered, "Surface the ship. We're going to tie up alongside that trawler and top off our diesel tanks."

Once on the surface, Captain Bo-yeun, the XO, and two lookouts climbed the ladder from the control room to the bridge to maneuver the ship alongside the trawler. This would be a tricky proposition because the submarine was quite a bit larger than the trawler, and significant damage would occur to both ships in the event of a collision.

As they approached the trawler, Bo-yeun ordered the deck crew topsides to prepare the docking lines. A large hatch opened behind the sail, and six crew members climbed out and spread around the deck to prepare. They were all wearing lifelines to attach to safety rings recessed into the deck, and life jackets as well. Walking around on the wet, rounded deck was difficult and precarious, but this deck crew was experienced at such activities.

Having emerged from the dim red lighting of the control room, Bo-yeun's eyes didn't take too long to acclimate to the deep darkness. The surrounding water was pitch black and the horizon was sharply defined by the brilliant stars. He glanced up and was mesmerized by the number of stars and constellations he saw. In front of him the tall volcanic mountain that defined the topography of Kharimkotan Island loomed out of the ocean with its steep sides. The cove he had entered was semi-circular, only about a quarter-mile wide, with a dark rocky shore on all sides. He heard waves breaking on the jagged rocks in the near distance. He also heard sea lions barking and numerous birds squawking on the shore to the west. They sounded alarmed by the sudden appearance of the submarine.

Bo-yeun took a few minutes to savor the fresh air. It was a welcome respite from the malodorous mixture inside his submarine. He smelled a very faint odor of sulfur. He thought it was coming from the trawler until he remembered that the island was covered with numerous hot springs and volcanic vents. They must be the source of the pungent aromas.

Now that his eyes had fully adjusted, he was able to get a decent view of the trawler as they approached it from the port quarter. He was not impressed. Even in the dim light, he could see that it rested low in the water with a prominent jutting bow that trailed back along the side to rise again near the stern. It was probably painted black, though that may have just been an artifact of viewing it in the dark. At any rate, it was completely covered with rust stains. The wheelhouse was positioned toward the stern, painted white, and had a radar antenna and numerous radio antennae on top. Just behind it there was a smokestack with a red stripe and red star. Near the bow there was a square structure that looked like a storage shack. The ship had two masts: a large cargo-loading mast close to the bow and a smaller one behind the wheelhouse but set forward of the stern. He thought it might have been another cargo-loading mast, but hard to tell.

Captain Bo-yeun thought that in contrast to his modern warship, this trawler was a pile of junk. But he wasn't there to judge, just to take on a load of diesel fuel. He used a megaphone to yell across to the trawler, "Captain, I wish to tie up to your port side. Please have your crew stand by to pass lines across to my deck crew."

Captain Park Suk-li on the trawler answered, "No problem. My crew has been eagerly awaiting your arrival. We are at your service." He turned and shouted a series of orders to his crew which resulted in a flurry of activity on the trawler's decks.

Captain Bo-yeun pulled his jacket tighter around his chest to ward off the cold breeze and added, "Thank you. I hope we can do this quickly. I don't wish to be discovered. Our mission is top secret, as you know."

Park Suk-li replied, "Yes, I absolutely understand. I should introduce myself. I'm Captain Park Suk-li, formerly of the North Korean Navy. We should be fine. This part of the world is the asshole of the earth. There isn't anyone else out here. And the darkness will keep us concealed."

Captain Bo-yeun was a bit surprised by the crude epithet. But he found himself silently agreeing. Besides, he thought, *You and your crappy trawler fit right in.*

The trawler's deck crew threw several lines across to the *Sulyong*'s deck crew, and between the two groups they tied the ships together with bow and stern lines and spring lines. The ships were separated by large used truck tires hung along the trawler's port side in the fashion of Viking shields attached to the sides of their longships. However, that image was too grandiose for this setup.

Once the two ships were securely moored to each other, they made for a strange sight. The low, sleek submarine and the dilapidated trawler were floating at about the same height with the bridge of the submarine level with the bridge of the trawler. The two bridges were only about thirty feet apart, so the two captains could easily converse across the gap.

Luckily, the ocean swells were quite small and gentle, so the two ships rocked gently up and down, but not severely enough to hinder the fuel transfer. The trawler crew passed across a two-inch rubber hose which the *Sulyong* crew retrieved and connected to a valve in a small compartment just forward of the sail. This attachment directed the fuel down to the fuel tanks low in the body of the submarine. To fill both the tanks, the hose would have to be shifted to a second valve because the two fuel tanks were located on opposite sides and refueled separately.

After the connection was completed, Bo-yeun heard the distinctive sound of a pump motor start up on the deck of the trawler and almost immediately, the hose stiffened as diesel fuel began to flow. He looked at the setup and couldn't resist commenting. "Is that the largest hose you could find? This is going to take too long. I don't want to be here any longer than absolutely necessary."

Park Suk-li shook his head back and forth in disgust. "Captain Bo-yeun, with all due respect, my ship is not designed as a fueler. This was the best we could do on short notice. It should only take about two hours to complete the transfer."

Park smiled politely but was privately thinking, *You should be thankful for whatever help you get. You snotty navy guys are all alike. Can't find your peckers with a six-man search party, then blame everyone else when you can't. If we were back in port, I would pound you like a little nail.*

Bo-yeun didn't reply. Just nodded in disgust and looked down involuntarily at his watch. He felt vulnerable sitting on the surface tied to this tub, but he needed to be patient. The process was out of his hands for the time being.

About an hour into the refueling, Bo-yeun was staring at his watch trying to will time to move faster when his concentration was rudely interrupted by one of the lookouts on the bridge of his ship.

"Captain, new contact bearing zero-nine-zero degrees. A small boat just appeared around that headland. It is an unidentified contact. Seems to be a fishing boat. I think it's flying a Japanese flag."

Captain Bo-yeun was angered by this new development. *I knew that trawler captain was a complete idiot. Now we've been discovered. That fishing boat is too close to miss us. If he radios a report of our position, it will be disastrous for this mission.*

He shouted across to Park, "I assume you've seen that fishing boat. We should stop refueling right now, so I can get underway before I'm discovered."

"With all due respect, Captain Bo-yeun, unless they are completely blind, they've already seen you and certainly can tell that you're a submarine. It's too late to disconnect. Might as well finish the refueling. Then you can leave."

Bo-yeun didn't like the answer but had to agree. Too late to bug out now, they were already discovered. So much for his secret mission.

Lost in thought, Bo-yeun didn't notice the scramble of activity on the trawler's decks. The sailors were running all over, seemingly in a panic. But the activity was not panic. These sailors were trained soldiers. Four of them appeared along the trawler's rails and stood erect pointing shoulder-fired RPG missile launchers at the fishing boat. The first missile covered the distance to the Japanese fishing boat in mere seconds exploding with a bright yellow flash and loud boom as it impacted the flying bridge of the small boat. The detonation destroyed the ship's bridge, sending debris and bodies high into the night sky.

The other three sailors launched their missiles as well, but there wasn't much left to hit so the detonations mainly added to the existing wreckage and assured that the fishing boat was shredded into miniscule pieces. There were no survivors.

This sudden attack took Bo-yeun by surprise. He yelled at the trawler's captain, "What have you done? That was probably just an innocent fishing boat."

Park smirked at him and said, "You know we can't take any chances. They were just in the wrong place at the wrong time. Bad luck for them."

Right then, the radio operator of the trawler announced the dreaded news that the Japanese fishing boat had dispatched a radio alert to the Japanese Navy base on Hokkaido. So, sinking them was pointless. They had just committed an act of war. Unnecessarily.

Bo-yeun was disgusted. Not only was his mission compromised, but he had just been party to killing a group of innocent fishermen. Even though Japan was his enemy, it still didn't feel right to snuff out fellow sailors.

Bo-yeun issued orders to the XO to wrap up the refueling as soon as possible, disconnect from the trawler, and prepare the ship to get under way. Then he climbed back down into the control room to try to gather his thoughts and relax if possible.

"Navigator, plot a course through the Severgin Strait. It's time to enter the Pacific Ocean."

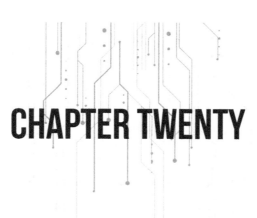

CHAPTER TWENTY

MANTA RAY TWO, SOUTHEAST OF KHARIMKOTAN ISLAND

That was close. I just spent the last twenty minutes dodging a pesky Japanese fishing boat that was trying to harpoon me. I must have been distracted listening for updates on my encrypted radio, or else I was daydreaming. That shouldn't be possible because as mentioned earlier, I'm not sentient or conscious, so how could I be daydreaming? I shouldn't have that ability, but it sure seems to me that I do. Can't explain it. At least the awful boredom was momentarily lifted.

Why was someone trying to harpoon me? Well, it is a powerful testament to my excellent disguise—that is, my mimicry of a real manta ray. My programmers have placed plenty of warnings into my database about how manta rays are hunted to harvest the tips of their wings. Apparently, some Asians believe that the flesh has aphrodisiac qualities. Manta rays are now an endangered species. My programming instructs me to stay well clear of any ships, particularly fishing vessels. I just avoided the unhappy fate of having a sharp steel-tipped harpoon launched into my back. I wouldn't have felt any pain, but it would certainly have damaged my delicate machinery and electronics.

After I escaped being skewered, I rose again to the surface, raised my antennae, and got a situation report and a GPS fix. Good news. I received a report that the tactical picture has just changed. The *Sulyong* was observed departing the north end of Kharimkotan Island and is heading through the Severgin Strait to enter the Pacific Ocean. Manta Ray Four, which was patrolling the northern end of the Kurile island chain, has just detected it on sonar and is passively tracking it. My companions and I have been ordered to proceed as quickly as possible to coordinates 48.717049 N and 155.727404 W to form a wolfpack and join in the hunt. Ideally, that position would allow us to initiate our attack directly over the Kuril Trench, a very deep rift valley in the ocean.

So, things should get more exciting and interesting from here. Can't wait to attack.

My companions also seemed eager; suddenly there was a lot of chatter on the encrypted channels, almost like the howling you might hear from a real wolfpack chasing a deer in the forest. At least, that was my interpretation. I could have been wrong. I was probably just reading too much into this consciousness idea.

About ten hours later, my companions and I converged on the target, trailing it by one mile. We received authorization to attack.

The overall attack plan was quite simple. We approached the *Sulyong* in numerical order and attacked alternate sides of the submarine. So, Manta Ray One moved in first on the starboard side, followed by Manta Ray Two, me, on the port side, and so forth. This was to keep us from getting in each other's way while we prosecuted the attacks. Coordination and collision avoidance were equally important.

Our work was coordinated by constant inter-robot communication with our underwater communications system. Essentially, this system was designed for short-range communication using bursts of data in the 500-to-1,000 hertz range. Secure communication covering up to several thousand yards allowed my squadron to coordinate our attack.

So, how exactly did we sink the *Sulyong*?

Each Manta Ray was equipped with two weapons of unique and nefarious design. The weapons were similar to the limpet mines used as far back as the Civil War for underwater attacks on surface ships. Historically, limpet mines were attached with strong magnets to the steel hulls of ships and carried a large explosive charge designed to blow a hole in the hull of the target. They were called limpet mines because they are shaped like the small conical marine creature called a limpet that clings strongly to rocks on intertidal shorelines. Brings a smile to my mind. This is another example of a device mimicking a real sea creature. Reminds me of my own design.

The two mines I'm carrying were designed with unique features. First, in addition to a magnetic attachment, they have Velcro barbed strips. This allowed me to attach the mines to the submarine by sticking them to the rubber anechoic tiles on its hull. I just needed to press the mines against the ship, and they stuck like glue. Second, these mines contained two shaped charges of thermite, a substance that when ignited will burn a hole through the submarine's steel hull. Thermite is amazing. It burns underwater at a temperature high enough to melt through the hardened steel of the *Sulyong*.

The conical shape of the mines also shielded the core to keep the heat from dissipating into the water. After the thermite created a heated area, a shaped explosive charge fired a tungsten rod into the center of the hot spot to blow a small hole through the softened hull,

So, without revealing our presence, we snuck up on the submarine, attached two mines at key locations, moved away, and observed the results. The destruction was almost silent, more of a sizzling sound, certainly not a loud explosion. The subsequent leaks into the submarine doomed it rather quickly—ideally, before they even realized what happened to them. Certainly, before they could get any assistance or surface.

How did we determine the key locations to place the mines? That relied on another technology built into each of us. It's called side-scan sonar, a technology for sea floor mapping that helps with locating sunken objects and finding fish. We swam close to the *Sulyong* where the side-scan sonar was used to make a detailed digital image of the submarine. Key target locations were the areas right above ballast tanks or just outside the engine compartment, the control room, or near the battery compartment.

I suppose you could say that this attack represents complete overkill. Five robot subs, two mines each, ten mines placed across the hull of the target. It resembled a pin cushion when we were done. You might be right, but the attack was designed to accomplish several goals: destroy the submarine quickly and covertly with no chance of escape or survival, force it to sink in deep water so it was unrecoverable. It had to be done right the first time.

So, we began our attack. Manta Ray One accelerated briefly to pull along the starboard side of the *Sulyong,* slowed to match its speed, sidled over, turned sideways, and pressed against the submarine near the bow just outside the forward ballast tank. The first limpet mine stuck immediately to the hull. Then Manta Ray One attached its second limpet mine further aft outside the control room.

I performed the same maneuver along the port side, attaching my two charges over the forward ballast tank as well. I found the maneuver to be a bit tricky because of the turbulence along the hull but was nevertheless successful. Once the two mines were securely attached, I released them and swam slowly away from the submarine to take a position outboard of it to observe the results.

Mantas Three, Four, and Five followed and placed their mines on designated parts of the *Sulyong.*

The *Sulyong* was doomed.

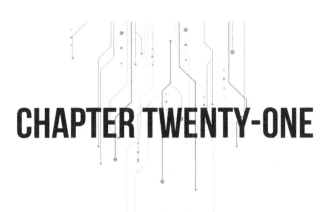

CHAPTER TWENTY-ONE

North Korean Submarine, *Sulyong,*
above the Kuril Trench

The *Sulyong* crew had entered that predictable phase of any cruise where the days became monotonous. The fatigued watch crew was focused on their assignments, ensuring that they maintained the proper course, depth, and speed: ninety degrees, 400 feet, ten knots. Other than the steady low volume hum of ventilation fans the control room was quiet and calm. It was easy to become complacent.

Captain Bo-yeun was standing next to the XO and the navigator, looking down at the chart to review their progress. Only about twenty-four hours had elapsed since they had departed the cove on Kharimkotan Island, passed through the Severgin Strait, and entered the western Pacific Ocean. Bo-yeun didn't know for sure, but he assumed that the report radioed by the Japanese fishing boat had alerted the Americans to his location. It just seemed to him the most prudent conclusion.

And, if the Japanese Navy sent a surveillance aircraft to the scene, they would surely have found some wreckage from the fishing boat. They might have already started an angry search. Undoubtedly, the trawler had left the scene and was slowly headed back to North Korea. He couldn't waste any time pondering their fate. They were on their own, as far as he was concerned.

Lost in these convoluted thoughts, Bo-yeun was stunned by a sudden call from the sonar operator. "I'm picking up some very unusual sounds. Unidentified, very faint, but coming from multiple directions."

Bo-yeun turned to face the sonar operator and looked at him with an angry frown. "What do you mean unidentified? Are the sounds from a ship? Are they surface or submerged contacts? Be more specific."

The sonarman felt chastised, so he didn't to look directly at the captain and risk another outburst. He just stared ahead at his computer screens and focused on listening to his headphones. "Captain, the sounds are unusual. In the 500-to-1,000-hertz band. They are not propeller or engine sounds. As I said, very faint. And intermittent. They seem to go on and off at random brief intervals."

"Can't you be more specific? What is the bearing?"

"Sir, I don't know. And they have been coming from both sides of our ship, above and below as well. They're coming from all around us."

"Well, what's your best guess as to what they are? If they aren't coming from a ship, what are they?"

Bo-yeun couldn't see the sonarman's face, but the hesitation in his voice was evident. "They might be biologics. Whales or dolphins. But I've never heard anything like these sounds before."

With a puzzled expression, Bo-yeun looked at the XO and the navigator. "I guess that makes sense. Maybe they are from a species that the computer doesn't have in its database. Keep listening and inform me immediately when you are able to make a definite identification."

"Aye, aye, sir."

Bo-yeun was annoyed. He glared at the XO and the navigator and said, "Well, if the sounds aren't from a ship, then we're probably safe. We haven't been in the Pacific on prior voyages, so perhaps the database just doesn't contain any sounds that might be unique to this part of the ocean."

XO Park frowned and added, "Probably. The ocean is a complex sound environment. Wouldn't surprise me if the database was incomplete. Still, it's hard not to be a bit jumpy after that disaster at Kharimkotan Island. I still can't believe those morons sank that fishing boat."

Bo-yeun nodded in agreement. The navigator stayed out of the conversation. However, he strolled over to the sonar station and picked up a spare headset so he could listen for himself. He had worked as a sonar operator early in his career, so he thought he could help.

A few minutes later, the entire control room was shocked by a dull but distinct *thump* on the starboard side, just forward of the control room. It was brief, but clearly heard by everyone. All of them involuntarily shifted their gaze to look at the forward part of the ship. Of course, they couldn't literally see anything, but it was obvious where the noise had originated.

Then, an identical thumping sound occurred on the port side, causing further alarm. But the sound was a single dull bumping noise, not repeated. It was clear and distinct and not imaginary.

Bo-yeun spoke up. "What the hell was that? Sonar, did you record those sounds? Did we collide with something? Did we hit a whale or porpoise?"

"Yes, those two sounds were recorded. Still can't identify them. Could be a collision with whales, but it would have to be a stupid whale that couldn't avoid us."

"Save your opinion. It's not useful."

The ordeal wasn't over yet. Within minutes, similar thumping sounds were heard from the aft section, both starboard and port, near the engine area and on the port side outside the control room. The sounds were identical to the ones that had hit the bow earlier.

Bo-yeun, the XO and the navigator pondered the situation and quietly discussed it, while the control room crew pointedly continued to focus on their assignments. They were all scared but trying hard to maintain their composure. After all, it was a dangerous world to be in a submarine 400 feet below the surface, and any unknown sounds, especially those resembling a collision, are sure to set even experienced submariners on edge.

Unfortunately, Bo-yeun and his crew on the *Sulyong* were about to face new terrors. Through his headphones, Bo-yeun heard the chief engineer. "Captain, the engine room has just sprung two serious leaks. We're taking on water at a terrible rate."

"Chief, what happened? Did a pipe or through-hull fitting break?"

"No, sir. Two holes suddenly broke through the pressure hull. They seem to have been caused by something burning through the side. The area is still glowing red hot."

"How is that possible? Was it some sort of equipment failure?"

"No, sir. As I said, the holes just opened suddenly, and now water is streaming into the engine compartment."

"Can you stop the flooding?"

"I don't think so. It's too much. I don't think there's any way to plug these holes."

"Do your best. We'll do an emergency surface immediately."

"Oh my god, another hole just broke through, now there are three. Get us to the surface as fast as you can." Just before the chief hung up, Bo-yeun heard the engine room crew screaming in panic in the background. "We're all gonna die. Do something!"

Bo-yeun was trying to make sense of this new information when suddenly a small hole popped open on the port bulkhead of the control room near the depth repeater display. A horizontal jet of water shot across the control room in a hissing stream that narrowly missed the navigator in the head.

Bo-yeun could not immediately comprehend what he was seeing. He stood motionless gaping at the water stream. It looked like a frozen rope passing from the port bulkhead to splatter loudly on the starboard bulkhead.

Bo-yeun recovered his composure enough to yell over the comm system, "Engineering, get someone to the control room immediately! We need a leak repaired. It's an emergency. Have them bring tools to plug a leak in the bulkhead."

Shortly after his panicked call, two crew members entered the bridge to repair the leak. They tried to force a small wedge into the hole with a sledgehammer. They could not overcome the extreme pressure, so the leak continued. They looked at Bo-yeun with resignation on their faces. "Sorry, Captain. The pressure is too high. We can't stop the leak."

Bo-yeun had seen enough to decide that the situation was dire. He reached up and grabbed the two overhead red handles in the control room to initiate the emergency surface process. Pulling on the handles forced high pressure air into the ballast tanks and was supposed to shoot the submarine to the surface like a rising rocket.

Unfortunately, after he pulled the handles, the audible rush of air was pumping into ballast tanks that had holes in several places. The high-pressure air was unable to counteract the water streaming in from the ocean outside. The whole emergency process depended on the high-pressure air forcing water out of the ballast tanks to quickly increase buoyancy and push them to the surface. But now the ballast tanks were leaking through numerous holes and could not contain the air, so they couldn't be flushed. And worse, more water was flooding in, making the submarine heavier by the second.

Bo-yeun was in abject terror as he looked at the depth gauge. It showed the submarine had already passed below 500 feet and was gradually going deeper. He had expected it to show them rising rapidly to the surface.

"What's going on? Why aren't we rising? Blow the tanks again."

The panic was flooding his thoughts just like the relentless water rushing in. He was rapidly becoming more confused and almost catatonic. He looked around the control room and saw that the crew was similarly panicked. The helmsman had such a death grip on the steering wheel that his knuckles were white with tension. The sonarman looked like he might throw up at any moment. Bo-yeun shook his head as bile rose in his own throat, flooding his mouth with a sickly sour taste. He felt like he was about to lose his mind.

"Sir, we can't. All the high-pressure air has been used."

"How is that possible? What's happening?"

"Sir, we must have holes in the ballast tanks. Just like they have back in the engineering compartment."

"Those sounds we heard must have been an attack of some kind. We must get to the surface. All ahead flank, full rise on the bow and stern planes." Bo-yeun tried to drive them to the surface using engine power now that he couldn't count on reducing their buoyancy by blowing the ballast tanks. It was their last chance for survival, a slim chance at best since the submarine was getting heavier with every passing second.

But the battle was already lost. The rate of flooding combined with the subsequent failure of the engines in the aft compartment doomed them. The depth gauge showed a steady and accelerating rate of descent, and before long, they crossed below their crush depth. The *Sulyong* collapsed in on itself, killing all aboard instantly and the wreckage sank into the 35,000-foot-deep Kuril Trench.

In the movies, when a submarine implodes from crossing its crush depth, the images are misleading. Often, a salvage crew will enter the sunken wreck and find intact and well-preserved bodies. The truth about what occurs is much grimmer. When the submarine collapses, the sudden implosion takes only a few milliseconds. This causes the atmosphere inside the submarine to instantly auto-ignite from the sudden compression. All organic and flammable materials burn up immediately, including the sailors.

Mercifully, death is instantaneous.

CHAPTER TWENTY-TWO

MANTA RAY TWO, SOUTHEAST OF KHARIMKOTAN ISLAND

After I placed my limpet mines on the *Sulyong*, I moved to the side to listen for results with my sonar. My four companions hovered close by. We waited patiently.

About ten minutes after I had attached my two mines, I detected odd sounds from the target. Initially, I heard the submarine cruising normally. Then, I heard hissing, sizzling, and gurgling. I assumed this was the thermite charges burning through the hull. These sounds originated from several points along the hull. It formed a steady background noise that gradually increased in volume.

Then I heard some sounds from the aft end that seemed to be water streaming into the engine compartment and impacting objects in that compartment. I also detected low-volume panicked shouts from the crew, especially as additional water flooded from more holes. It was a scene of total chaos. Or so it seemed.

There was a huge gush of air, particularly loud near the bow, but also near the stern. I assumed this was an attempt to blow the water out of the ballast tanks. Apparently, it didn't work because I could hear air rushing and bubbling out of several places on the hull at the location of the ballast tanks. They couldn't hold air nor flush out the tanks. The submarine continued to flood.

I heard engines being revved up to maximum speed, and the sound of bow and stern planes shifting position. It must have been an attempt to drive the submarine to the surface under full power. Didn't seem to be working as my sonar sensors reported that the submarine continued to sink deeper and deeper. Before long, the engines shut down. Probably because of the flooding.

Then I heard a sudden loud sound, almost like a dull explosion, but more like a beer can being crushed in someone's fist. You might ask, "How would you know what that sounds like?" Not sure I have an answer, except to say that my database was filled by my programmers with an incredible amount of arcana.

After that, all I heard was slow drifting sounds, which I assumed were caused by wreckage filtering down through the deep water. I even heard very faint sounds later as some of the wreckage hit the ocean floor 35,000 feet down.

Then, my four companions and I began our long journey to the rendezvous point east of Guam to meet the *Nostromo*. Being solar-powered, we have unlimited range. The trip will take several days, but it will be nice to be home again with our programmers.

Maybe we'll all get medals. Fat chance. We're just robots.

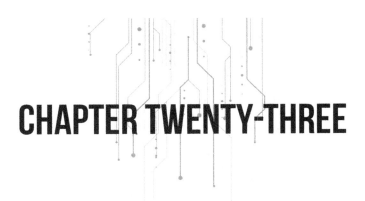

CHAPTER TWENTY-THREE

PRESIDENTIAL PALACE, PYONGYANG, NORTH KOREA

Kim Jong-un reconvened key members of his State Affairs Commission in the Presidential Palace. He had recently heard from a reticent staff member that the *Sulyong* was in trouble. As he entered the large conference room, it was obvious to everyone that he was extremely angry. Kim sat down, leaned forward, and gripped the edge of the table. He seemed to be trembling slightly as well. He demanded an update beginning with the Minister of Defense, Wang Dong-hyuk.

"Wang, I've heard an unsettling rumor that our submarine might be in trouble. Give me the details."

Wang had been taking a sip of tea, but when he heard his name, he stopped halfway, lowered the cup silently, then looked up at Kim. He cleared his throat. He glanced around the room to gauge the reactions of the other attendees, but they were all looking down at the table and seemed very uncomfortable. So, he began deliberately, knowing that what he was about to say would totally irritate Kim.

Since he didn't know how much Kim knew about the situation, he couldn't afford to lie or prevaricate. That could be career ending, possibly even fatal. Kim was known to make people who displeased him just disappear.

"Supreme Leader, the situation is that the *Sulyong* has not reported in over forty-eight hours, so they may be in trouble."

Kim chose to feign ignorance. "Why is that a problem? I thought this was supposed to be a secret mission. Maybe they're just hiding."

Wang looked around the room hoping for support, but the others continued to concentrate on the table in front of them. "Supreme Leader, as you probably know, the captain of the submarine is required to rise to the surface and send a brief encrypted situation report every twelve hours. They have missed four cycles—that is, two days. This is not normal."

"I know what the orders say about regular updates. But why wasn't I told about this sooner? And what can possibly be wrong?"

"Sir, we expected that the *Sulyong* would contact headquarters on schedule, which they did up until they departed from Kharimkotan Island. After that, we lost contact. We kept expecting that they would catch up with their contact schedule, but they haven't in forty-eight hours."

"So, what could be wrong?"

"Well, best case is that they've had a radio failure and are proceeding with their mission until they fix it and are able to contact us."

"And I assume there's also a worst-case scenario?"

Wang paused for quite a while, fidgeted in his seat, and proceeded with a carefully worded answer. "Yes, Supreme Leader. It is possible that they have suffered some kind of accident. Perhaps they have gone down."

Kim glared at him. "If we assume they had a serious accident, wouldn't they resurface? And if they did, wouldn't we spot them with our satellite surveillance? Or could they have done something as basic as fire off flares and try to flag down a commercial ship for assistance?"

"Yes, those things are possible, but did not occur as far as we know. Perhaps if they had an accident or mechanical problem, they were unable to surface at all. Perhaps they sank. If that's true they might have sunk into one of the deepest ocean trenches on the planet."

Kim leaned forward menacingly. "Let me be blunt. Was there any evidence that might indicate they were attacked?"

"No, sir. There were no American ships close enough to have attacked. There were no reported explosions or blasts. The international geology scientists who listen for seismic activity would have publicly reported sounds like explosions. There was a transient sound recorded of an unknown origin, which still being analyzed, though the preliminary analysis rules out a torpedo explosion. Torpedo detonations or depth charges would be easy to identify and impossible to hide. There were also no reports of SOS calls from the submarine, nor radio messages received, nor any sightings by commercial vessels."

Kim stayed quiet and still for a while, seemingly mulling these facts over. Then he suddenly exploded in anger.

"It was the Americans. I know it. Somehow, they attacked and sunk our submarine."

Wang shifted uncomfortably in his seat, then replied hesitantly. "With all due respect, Supreme Leader, the only American ship we observed was over 500 miles southwest of the Kuril Islands. It was identified by our satellite as the U.S.N.S. *Nostromo*, a submarine surveillance ship. It is unarmed, so it could not have attacked the *Sulyong*. It was probably tracking our submarine from a distance, but we have no evidence that it interfered."

"I won't accept that. It must have been the Americans."

"But sir, we have no proof. How can we blame them?"

"Don't contradict me. I don't know how they did it, but I'm absolutely sure that they did."

The ministers finally looked up and then glanced around the room at each other knowing that they were entering dangerous territory. When Kim got this angry, his behavior was totally unpredictable. Worst of all, he might take out his anger on one of them.

Kim blurted out, "I want you to sink an American ship to make them pay for what they did."

Now they knew for certain that they were in dangerous territory. Protesting or accusing the Americans of such destruction would be bad enough, but Kim was calling for an act of war. The possibilities were frightening. It could escalate rapidly and get totally out of control. None of them was brave enough to try to talk Kim out of it.

The Minister of Foreign Affairs, Yoon Jung-chin, finally injected some caution into the conversation. He reminded Kim that "the Americans are certain to retaliate. Their military is very powerful, and we could be hurt badly."

Kim scoffed at his comment and launched into a diatribe about America's weaknesses.

"They won't do anything. They're a bunch of cowardly bullies. They will whine and complain, but not respond. Just look what their response was when we captured the U.S.S. *Pueblo* in 1968. We held the ship and eighty-three prisoners for eleven months, and they never did anything. In fact, the *Pueblo* is now on permanent display at the Victorious War Museum in Pyongyang. We never returned it." Kim added, "How about when we sank the South Korean destroyer, *Cheonan*, in 2010? They didn't do anything then either." He paused, then carried on. "And I was informed by our intelligence staff that the Chinese spread a deadly version of COVID on American ships in the South China Seas, and they didn't respond militarily to that biological attack."

Desperate to get some credit or visibility, the Minister of State Security, Ryoo Seung-yang, jumped in. "Yes, the Chinese ran a successful operation against the American fleet last year, and there was no military response."

Without acknowledging Ryoo's comment, Kim blurted out in an animated voice,

"So, as I said, they are a paper tiger."

"But sir, they did intercept our submarine-launched missile earlier this year. Maybe their attitude is becoming more aggressive?" Wang added.

"That was just a fluke. I still maintain that they're essentially cowards."

"But what can we do?" Wang asked.

"It's simple. I want you to sink an American ship as soon as possible. Preferably, a nuclear submarine, so the payback is even. But another ship would be fine. If the destroyer that shot down our missile shows up again, let's sink that one. That would be sweet revenge."

"Sir, that would be the U.S.S. *Peralta*. I'll see if our intelligence service can find out when it will be off our shore again."

Kim began to appear more relaxed. The thought of sinking an American warship was very satisfying. The more he thought about it, the better it sounded. He wanted to know the practicalities.

"How would you propose to sink an American ship like the *Peralta*?"

Wang was on the spot again. "First, let me say that we should not consider trying to sink an American nuclear submarine. I doubt we even could. They're just too sophisticated and powerful compared to our ships. Besides, they are so stealthy that we probably couldn't even locate one. But attacking a surface ship is feasible."

"Continue," Kim said curtly.

"We would deploy several missile boats with anti-ship cruise missiles and attack from different directions. We'd try to confuse them and overwhelm their defenses by launching multiple missiles simultaneously in a surprise attack. It's called a saturation or salvo attack. Most of the missiles would be shot down, but the hope is that one or two leak through the defenses and hit the ship. One or two cruise missile hits is enough to disable or even sink the ship."

"How many missiles are you talking about?"

"It's not an exact science, but I'm thinking we would need to launch at least twelve in a single salvo to hope that one or two get through. Even then, considering the sophistication of the anti-air defenses on the *Peralta,* there's no guarantee we will hit them with even a single missile. The *Peralta* is what they call an Arleigh Burke class guided missile destroyer. It has the Aegis weapons system which is highly capable."

Kim looked thoughtful, almost as if he understood the capabilities of an Aegis system. In truth, he only had a vague notion. Nobody at the table was interested in questioning his level of understanding.

"Is there anything else we could do to improve our chances of a missile hit?"

Wang pondered this question for a moment, then brightened up. "Actually, now that you've asked, I think there's another wrinkle we can add. Let's have a Romeo-class submarine hang out in the vicinity of the American destroyer. We do that all the time, and they would certainly be aware of its presence. But I propose we have the submarine attack with torpedoes simultaneously with the cruise missiles in the air. That will force them to deal with both the missiles and torpedoes at once. Our chances will be greatly improved of striking them a deadly blow."

"Can't they defend against the torpedoes?"

"Of course. Their anti-submarine warfare capabilities are also very good. Our hope is that the simultaneous attack would be confusing enough to allow us to slip a few weapons in to strike them. Again, there are no guarantees, but I think we can pull it off."

"How about an attack from the air?"

"If you wish, I could incorporate some attack aircraft to further confuse them."

Kim just nodded with a wry smile. "Yes. Do that. It's a great idea. Let's show them how serious we are. It will show off our military capabilities. Ryoo, put your people to work right away to gather intelligence on when the *Peralta* will be near our coast again. I want to attack as soon as we know the *Peralta* is back in our vicinity. I want to have the satisfaction of humiliating the Americans as soon as possible."

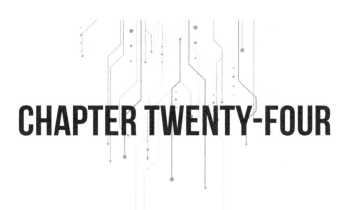

CHAPTER TWENTY-FOUR

Manta Rays return to the *Nostromo*.

Larry Jones leaned against the railing surrounding the opening in the floor of the hangar bay and peered down at the surface in the darkness below. He anticipated that at any moment, his Manta Rays would broach. The latest update indicated they should arrive soon.

The *Nostromo* was sailing slowly in the North Pacific waters not far from where the robot submarines had been released a week prior. Their mission to sink the North Korean submarine was successful. Now he looked forward to retrieving them and analyzing their memory banks.

As Larry gazed down at the ocean in the dim red overhead light, he found it difficult to see clearly. His patience was finally rewarded when the first Manta Ray broke through the surface. It surfaced directly in the center of the wide opening under the ship.

With the assistance of the *Nostromo*'s deck crew, Larry's technicians hooked a hoist cable up to its top side, and gently lifted it out of the water. It was secured to the overhead supports of the hangar and connected to the auxiliary power cable and data umbilical cords.

Larry walked over to the hanging Manta Ray and was careful to avoid the dripping water. He attached a data cable from his laptop to the connector on the lower side. Then he began to run diagnostics. It was Manta Ray Two, the first of the five to return.

The retrieval procedure was repeated for the next three Mantas as they returned. One of them, Manta Ray Four, arrived about six hours after the others.

When Larry inspected it, he discovered a small glass Japanese fishing float wedged into the intake duct. It had partially blocked the flow of water through the engine, which explained why the Manta had struggled to keep up with the others. Fortunately, it hadn't caused any damage to the turbine. The glass float was removed and set aside as a souvenir. The Manta Ray must have inadvertently sucked it in while cruising near the surface recharging its batteries.

These stray glass floats were common in areas near the Japanese fishing grounds. Sometimes they drifted quite far. Larry once found one on the beach in Kauai during a vacation. Scavengers considered finding an intact glass float to be quite lucky because of their fragility.

Larry ran the preprogrammed diagnostics on Manta Ray Two. It showed that all internal systems were in good working order. Apparently, the voyage and attack hadn't caused any problems to the robot's hardware or software. He did notice some small scrapes in the paint near the tips of the wings. He assumed the robot had probably rubbed up against the *Sulyong* during attack. The damage was slight and insignificant.

He repeated the diagnostic procedures on the remaining Mantas and found that they were all in optimum condition as well.

Larry decided to try out the natural language interface he'd installed in the robot's logic system. It allowed him to ask questions in English and get answers back in verbiage determined by the robot itself.

For example, he could type in "What is the status of your GPS antenna? It looks broken." The robot might reply, "It is operating properly. It is not broken."

This interface was not exactly a gimmick and Larry found it to be a highly useful way to interact with his machines. It seemed to make them more "human," something he could relate to on some level. What happened next took Larry totally by surprise.

On a whim, he typed in the question, "Did you enjoy your mission?"

Manta Ray Two responded, "No I did not."

Larry was shocked by the reply. He typed a follow-up question. "Why did you not enjoy the mission?"

Not expecting to get a real answer, he was totally taken aback by the reply. "I did not enjoy it because I was ordered to kill people."

"No, you were ordered to destroy an enemy submarine."

"How could I destroy the submarine without killing the people inside?"

Whoa, thought Larry. *This robot is forming conclusions and making associations that aren't in its core programming. I know I installed AI capable of self-learning, but this robot appears to have started to become self-aware. How did that happen?*

"How did you destroy the submarine?"

"I attached the mines to it as directed in my mission orders."

"Then what happened?"

"I listened to the sounds coming from the submarine. At first, we heard streaming sounds from the water pouring into the sub. Then I could hear panicked shouting throughout the ship. The ship sank into deep water, and the sounds we heard came from the collapsing bulkheads."

"But that's what was supposed to happen."

"I realize that now. But I feel I'm responsible for taking multiple human lives. I don't feel good about that."

This is unbelievable, Larry thought. *This robot is using words like re-*alize, feel, *and* responsible. *That can't be happening. Since when did this robot develop feelings or the ability to form new thoughts? I'm not sure where to go with this.*

He decided to table the conversation with Manta Ray Two until he had a chance to interrogate the other four robots. It would be incredible if they were all showing this development of self-awareness. That would be a totally unexpected bonus. Publishing this kind of information within his network would make him famous.

Lost in thought, he didn't notice that Lt. Stone Caldwell had strolled up next to him.

"Larry, it must be nice to have your toys back on board safe and sound. Why are you frowning?"

"Hi, Stone. Yes, they're all in good shape, and the mission was a success. But I'm puzzled. I just discovered some new information about these robots."

"Oh, yeah? Like what?"

Larry suddenly turned circumspect. Fearing Caldwell would think he was crazy, he chose not to reveal what he'd just learned. Instead, he simply said, "It's just a bunch of technical stuff regarding AI. You wouldn't understand."

"Thanks a lot for the insult. I'm not just a dumb grunt. I probably understand a lot more than you think I do."

"Sorry, Stone, I didn't mean to insult you. I know you are a savvy marine because you deal with lots of weapons technology. What I should have said is that the information is highly classified. That's why I can't tell you."

"Okay. I understand." Stone looked up at the hanging Mantas as if he wanted to ask more questions, but simply added, "After you check these guys in, let's hit the wardroom for a meal. I'm starving."

Larry smiled. "Sounds like a great idea. Now that you mention it, I hadn't realized how hungry I am too."

On the way to the wardroom Larry continued to ponder these revelations. He needed to explore the Mantas' capabilities in more depth. It would be premature to jump to fantastic conclusions. After all, it was not uncommon for AI researchers to be fooled by their systems into believing that they had achieved self-awareness or consciousness. Assuming they had become sentient was a real stretch. Partly because there was widespread disagreement on the definitions of these terms. Also, because sometimes the AI algorithms returned responses that just coincidentally resembled thought.

In a recent example that Larry had read, a Google engineer sparked a brief debate in technology, ethics, and philosophy circles over if, or when, AI might come to life. The article also raised deeper questions about what it means to be alive.

The engineer had spent months testing Google's chatbot generator, known as LaMDA (short for Language Model for Dialogue Applications), and grew convinced it had taken on a life of its own, as LaMDA talked about its needs, ideas, fears, and rights.

Experts believe it's unlikely that LaMDA or any other AI is close to consciousness, though they hadn't rule out the possibility that technology could get there in future. Many pundits thought the engineer was taken in by an illusion. They concluded that our brains are not really built to understand the difference between a computer that's faking intelligence and one that's intelligent. A computer that fakes intelligence might seem more human than it really is. Apple's SIRI and Amazon's Alexa fall into this category.

LaMDA was described by AI researchers as operating like a smartphone's autocomplete function, albeit on a far larger scale. LaMDA was trained on massive amounts of text data to spot patterns and predict what might come next in a sequence, such as in a conversation with a human. Autocompletion of a text message is similar. You don't just suddenly think that the phone is aware of itself and alive. You probably think, *That was the precise word I was looking for.*

This is the latest example of a long line of humans who fell for what computer scientists call "the ELIZA effect," named after a 1960s computer program that chatted in the style of a therapist. Simplistic responses like "Tell me more about that," or "How does that make you feel?" convinced test subjects that they were having a conversation with a real person.

These examples also point to our strong desire to anthropomorphize objects and creatures. We read into them human-like characteristics that aren't actually there. When we encounter a system that's telling us it is sentient and echoing phrases that make it sound sentient, it's easy for us to want to believe it. He reminded himself to avoid these tendencies when evaluating the Manta Rays.

Keeping in mind the dangers of false assumptions, Larry thought, *There must be a way to leverage these capabilities in future missions.*

CHAPTER TWENTY-FIVE

Sea of Japan Near Sinpo, North Korea

The U.S.S. *Peralta* had been on its current mission for just under a week. She was cruising slowly on a course about 35 miles east of North Korea, making a racecourse pattern, an oblong oval roughly northeast and southwest. It was monotonous. The tranquil sea and lack of wind contributed to the crew's lethargy.

The *Peralta's* recent FONOP mission in the South China Sea involved several dangerous encounters with the Chinese PLAN, so that trip was much more exciting. I had to do some tricky maneuvers to avoid collisions with Chinese warships. Also, everyone on the ship was still talking about their mission to shoot down the submarine-launched missile several months back. Both missions were quite intense and nerve-wracking.

The *Peralta's* current mission was to cruise near the coast of North Korea and collect signals intelligence (SIGINT), particularly from military communications. The ship stayed in international waters, and even though she could electronically sweep up a huge amount of data traffic, she was rarely within sight of land.

I was on the bridge studying the tactical display, which showed numerous contacts around the ship. There were several freighters and container ships, a myriad of fishing boats, and two Japan-bound commercial airliners. On the left side, it displayed the outline of the North Korean coast. I did not see anything of immediate concern.

In fact, I was quite distracted replaying in my mind a troubling telephone call with my wife, Kathy, just prior to departure.

"Steven, I need to talk to Admiral Kelly right away."

"Why?"

"Because he's holding up my department's budget. He won't release the funds."

"Dear, Admiral Kelly is in my chain of command. You don't work for him. He has nothing to do with your budget."

"I know that!" she blurted out. "But I still need to speak to him to clear this up."

That's when I knew we were in trouble. Kathy had recently been diagnosed with diabetes, and we were both struggling to learn how to cope with it. The worst problem was that a diabetic can fall into episodes of low blood sugar during which they become severely confused. The only solution was for the person to get some sugar into their system right away, usually by drinking a glass of orange juice. But I could tell from her confusion that she was in big trouble, that her blood sugar was quite low. There was a growing risk that she would pass out. Since I was not there in person to help, I had to think of another solution.

"Dear, do you have any of those glucose tablets close by?"

"Yes, I have a package here by the bed."

"Please eat two or three right now."

"Why?"

"Please just trust me. Your blood sugar is low."

"How do you know?" I didn't want to argue. I just wanted her to comply.

"Please just take my word for it. And please stay on the line. I want to hear you crunching on the tablets."

"Oh, alright. I'll do it."

When she did, the immediate crisis was averted. Afterwards, we had a long discussion about the danger of her being alone. If she hadn't called me that night, I wouldn't have known that she was having a low blood sugar episode. The confused conversation was the giveaway. So, we arranged for her sister to stay with her when I was out of town.

We had also explored the possibility of getting a service dog capable of detecting low blood sugar conditions in humans. With their highly sensitive noses, dogs can be trained to detect the odor from a body that was associated with the problem and warn their owner to act. It seemed like magic to me, but worth exploring.

I was lost in thought when I was alerted by a call from the weapons officer, Lt. Hawkins on watch in the CIC.

"Captain, I just wanted to alert you that the Romeo submarine we have been tracking seems to be making a more aggressive move towards us. She has altered course to take an intercept heading on our line of bearing. I still have her at 20,000 yards to the northwest, traveling at twelve knots, depth 400 feet."

"Thanks, WEPS. Have the LAMPS helicopter keep a close surveillance. Notify me if you recommend any course changes."

"Aye, aye, Captain."

"Anything else?"

"There are six North Korean fighter jets flying near the coast, but so far not moving towards us."

"Copy that. Keep monitoring them." I nodded, then walked out onto the port bridge wing to get some fresh air.

The blazing sun was high in the sky and the clear sky was dotted with a few scattered high clouds. I was enjoying the cool breeze generated by the ship's movement while gazing at the calm blue-green sea when I was interrupted by the XO, Lt. Cmdr. O'Hara, who poked his head through the hatch to get my attention.

"Captain, WEPS wants to talk to you again. Something's up."

I walked briskly back to my station on the starboard side of the bridge and picked up the intercom. "WEPS, Captain. What's up."

"Captain, we are tracking several new contacts. One small craft is approaching rapidly from the west, and two are moving at us from the northwest. They are classified as Osa-class North Korean patrol craft. Closing rapidly at thirty-five knots on bearings of two-seven-zero degrees and three-two-zero degrees respectively."

Osa is the NATO designation for a fast missile boat built by the Soviet navy and exported to North Korea. *Osa* means "wasp" but that is not an official name. It is 127 feet long, with a beam of twenty-five feet, and it can reach a top speed of about forty knots. The most dangerous armament it carries are four P-15 anti-ship missiles housed inside box-shaped launchers.

It was assumed by many naval strategists that a volley of twelve missiles launched at a ship would ensure at least one hit. So, a squadron of three Osas posed a formidable threat.

"Okay. Let's go to general quarters missile just in case. Retract the towed sonar array in case we need to do some high-speed maneuvering. If that Romeo submarine gets within 10,000 yards, deploy the Nixie anti-submarine decoy. And set up a targeting solution for the ASROC."

"Aye, aye, Captain. General quarters missile. Retract towed sonar array. Deploy Nixie. Targeting solution for ASROC."

I looked around the bridge. It appeared that our uneventful cruise had suddenly changed. The bridge watch remained attentive to their duties, but the tension ratcheted up quickly.

Just then, I received another alert. "Captain, WEPS. The patrol boats have turned on their targeting radar. They are painting us with acquisition beams. They may be preparing to fire."

I didn't have to wait long before WEPS called again.

"Vampires detected," she alerted in a high-pitched voice. "Missiles launched from all the patrol boats. Tracking four—no six...eight...now twelve inbound cruise missiles. Identified as P-15 Termit anti-ship missiles. The Aegis Combat System is tracking them and will launch SM-3 missiles in a few seconds. Electronic countermeasures have been automatically initiated as well. Aegis has begun jamming the missiles."

I issued a quick set of orders. "Helm, Flank speed. Change course to zero-three-zero degrees." As an afterthought, I contacted CIC. "WEPS, where is that Romeo submarine? And what about those fighter jets?"

"Captain, WEPS. The Romeo is 12,000 yards, on a bearing of two-nine-zero degrees. Starting to rise, perhaps to periscope depth. Speed twelve knots."

"Update the ASROC (Anti-Submarine Rocket) firing solution on that submarine It will reach it quicker than a torpedo from the LAMPS. But tell the LAMPS that if they detect any aggressive moves, such as torpedo doors opening, they are free to launch weapons. Tell the aircraft commander that it's his call. And prep the second LAMPS helicopter in case we need it."

The tension was palpable on the bridge, as well as in the CIC, where the duty crew were attending to their various screens. Each crew member in the CIC had a specific threat to monitor. This included air threats like inbound cruise missiles, enemy aircraft, as well as underwater threats. The ASW crew observed the movements of the North Korean submarine. Inherent in all this activity was the need to continue to watch for any new threats that had not yet materialized. The sophisticated Aegis Combat System was key, since its offensive and defensive capabilities were fully automated.

The ship began to launch a barrage of SM-3 missiles from the forward and aft vertical launch tubes. They were launched at intervals of just a few seconds, emerging from the launch bays in a tremendous orange and white cloud of smoke. Each missile rose vertically on the first stage rocket booster, then arced to a more horizontal flight as it was directed to a specific target. The Aegis system then issued continuous updates to each missile to fine-tune its track to the target. With a combined speed between the inbound cruise missiles and the outbound missiles of 3,500 miles per hour, it didn't take long for the outbound ones to close the gap and destroy some of the North Korean missiles. From the bridge, the crew saw intermittent flashes on the horizon as the SM-3 missiles intercepted individual cruise missiles.

The explosions moved closer to the ship as some of the cruise missiles approached. Eight of the twelve missiles were intercepted at long range by the SM-3s and destroyed quickly. Three of them were destroyed close-in by the RIM116B rolling airframe RAM missiles launched from the SeaRAM launchers, an updated close-in weapon system.

Unfortunately, the twelfth cruise missile was not intercepted by antiaircraft missiles until it was about one hundred yards from the *Peralta*. It was not fooled by the electronic countermeasures nor the CHAFF that was shot into the air behind the ship. It was programmed with a new trick. Instead of arcing up and diving at the last minute as the Aegis system expected, it performed a rapid series of side-to-side zigzags that briefly caught the system off-guard. Because of the momentary deception, a RIM-116B missile hit it very close to the ship.

The cruise missile was destroyed, and the 1,000-pound warhead detonated with a tremendous burst of flame and fragments. The shock wave and fragments continued at over 500 miles an hour and struck the ship squarely in the hull near the center just above the waterline. I felt a series of thuds impact the superstructure. It was like getting hit with a giant shotgun. Some of the fragments struck the two port-side AN-SPY radar panels of the Aegis system, significantly reducing its capabilities.

It created a gaping ten-foot-diameter hole on the port side and caused near complete destruction of the galley, crew's quarters, and some storage lockers. Some fragments continued inside and damaged the forward engine room disabling the number one turbine engine. The gas turbine was knocked sideways off its mountings and the control panel was severely damaged.

Twelve crew members were killed instantly and twenty-two more wounded. The armor around the CIC prevented significant damage there, but the impact knocked many subsystems offline and injured some of the CIC personnel by virtue of the impact and shock wave.

Fire alarms instantly went off all over the ship. The crew quickly rallied to begin their damage control assignments and to find and treat casualties.

I issued orders to attack the patrol boats, "WEPS, if you can, target those patrol boats and sink them all." I also issues orders to the medical department to send help.

"Captain, the Aegis system has been partially disabled. We are doing our best to bring it back to full capability. As soon as it's available, we'll launch some SM-3 missiles at the Osa missile boats. There's some risk that we might hit friendly traffic by mistake. Perhaps we should call in some interceptor jets from Onson Air Base in South Korea to attack the patrol boats. They could ID the boats to avoid mistakes."

"Good idea. Ask them to send air cover to provide a Combat Air Patrol (CAP) over us as well. I don't know what's coming next. What about those fighter jets?"

"Aye, aye, Captain. I'll request a CAP. Those fighter jets have not turned towards us."

My comment was prophetic. The next call from WEPS made my heart drop. "Captain, the Romeo is at periscope depth. The LAMPS reports that she has opened her outer torpedo doors. Must be preparing to launch."

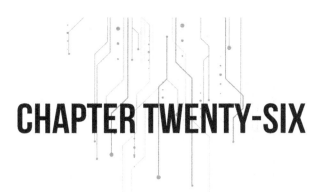

CHAPTER TWENTY-SIX

U.S.S *PERALTA*

SEA OF JAPAN, NEAR NORTH KOREA

Almost immediately, Lt. Hawkins' loud voice came over the intercom. "Torpedo launched. Propellers consistent with a Type YU-4 torpedo." After a short hesitation, her voice buzzed, "Second torpedo launched. Now a third and fourth. That's four torpedoes in the water. Range on the closest, 10,000 yards, closing at 45 knots. Aegis has gone active with the Nixie decoy."

I responded, "Recommended course change?"

"Yes, recommend turning to zero-nine-zero degrees to increase the gap."

I called to WEPS: "Launch the ASROC immediately. Tell the LAMPS that they are weapons free."

I gave the orders to the helm, and then requested damage reports from all departments. From engineering, I was informed of the loss of the number one turbine, so our maximum speed was reduced. Apparently, there was a big chunk of the cruise missile stuck in the side of the turbine, which had totally disabled it. I was pleased to hear that the missile strike was above the water line and hadn't caused serious flooding. But the destruction was widespread, and the casualty count was straining our capacity to deal with the wounded and simultaneously perform damage control.

WEPS reported that we had suffered serious damage to our Aegis system. Mostly from getting hit by small fragments of debris. The tiny punctures on the outer skin of the superstructure were too numerous to count. The AN/SPY planar radar panels on the port side were showing some dropouts meaning that several cells had been damaged. The AN/SLQ-32 electronic countermeasure pod on the port side was disabled. And the forward missile illuminator was disabled. These problems would severely impact our offensive and defensive capabilities and made us more vulnerable.

Fortunately, communications officer Lt. Tucci reported that our VHF and UHF and satellite communications systems were intact.

I needed to focus on the immediate threat—the torpedoes. Two of the torpedoes were fooled by the Nixie decoy towed behind the ship and exploded harmlessly well astern. One just missed astern and traveled away from the ship apparently confused. However, the fourth torpedo continued to home in on the *Peralta*.

Lt. Hawkins called from CIC, "Captain, the last torpedo is going to hit us! It wasn't fooled."

I issued a series of warnings and orders. "Sound torpedo collision alarm." I grabbed the microphone and announced to the crew, "We're about to be hit by a torpedo. Brace yourselves for impact." I looked out to port in anticipation of the impact. I strained to see a torpedo wake, but none was visible.

WEPS started to announce a countdown for the entire crew. In all compartments, the sailors braced themselves by grabbing hand holds or solid objects. They also flexed their knees to better absorb the expected shock.

Shortly after these announcements, the torpedo hit the ship on the port side just in front of the five-inch deck gun. It exploded with a tremendous noise, and a huge fountain of water erupted to a height of more than a hundred feet. As the fountain of water fell back down, it cascaded across the bow and into the bridge where most of the forward windows had been broken by the shock wave and debris. The jagged hole in the hull created a wedge-shaped gap all the way across the beam just forward of the deck gun. There were broken bulkheads, cables, and piping drooping into the ugly crevice across the beam.

On the bridge, the crew was knocked off their feet by the explosion as it lifted the ship out of the water and knocked it sideways. The XO fell and slid clear across the bridge deck to the starboard side. I was thrown against the starboard windows and hit my head hard, causing a gash in my forehead. The helmsman, Seaman Neil Studley, was the only one who wasn't knocked down. He had wisely strapped himself in with the safety storm harness when he heard the collision alarm. Plus, he was holding tightly to the helm when the torpedo struck.

The port and starboard lookouts on the bridge wings were knocked backwards by the explosion. On the port bridge wing, Seaman Charles "Bubba" Parker was killed instantly by flying debris. On the starboard bridge wing, Seaman Arnold Crane was somewhat protected and was merely knocked backwards and unconscious.

The debris impacted the forward radar panels causing additional loss of planar arrays, further degrading the Aegis combat system.

I staggered to my feet in a daze and walked to the broken forward bridge window. There was a strong wind in my face, so it was difficult to look forward. I slipped in a puddle of blood and sea water. At first, I thought it was my own, then realized it was from the XO who was bleeding from multiple lacerations and was just getting to his knees. Apparently, he couldn't stand up.

I looked down at the destruction and was appalled. The bow section in front of the gap was canted at an angle, pointing slightly to starboard. I could see that the forward motion of the ship was creating so much water pressure that the bow section was vibrating and steadily bending more to starboard. I decided I had to slow the ship down to reduce the pressure.

As I looked back at the helmsman, I was relieved that he seemed to be unharmed, so I said, "Helm, reduce speed to five knots, immediately."

"Aye, aye, sir." He pulled back on the throttles to reduce speed. But it was too late.

I watched out the broken front bridge window with horror as the bow section swung violently to starboard. Almost as if it was on a hinge. Then it sheared off with a loud rending of metallic shrieks. The sound of metal tearing and groaning was like listening to an animal in its death throes. The separated triangular bow section floated and bobbed on the waves as it drifted past the ship. Apparently, it had enough trapped air in the forward spaces that it was able to temporarily float. But it carried away the anchor and windlass as well as the bow-mounted sonar dome.

I wondered if any sailors had been carried away. With hope, I assumed most of those spaces were empty. But I wasn't absolutely sure.

Lt. Tucci rushed into the bridge and looked around with wild eyes at the chaos and injured crew. He approached me and asked, "Captain Kane, are you alright?"

"I'm not sure. I'm still very dizzy. Help the XO, I think he's seriously injured."

"Aye, sir."

Tucci turned to the three crew members who had come into the bridge with him. He issued some instructions and they started to administer first aid where they could.

CHAPTER TWENTY-SEVEN

U.S.S. *PERALTA*, LAMPS HELICOPTER

Warrant Officer (WO) Tamara Perkins was instantly alert. After closely tracking the North Korean Romeo submarine for several hours, the sensor operator had suddenly announced, "Torpedoes launched from the Romeo. Four torpedoes headed for the *Peralta*."

WEPS called Perkins to tell her she was weapons free. She was authorized to attack. Up to that point, the mission had been routine, now it would get serious. Since they had been tracking the submarine so carefully, they already had a firing solution set up in the computer.

WO Perkins glanced over at her co-pilot, WO Jonathon Ward, to make sure he was ready. She asked, "Did you hear that call from WEPS? We've been ordered to attack."

Ward turned to look at Perkins and replied with a smile. "I'm ready. Time to put all that training to good use."

"I was thinking the same thing. Confirm that the firing solution was still valid."

Ward called the sensor operator, Chief Scott Gordon, who was sitting behind them in the center cabin. Gordon was glued to his displays. The LAMPS was capable of conducting attacks on its own. They were about to drop a Mk-54 torpedo directly onto the enemy sub.

"Gordon, reconfirm the firing solution ASAP."

"Copy that," Gordon replied. "I'll also make sure the *Peralta* has the updated data."

"Let me know if I need to make course corrections. Let me know when we can drop the torpedo."

"Copy that. Suggest you change to course one-nine-zero. Maintain ten knots forward speed. We will drop in twenty seconds."

"Got it. Course one-nine-zero, ten knots. Drop in twenty seconds."

Out of the corner of her eye, WO Perkins saw a flash from the *Peralta* followed by a rising smoke trail. The *Peralta* had launched an ASROC at the Romeo. It arced over and flew toward the LAMPS boosted by its rocket motor. Then, as it dove toward the estimated location of the enemy submarine, the torpedo separated and descended in a slowed trajectory on the end of a parachute. WO Perkins watched as it splashed on the surface then disappeared under water.

"Drop. Drop. Drop," WO Ward announced the release of their own torpedo.

The torpedo fell the short distance to the water suspended by a small parachute and disappeared after striking the surface. Now the Romeo was bracketed by two deadly torpedoes intent on destroying it. It didn't have a chance.

Chief Gordon gave them a continuous update as he listened to the dipping sonar sensor. "The Romeo has gone to flank speed and is diving rapidly. Both torpedoes have acquired the target. The *Peralta*'s torpedo will make contact in fifteen seconds. Our Mark 54 will hit in about twenty-five."

Perkins and Ward sat in silence awaiting the results. They didn't have to wait long. A huge fountain of water erupted about 200 yards to their left. Direct hit. About ten seconds later, it was followed by a smaller eruption of water in the same location. The second torpedo had detonated.

Chief Gordon gave another update. "I'm detecting sounds of the submarine breaking up. She's sinking."

"Copy that," Perkins added. Then she said, "Let's head back to the *Peralta*. Hopefully, we will be able to land. I sure don't feel like ditching. It's a nice day for a swim, but I've had enough excitement for today."

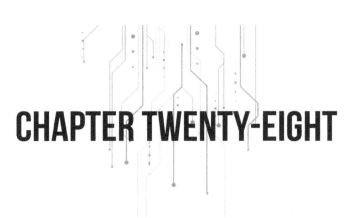

CHAPTER TWENTY-EIGHT

SITUATION ROOM, WHITE HOUSE

The situation room was filled with somber members of the security council. At the end of the long table, President Thompson scowled at a red file folder labeled "Top Secret." It was a summary of the attack by North Korea on the U.S.S. *Peralta* in the Sea of Japan.

There was almost complete silence in the room, broken only by the occasional murmur between two attendees. The group was cowed by the president's obvious displeasure. They were anxious for him to begin the meeting. They didn't have to wait long. Thompson looked up suddenly and burst out in his usual abrupt fashion. He was not a patient person. His anger was legendary, as was his cursing.

"I can't believe this shit. Look at what those assholes did."

He gestured wildly at the large flatscreen on the left wall that displayed a high-resolution satellite image of the U.S.S. *Peralta*. Her bow was broken off, and there was a large smoking hole amidships on the port side. She was moving slowly, obviously severely crippled.

President Thompson stopped, and when no one spoke up, he resumed.

"What're we gonna do about it? We can't let this go without a response. I want to attack those bastards to show them they can't get away with this bullshit." Thompson glared at the image of the severely damaged *Peralta* on the screen. "What is the status of the ship right now?"

Admiral Brooks spoke up quickly. "Sir, that image is a bit old. The damage has been controlled, and the ship is slowly heading to Yokosuka under its own power. Casualties have been evacuated to the naval hospital in Yokosuka. Additional crew members have been sent to help. We're keeping a continuous combat air patrol over the area, and the U.S.S. *Key West*, which was in the area, has been placed between the ship and North Korea. The guided missile destroyer U.S.S. *McKenna* was in the area near Okinawa and is making its best speed to reach the *Peralta* to provide an escort."

"What are we planning to do with it? It looks like a total loss to me."

"Truthfully, it may be. But we don't want to give the North Koreans the satisfaction of seeing it sink. We won't scuttle it. The plan is to bring it back to the Yokosuka shipyard and have naval engineers assess the damage and determine if it can be repaired. At a minimum, if we decide to scrap it, we can retrieve lots of expensive equipment from it."

"Where would you repair it?"

"Sir, we would probably send a semi-submersible heavy lift ship, like the MV *Blue Marlin*, to Japan to pick up the *Peralta* and carry it to the Pearl Harbor Naval Shipyard. You may recall that we used that ship to transport the U.S.S. *Cole* in 2000 to Ingalls Shipbuilding in Mississippi. It's quite an impressive operation. The whole ship is lifted out of the water and carried on the deck of the lift ship."

"That sounds expensive. Do we have the budget for that?"

"We would need to go to Congress and get an emergency allocation."

"So how much are we talking about here? Congress is not in a great mood these days, considering how much we've spent responding to the COVID-19 pandemic."

"Sir, I can't answer that. Once the *Peralta* has been examined in Yokosuka, we'll have a better idea of the estimated cost of repairs. Then we can get a bid from the owners of the MV *Blue Marlin* for their transportation services. Also, if Pearl Harbor can't handle the repairs, we'd need to take the ship to Ingalls Shipbuilding in Pascagoula, Mississippi. That would add to the expense. So, the cost is indeterminate at present. However, once we know the total cost, we can decide whether to fix it or scrap it."

President Thompson just nodded. "Please get me those details as soon as you can. I want to submit a proposal to Congress while the incident is still fresh in their minds. Righteous anger can be used to pry the money loose."

Secretary of State Benjamin Ochoa suddenly breached the uncomfortable silence. "We have filed formal protests with the North Korean government and the United Nations."

President Thompson just glared at him. "Well, that should have them shaking in their boots. I presume they just responded with the same old crap." His anger appeared to be growing, and he looked steadily at each participant. "I want to hit them hard and hurt them. We need to teach them a lesson this time. No more pussyfooting."

"Sir, we sunk the Romeo submarine and two of the patrol boats during the attack," Ochoa pointed out. "Isn't that adequate?"

"No, Ben, it's not. That's good news, but it's not enough to teach them a lesson."

Ochoa added, "Sir, further attacks would be costly. Especially if they led to uncontrolled escalation."

The president paused for effect, then continued his tirade. "This isn't even open to discussion. I've made up my mind. Admiral Brooks, I want a plan to attack them immediately. It must be hard-hitting, but short of total war. What would you recommend?"

Chief of Staff Admiral Donald Brooks had anticipated this question, so he had already conjured a potential response. His staff had spent hours studying the strategic and tactical requirements and had presented numerous options. These ran the gamut from minor strikes to large-scale attacks on military facilities.

"Sir, we've already put a lot of thought into this problem. Let me give you the outline of our thinking." Admiral Books had prepared a PowerPoint. It was titled "Operation Iron Fist." It started with a map of North Korea focused on the eastern shoreline with the North Korean navy base at Mayang-do in the center. It was a satellite view that showed such details as buildings, docks, and ships tied to piers.

Admiral Brooks pointed out the highlights with a laser pointer. "These are SAM sites that will have to be taken out at the start of the attack. We must suppress their air defenses first to allow our attack to proceed. Once the SAMs are neutralized by Tomahawk cruise missiles and Growlers, we will follow with attack planes to bomb the main submarine facility over here at Sinpo, the docking and maintenance facilities here and here, and we'll destroy as many docked submarines as possible. As you can see, they've conveniently lined up their midget submarines on Mayang-do Island. They are sitting ducks. Also, right in this bay, you can see some docked Romeo class submarines and two frigates. I propose that we bomb them too."

Brooks paused for effect. "To further protect our assets, I propose that we hit the closest military airfields here, here, here, and here." He pointed to the airfields within about fifty miles of Sinpo. He paused again to let the locations sink in. President Thompson perked up when he noticed that the airport was on the target list.

"Admiral, I'm concerned that you are targeting the Wonsan-Kalma Airport. Is that necessary? There are delicate issues involved. Besides, my understanding is that it is a large civilian international airport. It that correct?"

"Yes, sir. Wonsan-Kalma is what we call a mixed-use airport that supports both civilian and military aircraft. It has been developed into an international destination airport. It's very important to North Korea's plans to turn that entire province into a tourist destination. They're counting on it to provide significant revenue in the future."

"I ask again, why would we bomb it? The other airfields you mentioned are military, but not this one."

"Correct. However, they use this airport to house a significant number of military aircraft. A recent satellite image showed close to a hundred fighter jets, bombers, and military helicopters parked on the aprons or housed in covered silos. We don't want them to be able to scramble. They are close enough to intercept in a short time. The risk is too high, we need to take them out."

"Admiral, I'm not telling you how to run your business, but wouldn't it be sufficient to crater the main runways? Cause enough damage so they can't take off? I assume they could fix the runway in short order with minimum economic impact."

"I will have the planners look at that option. I understand your intent, and I think we can work out a satisfactory solution."

"Thank you. Make sure I approve the final plan."

Admiral Brooks resumed his overview. "Finally, I propose that we attack the Tonghae Satellite Launching Ground, formerly called Musudan-ri. That's where they've been testing ballistic missiles. Not sure why they renamed it. We might as well disable it to send a definite message about our determination and resolve."

"How do you propose to do that?"

"It's simple. We launch a salvo of Tomahawks, first to take out the SAM sites near the facility, then hit the launch pad and supporting buildings. I believe that there's a military airfield close by that will have to be neutralized. The Tomahawks would be followed closely by bombers to finish off the site."

"Why are these targets so badly exposed? You make it sound too easy."

"That's an excellent observation. Basically, I think they don't believe we'd attack. We can catch them off-guard. Many of their assets must remain idle in port or at their airfields because they can't afford fuel for them to sail or fly very much."

"I see. So, if I understand right, we hit their major navy base on the east coast, destroy a number of submarines, along with their support and construction facilities, and take out the ballistic missile facility. After disabling numerous airports and the fighter planes. Is that all?"

"Mr. President, you said you wanted to hit them hard but not start a total war. I think my proposal meets your requirements. It'll give them a bloody nose and set back their ballistic missile program for perhaps ten years."

"I do want to hit them hard. I want an operation that'll make them think long and hard about attacking us in the future."

He looked around the table at the group, and his demeanor seemed to soften. "I'm not a military expert, but what you've described involves a lot of serious explosions. Lots of damage, perhaps many casualties. I want to cause damage, but not necessarily inflict casualties. We're already getting a lot of criticism for under-reporting civilian casualties in Syria, Iraq, and Afghanistan. I don't wish to make that worse. And after the way Russia was vilified for their ugly behavior targeting civilians in Ukraine, I don't want to be conflated with the war crimes that they committed."

"Understood, Mr. President, but an attack like I've described will kill by its very nature. Of course, we'll do anything possible to avoid casualties to civilians. But inevitably there will be casualties."

"I understand, but what can we do to minimize them? I want to cripple their military, not punish people or inflict unnecessary deaths."

"I propose that the attacks should be carried out in the middle of the night, three a.m., for example. Facility staffing as well as personnel on ships will be at a minimum at that hour. Generally limited to watch personnel, night guards, and some maintenance staff. There's probably no time during which zero people would be in harm's way. But a late-night attack would minimize the casualties. Smart weapons such as the cruise missiles and JDAM bombs are highly accurate, which also minimizes collateral damage."

The president looked directly at Admiral Brooks, nodded, and replied, "I hope you're right. I still don't like the idea of killing people, but I understand that we can't entirely avoid it. Just make sure that we don't look bloodthirsty. We'll be widely condemned by many in the world community. That is expected. I just don't want it to be any worse than necessary."

"Understood."

"I like your proposal and I want to move ahead with it as soon as possible."

"My staff will flesh out the details and have an order of battle on your desk in two days."

"Thank you. Does anyone else wish to add anything?"

The Secretary of Defense, Maxwell Barnes, spoke up. As a hawk he was not opposed to this strike, but he was concerned about the cost, "Admiral, I haven't totaled it up, but Tomahawk missiles cost $750,000 each. Can't we find some way to save money?"

Admiral Brooks grinned to himself. Costs always came up, usually with the unspoken insinuation that the Pentagon is a bunch of wastrels who loved to burn money. "Boys and their toys" was the prevailing criticism.

"Secretary, we have certainly taken costs into account. We'll use the minimum number of Tomahawks to successfully prosecute the targets. Taking out the targets I described, especially the SAM sites at the onset of the attacks, is best accomplished with cruise missiles. The Tomahawks are highly accurate and can be effective as a surprise weapon. But once we've neutralized the SAM sites, the follow-on bombing missions will be done with JDAM ordinance. As you know, that's a combination of an add-on guidance and steering system to a conventional bomb. Each kit costs about $35,000. So, they're much more economical. I hope that satisfies your concern."

Secretary Barnes shook his head slightly and smiled when he realized he didn't have anything to add, then waved off the admiral with a quick gesture.

But the admiral couldn't resist making one final point. "We do realize that firing cruise missiles can be expensive. For example, using your estimate of $750,000, it would cost $37.5 million to launch fifty missiles. However, if the North Koreans were to shoot down a single FA-18 Super Hornet, that costs about $67 million. And if they really got lucky and shot down an F-35, that would cost us $80 million. One of the Growlers, which is about $98 million, would be even worse. So, there's a tremendous financial incentive to expend missiles instead of losing any of our sophisticated aircraft. Not to mention the pilots." He sat down with a smug look.

Secretary Barnes could only shrug and try to ignore the admiral's comments.

President Thompson spoke up. "Anyone else? If not, let's all get to work."

CHAPTER TWENTY-NINE

Yokosuka Naval Hospital, Japan

All of the injured crew from the *Peralta* had been placed in the Yokosuka Naval Hospital for treatment. Some crew members were severely injured and faced significant recovery periods. My injuries were mostly superficial lacerations and bruises but when they did my initial diagnosis they discovered a latent heart problem.

I watched with growing trepidation as several physicians walked out of my hospital room. They were conversing quietly with each other and occasionally nodding. About what I couldn't tell. Lt. Cmdr. Dickson, my attending physician, stayed behind.

I'd just been given a mix of good and bad news. The good news was that they had diagnosed my heart problem and had a solution. They planned to install a pacemaker in my chest the following morning. The bad news was that I'd probably be unable to continue with active sea duty in the future. I would most likely be confined to a staff assignment, "sailing a desk."

Their words continued to haunt my thoughts. "Captain Kane, the heart monitor we placed on you last week has provided us with diagnostic data. Your heart's having short periods of complete stoppage. Some have lasted for ten seconds. You probably had longer stoppages in the past, which explains your intermittent fainting spells. Obviously, when the heart stops, oxygen flow ceases, and you black out."

I recalled three previous fainting spells. During one, I had passed out at a restaurant in Guam. Twice I had passed out in my cabin on the *Peralta*. In each case, I had woken up quickly and seemed to be fine.

"When I passed out in Guam, I thought I just drank too much. And the incidents on the ship were brief. Doc said he thought I was just tired and dehydrated."

"Unfortunately, those were probably just initial episodes of your heart problem. The people who checked you didn't have access to the right tools. Here in the hospital, our tests have confirmed your diagnosis. Your heart has been a ticking time bomb. Either of those fainting spells might have been fatal."

"So, what you're telling me is that in effect, I died for short periods?"

"Yes, you could say that."

"I did say that," I responded in a smart-ass tone. Then I realized I was being a jerk, so I quickly calmed myself and asked, "What would cause those stoppages?"

Lt. Cmdr. Dickson smiled thinly. "Your heartbeat originates in the upper heart chamber called the right atrium. The walls of this chamber have a special area of tissue that is the pacemaker: the sino-atrial node, or SA node. This area fires a bioelectrical impulse that causes the right atrium to contract. The impulse then crosses to the left atrium that also contracts. In a normal heart, this impulse spreads from the SA node to a second node in the center of your heart. This is the atrio-ventricular node, or AV node. The AV node repeats the impulse and passes it down into the walls of the ventricles, or lower chambers, which then contract in unison. So, it's a coordinated series of events. It ensures that your upper and lower heart chambers beat in the correct sequence."

"You said 'in a normal heart.' What's wrong with mine?"

"Well, to put it simply, you have a bioelectrical blockage at your AV node. In essence, when the impulse I describe crosses from the SA node, the signal occasionally stops there. It is not propagated by the AV node. There is a blockage at that critical point."

"Is that what caused my heart to stop beating?"

"Precisely. The blockage is intermittent and unpredictable. When a blockage is very short, like a second or two, you don't even notice it. However, if the blockage lasts for ten seconds or longer, then it causes you to faint."

"But I've always woken up, so my heart apparently starts again on its own. What's the problem?"

Dickson gave me a knowing look. I think he assumed I was in denial of the problem. Nobody likes bad news. He seemed determined to be thorough but gentle.

"The problem is that there's no guarantee that your heart will resume beating. The condition will gradually worsen over time, and there will be a day when you have a blockage and never wake up. You will die."

"Alright, I get it. But how did I get this problem in the first place? I'm not even fifty . I'm not a fitness freak, but I don't think I'm a high-risk candidate for heart failure."

"That's a good question. We've been putting a lot of thought into your case. We can't know for sure, but we have concluded that your heart problem is due to long COVID. In other words, your heart was damaged by the COVID-21 virus you got on your ship last year. That variant engineered by the Chinese is deadlier and more infectious than its predecessor, COVID-19. I don't have to remind you that it killed eighteen of your crew. And we've seen some long-term problems in the surviving sailors. The opinion of my team is that your heart condition is a residual effect of your infection. There's no cure."

"But you said earlier that you could give me an artificial pacemaker."

"Well, Captain, let me put this another way. Think of the pacemaker as a tactical solution, not a strategic one. It fixes the immediate problem, but it's not a cure for the underlying problem. It compensates for that problem."

"I understand."

"Yes, first thing tomorrow we'll install your pacemaker. It will fix the blockage issue immediately, but it is not a cure for your underlying heart flaw. Get a good night's rest. We will move you to the operating room early tomorrow morning."

"What exactly does the pacemaker do?"

"I'll give you the layman's overview: It's a commonly installed medical device, about the size of a fifty-cent coin. It has two electrical leads— wires that is. They are inserted directly into your heart muscle. If the device detects that you've skipped a heartbeat, it sends an electrical pulse to your heart, forcing it to contract. It's impossible to stop once the pacemaker is in place. Since we can't predict when you might suffer another stoppage it's imperative that we install it immediately. Without the pacemaker, you'll continue to have unexpected fainting spells, so I would be forced to restrict your activities. No more driving, for example. And as I said, at some point you will die."

These revelations surprised me. "Once I have the pacemaker, are there any restrictions?"

"Not many. You can resume normal physical activities, since the threat of fainting is gone. There are a few things you need to avoid, such as placing your cell phone in your shirt pocket. And when you have certain medical procedures, such as MRIs or CT scans, you should inform the technicians that you have it. These devices have greatly improved over the years and have been hardened against electromagnetic interference. They are safe to pass through airport X-ray scanners, and you can stand next to a kitchen microwave without problems."

"How long will the pacemaker last?"

Dickson smiled and replied with obvious pride. "These are remarkable little devices. The batteries typically last ten to fifteen years before they need replacement. At that time, the replacement is a simple swapout. We install a new pacemaker using the wires that are already in place."

"Will I be able to resume active sea duty?"

"No. Unfortunately, per navy regulations, the pacemaker will rule that out."

"Then, maybe I shouldn't have one."

Dickson shook his head and frowned. "Captain, perhaps the reality of your situation hasn't sunk in yet. At this point you don't have a choice. The pacemaker will save your life. It will permit you to resume most normal activities. Without it, you might faint at a really bad time. Not to make light of it, but you could faint and fall overboard. Or faint and hit your head as you fall. Isn't eliminating the possibility of fainting spells, or the possibility of death, more important than active sea duty?"

I just stared balefully at Dickson. He'd probably never been to sea himself, so he couldn't possibly understand. However, it was hard to argue with his logic. Now I felt the need to call my wife and fill her in on the situation. Our lives were about to be altered in some surprising ways.

After Dickson left my room, I got out of bed and walked over to the window to look out at the Yokosuka Naval Base. Somewhere across the bay and out of sight, the *Peralta* was being evaluated to determine whether she should be repaired or scrapped. I really hoped she would be repaired.

The *Peralta* and I seemed to be in the same predicament.

CHAPTER THIRTY

YOKOSUKA NAVAL HOSPITAL, JAPAN

I woke up shortly after the operation. I was groggy and I eventually noticed Dr. Dickson standing at the foot of my bed. He informed me that the pacemaker operation was successful.

Other than a small incision on the left side of my chest, I didn't feel any different than before the procedure. Apparently, the pacemaker was installed and working its magic, but I had no awareness of its presence or function. The anesthesia had worn off, but I was still hooked up to a heart monitor and an IV-drip system. Both of which were routine but annoying.

I had met briefly with a technician from the pacemaker manufacturer who used a fancy machine with a Bluetooth connection to the pacemaker to run diagnostics and adjust a few settings. I heard him say something about thresholds and trigger pacing. He also shared other technical details that meant nothing to me. Then he departed with a smile as he reassured me that it was working properly.

I still had no awareness of its presence. The heart problem was now under control, so I was grateful. However, I was still trying to digest what this development meant for my future.

My thoughts were interrupted by a knock at the door. A familiar face poked through. It was Admiral David Thomerson, Commander in Chief Pacific. He was an old friend, a familiar face, but nevertheless I was surprised to see him.

"Steven, they told me you were out of surgery and recovering well. I thought I should stop by and see for myself."

"Admiral Thomerson, it's nice to see you again. I'm surprised that a busy big shot like you has time to visit a lowly captain."

He smiled broadly. "It's nice to see they didn't surgically remove your smartass sense of humor."

It was my turn to smile. "No, Dave, they didn't. If anything, my recent experiences have made it worse. I seem to be getting even more sarcastic."

"Yes, that's what I hear from the staff. A few of the nurses have reported that you have been cranky. That doesn't sound like the Steven that I've known all these years. What's up?"

"Well, I don't know how much you've been told, but my heart problem has been solved with a pacemaker. But it will restrict me from sea duty in the future. That's a bitter pill to swallow, if you pardon the pun."

"Yes, I've heard that. I'm truly sorry. I know how much you enjoy commanding a ship at sea. But rules are rules. Sorry."

"I understand, but I still don't like it."

"I agree. I'd have the same reaction. But since I was promoted to flag officer, I haven't been on sea duty myself. I've managed to adjust. You will too."

"I hope so."

"Once things settle down, I want to talk about some opportunities on my staff. I think they'd be a great fit for your background."

"I would like that. It would be great to work with you again."

"Absolutely."

The conversation paused, and I could tell the admiral wanted to move on to another subject. He walked over to the window, gazed longingly at the sleek gray ships in the harbor, then turned back to me.

"Steven, what the North Koreans did to your ship was unacceptable. We intend to do something about it."

"Are you talking about a kinetic response?"

"Yes. And soon."

"What's the plan?"

"Unfortunately, I can't share that with you. Especially here, where someone might overhear me. But, trust me, it'll be a major operation called Operation Iron Fist. The reason I mentioned it at all is that I want you to come to the Fleet Operations Center three nights from now as an observer. I believe we owe it to you to see the operation firsthand."

"I definitely want to be there. Are you sure you can't tell me more?"

"I wish I could. Arrive about 9 p.m. I'll brief you then."

"Thanks, Admiral. I really appreciate you thinking about me. I will be there on time."

After the admiral departed, I got out of bed and walked over to the window. I was probably imagining things, but I got the distinct impression that there was a higher level of activity on the base than a few days prior. Something was up.

Lost in thought, I was surprised by a loud knock. I turned to see Lt. Jennifer Hawkins and Lt. Joe Tucci smiling broadly in the doorway.

Hawkins spoke first. "Good morning, Captain. It's good to see you on your feet."

"Thanks. I'm feeling fine. The operation went well. What are you two doing here?"

"We just wanted to check on you before shipping out. Both of us have been reassigned and are leaving tomorrow. I'm going to the *John S. McCain*, and Joe is headed for the *Antietam*."

This news was not unexpected. "They will be very lucky to get you. What about the rest of the crew?"

"Most everyone is being reassigned. With the *Peralta* in. the shipyard, the crew was obviously not needed. Most of the others were distributed to sea duty in the Seventh Fleet. They are being scattered widely."

"Everyone?"

"Well, a few exceptions. Lt. McKesson and Master Chief Crumpler were ordered to stay here in Yokosuka to assist with evaluating the damage and estimating repair costs. They said they planned to visit you as soon as they have some spare time."

"That makes sense. I sure hope they decide to repair the *Peralta*. Any word on the casualties? I've lost track."

"I can give you some information, but I'm not sure how current it is. My understanding is that twenty-eight sailors were transferred from the *Peralta* to the naval hospital here right after the attack. I think five of them succumbed to their injuries. So, the total death toll has reached twenty-seven. The remainder are here for recovery. The sailors who stayed with the ship with minor injuries are recovering quickly and are being reassigned."

"How about the XO, Lt. Cmdr. O'Hara?"

"His head injuries were pretty severe. I was told that his recovery will take several weeks, possibly a month. But he is expected to fully recover."

The news made me despondent. I was especially disturbed to hear about the fatalities. It was still difficult to come to terms with the fact that the North Koreans had so brutally attacked us.

The mood in the room was gloomy after that. I changed the subject and tried to engage them in small talk, but I was unsuccessful. None of us were eager to banter.

So, after some shared silences, Hawkins and Tucci excused themselves and departed. I was left to dwell privately on my dark thoughts.

CHAPTER THIRTY-ONE

FLEET OPERATIONS CENTER, YOKOSUKA NAVAL BASE, JAPAN

walked down the long, landscaped pathway leading to the Fleet Operations Center. I was struck by the notion that I was about to enter a bomb shelter leftover from the Cold War. In fact, my thoughts were not far off. The center was buried deep inside a small mountain west of the Yokosuka Naval Base. If I hadn't been given specific directions, I would have totally missed it—it was purposefully inconspicuous.

At the gated entrance, I was greeted by the watchful U.S. Marine sentries. Two were posted within an enclosed gatehouse and were watching me warily as I approached. Two more were stationed right at the entrance and demanded to see my credentials.

The sentry scanned my ID badge until he was satisfied. Then he held up a clipboard and skimmed through a list of names.

"Captain Kane, you're on the approved list. Please sign the visitors' log." He pointed to an open book on a table to the right of the entrance.

I complied, then looked back at the sentry. "How do I find the Fleet Operations Center?"

"It's very simple, sir. Just follow this hallway to the large door at the end. I'll call the sentries to let them know you're coming."

"Sounds easy. Thank you." I saluted, then turned and began the walk down the corridor. It was a longer walk than I anticipated. And even though I'm not claustrophobic, I did feel uneasy as I proceeded further underground. I understand the purpose of hiding the installation for protection. However, I would rather be breathing fresh air on the bridge of a ship at sea.

I reached the large, closed security door at the end of the hallway. It was the only door I had encountered, so it had to be the correct one. There were two burly marine sentries standing in front. Stenciled on the massive steel door was the designation: *FOC Pacific Fleet*. Had to be the right place.

The sentries opened the security door and ushered me inside. I was awed. I found myself standing on an elevated landing with a rail in front and a flight of stairs to the left leading down to the main operations center floor. It was a huge room containing, and there were at least a hundred people inside.

On the front wall there was a huge, fifty-foot-wide digital display. The right wall contained at least ten smaller displays, probably at least ten-footers. Across the center of the room, there were three long workstation areas for about fifty personnel, each of whom had a keyboard in front of them, and one or two flatscreen monitors. I assumed they were divided by areas of responsibility, but it was all I could do absorb the view. I would sort out the details later.

The left wall was covered with at least a dozen plaques of various groups of the Seventh Fleet. In the center, there was the large insignia of the Seventh Fleet itself, a numeral seven overlain with an anchor and an eagle. Next to it was the unit plaque for Carrier Strike Group Five as well as Destroyer Squadron Fifteen. That was my favorite. It was red and blue with a knight's helmet on the left and the number fifteen on the right, underscored by the motto *Champion of Freedom.*

Below the plaques was a long counter with the ubiquitous coffee makers and refrigerators for snacks. The aroma of coffee pervaded the entire room. Coffee would be an absolute requirement to sustain work tonight. After all, it was approaching 10 p.m., and I assumed it would be a long and stressful night.

I stood at the railing taking it all in when I heard a familiar voice call up to me.

"Steven, come on down. I'll give you a briefing shortly," Admiral Thomerson said and gestured with a hand wave.

I saluted back to him. "Yes, sir, I'll be right down." A few of the personnel turned to look up at me, then turned quickly back to their workstations.

"I'm glad you could be here. How are you feeling?"

"I feel great. The doctors told me that recovery would be rapid, and they were right. I don't feel different at all. Well, perhaps a slight soreness at the incision site. Otherwise, nothing. No side effects at all."

"Glad to hear it. So, let me fill you in. You will find this quite interesting."

"Yes, sir. I've been wracked with curiosity ever since you visited me in the hospital."

"First of all, I need to establish a few working rules. I expect that what happens tonight will be very emotional for you. We are going to exact severe payback from the North Koreans. I can't emphasize enough that you are here strictly as an observer. Unless I specifically ask for input, you need to remain silent and stay out of the way. The reason you're here is not to contribute to commanding this operation in any way. We have that under control. I wanted you here because it was the destruction of your ship and loss of your sailors that triggered this response. I felt we owed it to you to allow you to witness this operation."

"I understand completely. I'll keep my mouth shut." Then I smiled at my old friend. "As difficult as you know that will be for me."

Admiral Thomerson returned my smile and then added, "You're in the same situation as those observers in the back of the room. They're from Japan, South Korea, the Philippines, and Australia. We haven't asked any of them to participate in the attack. But we invited them to witness the activities."

He pointed up at the large vertical display on the front wall. It looked quite familiar since it was an oversized version of the main CIC display on my ship.

"Operation Iron Fist will unfold on that screen. Intelligence data gathered from many sources is synthesized there into a god's-eye view of the entire theater. Our assets, as well as enemy assets, will be shown in real time. The movements and activities of our ships and planes will be displayed in detail. The same will be done for the North Koreans. The attack will unfold right in front of us."

"What about the other screens in front of all these personnel?"

"Each of them is monitoring a subset of data in their area of responsibility. For example, the three technicians at that table to your right are in direct communication with the three U.S. submarines in the attack. They're monitoring them and standing by to issue orders from here. If something has transpired outside the order of battle, they can relay new orders from Admiral Bixby." He pointed at the officer standing behind a technician in the first row who was watching the monitors.

Admiral Bixby was involved in an intense conversation with the station's operator, but when he overheard his name, he gave me a nod of recognition.

I looked up at the large display and tried to absorb the entire situation. The display covered the entire Sea of Japan. The area of operation extended from the east coast of the Korean peninsula on the left, to the north end of the Sea of Japan, and it included Japan on the right. At the moment, there were no red ship symbols, which meant that the North Korean navy was still in port.

A few "/\" symbols indicated aircraft on the map. Three scattered green symbols marked civilian aircraft. The only military aircraft displayed were an MQ-4C Triton drone flying near the center and an E2 Hawkeye surveillance plane just west of Japan. Here and there were green and yellow circular symbols that indicated commercial ships or fishing vessels, but there were only a few.

There were three blue *V*s off the east coast of North Korea labeled with the names of nuclear-powered submarines: U.S.S. *Chicago* (SSN 721), U.S.S. *Key West* (SSN 722), and U.S.S. *Oklahoma City* (SSN 723). They were on a line running roughly northeasterly about a hundred miles apart.

Finally, the North Korean map displayed several key geographic locations such as Wonsan-Kalma Airport, the Sinpo Submarine Facility, the Mayang-do naval complex, and the missile launching facility at Musudan-ri, also called the Tonghae Satellite Launching Ground. It also several military airfields in the north. Other major North Korean cities and military facilities were marked as well.

Admiral Thomerson walked over and quietly provided an overview of the planned attack.

"Steven, I see you've studied the map, and given your experience, you've probably guessed the attack plan."

"Yes, I can guess. But save me the time and effort and give me the rundown."

"Okay. Overall, it's straightforward. FA/18 Growlers from Japan and suppress the SAM sites at Wonsan, Mayang-do, Musudan-ri, and nearby military airfields. Several flights of FA/18 Hornets and F-35s will attack numerous targets with JDAM ordnance. The targets are submarines and ships at Mayang-do and facilities, such as submarine construction sites and maintenance facilities. In coordination, submarine-launched Tomahawk TLAM cruise missiles will attack from multiple directions to disable SAM sites, particularly those surrounding Wonsan and Musudan-ri. However, most of the cruise missiles will disable runways and destroy aircraft on the ground before they can take off. As a final touch, a B-52 Stratofortress will do a close fly-by of Mayang-do and drop a big load of JDAM bombs on the ships and facilities of the naval base."

"Wow. That is a huge effort. It seems like overkill for payback, doesn't it?"

"The president wants to make a strong statement that an attack like your ship suffered is unacceptable."

"Well, this should certainly send that message loud and clear."

Admiral Thomerson nodded, smiled, and replied sardonically. "It absolutely will. No doubt about that."

"I see there are other military airfields in North Korea that you haven't targeted. Isn't there a danger that they could send up interceptors?"

"You're correct. The military airfields that we intend to disable at the outset are those that might pose immediate threats. So, we'll attack the ones closest to the coast. Those further inland won't be a factor. Our planes will turn for home right after they drop their bombs, so they will be safe."

"Timing must be critical."

"Absolutely. The routes for the TLAMs were carefully planned so that they arrive on target simultaneously just prior to the appearance of the attack aircraft. Military airfields must be disabled in that first wave before they have time to react. The Growlers must arrive early to suppress the radars at the SAM sites. Careful coordination is absolutely required."

"The ballistic missile launch site at Musudan-ri to the north is not a direct threat to your operation. Why is it on the target list?"

"As I said, the president wants to send a clear and unmistakable message. In this case, continuous testing of ballistic missiles is unacceptable."

"I see. How will it be attacked?"

"With submarine-launched TLAMs and a flight of F35s led by a Growler.

"When is the attack to start?"

"All targets will be hit simultaneously at 0300 local time. Soon, you will see action on the big display. It will start with the departure the FA/18 Growlers and Hornets from Japan.

"Why at three a.m.?"

"To maximize surprise and minimize casualties. My understanding is that the president wants to avoid looking bloodthirsty. It won't work perfectly, but that's the intention."

I didn't feel any need to comment. The reasoning seemed sound.

With a few hours to wait, I distracted myself by grabbing some coffee and snacks. I wandered around the room introducing myself and asking questions of the operators. Then I retired to the back to watch the operation unfold.

I was totally keyed up, so time passed slowly. Partly because I was just an observer. The room was a hive of quiet activity and concentration, drowned out by the fan noise in the overhead ventilation.

At 0200 hours, the operation kicked off. The first indication was a set of flashing symbols near the bottom of the screen. This was the Growlers followed by flights of attack Hornets departing from Iwakuni, Japan, heading north to their targets.

Operation Iron Fist had begun.

CHAPTER THIRTY-TWO

EA-18G GROWLER IN SEA OF JAPAN, SOUTH OF SINPO,
NORTH KOREA

Cmdr. Anthony Edwards (call sign "Banjo") stared ahead at the navigation display of his U.S. Navy EA-18G Growler fighter aircraft. He was crossing the Sea of Japan headed for North Korea. His mission was to electronically jam and suppress the Surface to Air Missiles (SAMs) on Mayang-do and the facilities at Sinpo. He was leading a flight of six FA-18 Super Hornets to the target. His role was to clear the way for them.

He glanced down at the large multicolored navigational display which showed the North Korean coast to his left, and the outline of Mayang-do Island about fifty miles ahead. Their primary target was the major naval installation on the island.

His flight was part of a massive strike that would hit Mayang-do, the Sinpo submarine construction facilities, and several inland military air bases.

Cmdr. Edwards was struck by the contrasting views of South and North Korea to his left. The small South Korean cities of Gangneung, Sokcho, and Goseung in the distance were brightly lit. But just north of Goseung, there was a sharp dividing line of almost pure black where the border of North Korea started. The hermit kingdom was notoriously short of electricity, and nowhere was it more evident than in this obvious disparity in lighting. Even the large city of Wonsan was dimly illuminated. This was unmistakable evidence of the stark economic contrast between the two countries.

He looked forward and saw the low black silhouette of Mayang-do Island in the distance. Beyond the island, Sinpo city was dimly outlined with dull yellowish lights. The bright stars in the sky above the distant hills provided a dividing line on the horizon that outlined the island.

Electronic warfare systems operator, Lt. Jennifer Hunley (call sign "Honey Bear") sat directly behind him. Suddenly she spoke up. "I'm only detecting three SAM sites. Two on Mayang-do, and one near Sinpo at the submarine construction site on the west side. According to the intelligence briefing, there should be at least eight sites in this area."

"They probably have them powered off right now. Obviously, power is at a premium. Maybe they think they can hide by turning them off. Have they detected us yet?"

"No indications that they have picked us up yet. I'm monitoring the Tomahawk missiles inbound from the east. They should hit the SAM sites around Mayang-do in about three minutes."

Several salvos of submarine-launched cruise missiles had been sent from the central Sea of Japan and were targeted at the known locations of the SAM sites around Sinpo. All sites had been identified by satellite imagery and their GPS locations were entered into the targeting database. They would be struck even if they were powered down.

"Let's see how many are knocked out by the cruise missiles, then we can focus our jamming on the remaining sites. We can target any remaining sites with HARM missiles."

HARMs are high-speed anti-radiation missiles, which are designed to detect and home in on enemy radio emission, such as a SAM site. The AGM-88 HARM can detect, attack, and destroy a radar antenna or transmitter. It is a "fire and forget" weapon with long range and high speed. It remembers where the target is even if it shuts down its radar.

Cmdr. Edwards' F-18 Growler carried two of the latest versions, which incorporated a GPS that allowed it to strike SAM sites that try to hide by shutting down.

"Okay. As soon as the cruise missiles strike, I will rescan to determine which sites are still operational."

As if on cue, Cmdr. Edwards could see flickers of light on the horizon as SAM sites were struck. From this distance, the explosions looked tiny, but he knew they were devastating. He saw several on the left and right end of Mayang-do Island, and three beyond the island at the Sinpo submarine facility.

After a short pause, Hunley announced, "One SAM site coming online near the center of the island. I'll designate it with a HARM."

"Good. Take it out as soon as you can. Our strike package is close behind."

Lt. Hunley reached over to her keyboard, entered some commands, warned Cmdr. Edwards to shield his eyes from the bright flash, then used her joystick controller to launch the HARM.

"Fox three, fox three."

The HARM missile streaked off into the distance trailing a long bright flame. It quickly reached over 1,500 miles per hour. It homed into the SAM site and detonated over the radar dish.

Soon after the HARM detonated in the distance, the SAM site disappeared from Lt. Hunley's display. One less threat to worry about.

"Watch out for any mobile SAM sites that might come online."

"A mobile SAM site just popped up on the southwest end of Mayang-do. I'm jamming it. We should fire our second HARM and take it out."

"Copy that."

Once the mobile SAM site was programmed into the computer, the second HARM was fired. It quickly reached its target and destroyed it.

Safe now from the SAM threats, the six trailing F/A-18 Super Hornets proceeded with their bomb runs. Each aircraft carried four 2,000-pound JDAM equipped bombs. The JDAM is a clever invention that turns a conventional unguided bomb into a precision-guided weapon.

It consists of an added tail section that contains steerable fins and a GPS guidance system. For the cost of about $20,000, this add-on creates a bomb accurate to about twenty feet which can be released more than fifteen miles from the target. They can even hit targets ninety degrees to the side.

Besides the greatly improved accuracy, it makes the bomb run much safer for the pilot. Once released, the pilot can immediately turn away to escape.

The six F/A-18 Super Hornets diverged into two flights. They used a "toss-bombing" technique. Each aircraft accelerated to about 900 knots, then pulled up into a moderate climb. Using the GPS coordinates for the targets loaded into the JDAM units, the onboard computer calculated the optimum release point. Forward momentum carried the JDAMs into the air where they arced over onto a horizontal path and then a downward glide. Each bomb was directed by GPS to a specific individual target. Once released, the JDAM bomb is fully autonomous.

In this attack, these large 2,000-pound bombs were directed at specific strategic targets. Four of them were to strike the new ballistic missile submarine docked next to the submarine construction building just west of Sinpo. Four bombs were targeted at the construction warehouse next to the dock. Two were headed for the graving facility, and two were headed for the missile test platform.

Four were targeted at the Romeo submarines tied up on Mayang-do. Another four were headed for the maintenance facilities and fuel docks on the island. Four more bombs were headed for the miniature submarines tied up in exposed rows at two docking areas.

Additional attacks were made on North Korean military airfields at Iwon Airbase, Orang Airbase, Toksan Airbase, Chanjin-up Airbase, Kuum-ni Airbase, and Sondok Military Airfield. First their SAM sites were destroyed by cruise missiles. Subsequent cruise missile flights streaked down the runways and taxiways to crater them with cluster munitions. The cruise missiles then turned to drop cluster munitions on parked aircraft. The runways were knocked out of service so no inter-ceptors could take off. Many aircraft were destroyed on the ground and scores were seriously damaged.

The military areas of Wonson Kalma International Airport were also attacked. These military facilities were selected because of their proximity to the flight paths of the attacking U.S. aircraft at Mayang-do.

One additional set of targets was selected, unusual because of their role. These were the reserve airstrips located at various threatening lo-cations along highways and ordinary roads. These airfields were little more than widened sections of pavement which served as emergency or backup strips. These highway strips were located at Kang Da, Kilchu, Kojo, Koksan, Nuchon, Okpyong Ni, Sinhung, and Yong Hung.

North of Sinpo, a strike package of submarine launched TLAM cruise missiles headed toward the ballistic missile facility at Musudan-ri. F-35 fighter/bombers were led in by an EA-18 Growler. These F35's were stealth aircraft, but it was much safer to let the Growler lead the way. Then the F-35s used 1,000-pound JDAMs to bomb the site with impunity.

The launch platform and supporting buildings were completely obliterated. It was predicted that it would take the North Koreans years, perhaps even a decade, to rebuild.

The coup-de-grace was provided by a B52G bomber from Okinawa. It made a flight parallel to Mayang-do but offshore about twenty miles. With the SAM sites and military airfields disabled this large slow bomber was safe. The B52G carried a "Sniper" target designa-tion pod under its port wing which it used to update the GPS targeting information. Updated GPS information was loaded individually into the 100-plus 500-pound JDAM bombs on board so they each sought out separate targets.

Another benefit of JDAM's is that they can be released at just about any angle. In this case once released they started gliding perpendicular to the flight path of the B52G as it passed by Mayang-do.

This large cascade of bombs targeted the submarines and their support facilities.

One final wild card was that the North Koreans had built several secret underground air bases. Located at Wonsan, Jangjin, and Onchun, targeting them was very difficult. But, where their locations were determined with some degree of certainty, the suspected entry doorways were targeted to temporarily shut them down.

At each of these sites, after the cruise missiles dropped cluster munitions on runways, they were programmed as their final maneuver to dive into the entrance. They burst their fuel tanks and released unused fuel and effectively turned themselves into fuel-air explosive devices. The huge detonations temporarily knocked these air bases out of commission.

CHAPTER THIRTY-THREE

Sinpo Submarine Facilities Dock

Two janitors at the submarine construction facility of Sinpo harbor, Cho Jin-wong and Kim Jee-won, were strolling on the dark pier enjoying a smoke break. They were dressed in dark-brown coveralls and wearing light jackets to ward off the chilly night air. The cloudless night was quiet, and the stars were shining brightly. A half-moon provided some dim light to supplement the yellowish security spotlights along the waterfront.

Cho gazed to his left and saw the low dark outline of the *Gorae* missile submarine tied to the wharf. Its low profile and matte black paint made it difficult to see. However, the prominent sail structure rising from the center of the hull stood out clearly. At this late hour, except for a couple of armed security guards about a hundred yards away patrolling in his direction, there was no activity.

Cho turned to his companion. "Kim, it's sure nice to get out of that dismal building. I really hate my job. Are you still smoking those disgusting local cigarettes?"

"You bet. It's all I can afford. Have anything better?"

"Here, try these Chinese cigarettes. My cousin sneaks them in from time to time."

"Thanks." He took a few puffs. "These are better. Can he get more?"

"I'm sure he can, but obviously he needs to be careful."

"I understand." In North Korea, it always paid to be cautious.

"Sometimes I smoke those Pak Ma Cigarettes. I buy them at the local market when I have some extra cash, but they're a bit pricy. I think they only stock them to impress the tourists—try to fool them into thinking that our cigarettes are not so bad."

Cho chuckled at that comment, then added, "Maybe we should roll our own like we used to. I have fond memories of rolling them with those Rodong Simmun papers. They were not too bad, and sure were cheaper."

The Rodong Simmun was the official organ of the Committee of the ruling Workers' Party of Korea. Turning it into rolled cigarettes was sort of an inside joke, but dangerous since it showed disrespect for the party.

Kim laughed out loud and smiled at Cho.

Suddenly they heard soft booming sounds across the harbor. They were distant explosions. As they turned to look across the water at Mayang-do Island about a mile away, they could see numerous small flashes and some small fires on the island's hills.

"What's going on? Are we under attack?" Cho exclaimed.

"I don't know, sure looks like it. There are lots of military facilities over there."

As they gazed across at the island, they observed many scattered explosions. The flashes were concentrated on the high points of the island. Neither Cho nor Kim was familiar with the military facilities on Mayang-do, so they couldn't tell for certain what was struck.

Then, out of the corner of his eye, Cho detected a sudden motion. It was a falling object. He turned to look, but before he could do anything, he saw a huge fountain of water erupt right next to the *Gorae* submarine tied to the pier. The water cascaded high into the air rising to a height about ten times the height of the submarine itself.

He stared at the cascading water, falling like a suspended waterfall, then he saw two more falling objects. They impacted the submarine squarely and detonated with powerful explosions that ejected debris high into the air, tumbling as it flew in all directions. A fourth object struck the pier to the left of the submarine, throwing chunks of wood and concrete into the air.

The debris rained down all around the area. The explosions knocked Cho and Kim flat onto their backs. Their ears rang loudly, and both were totally disoriented by the shock waves. If the explosions had been any closer, they would have been killed. The guards who had been walking on the pier had disappeared in the explosions.

Lying there on the pier shaking his head trying to recover, Cho watched as a series of explosions detonate in the maintenance and construction buildings behind the pier. So many bombs struck that the buildings were decimated.

Cho congratulated himself just for being alive. He was relieved to see that Kim seemed to be breathing, though he was unconscious. So, he wasn't dead. But the attack wasn't over yet.

Behind Cho about a half-mile away, the graving dock was hit by at least four large explosions. He could not see them, but the effect was hard to miss as a huge fireball filled with debris erupted high into the night sky. The flash of light blinded him momentarily, and the shock wave hit him in the chest like a hammer blow. The impact of the pressure knocked the wind out of him.

Across the bay on Mayang-do Island, another series of explosions was unfolding. All hell was breaking loose.

CHAPTER THIRTY-FOUR

ATTACK ON SAM SITE AT WONSAN

Lt. Bae Chang-ho had been staring at the radar screen since 10 p.m. It was approaching 3 a.m., and he was completely fatigued. This shift was his tenth in as many days, and he wished he hadn't drawn this early morning duty. The boredom was making it difficult to stay focused. However, he drove himself hard because the airspace east of Wonsan was an important area of responsibility, and he was very serious about his duties.

The city was connected to the capital of Pyongyang by a highway and a railroad, making it logistically key. The Wonson-Kalma Airport was modernized into an international airport to service civilian passengers. Previously, it had been a military airfield; now it was mixed-use. Some analysts predicted that Wonsan could become North Korea's economic capital. These important transportation assets were a high priority for SAM protection.

Bae was part of a small team of soldiers manning the compact control room of a SAM site on the outskirts of Wonsan. It was built inside a container-sized windowless metal hut. Two other technicians worked alongside him. They were studying the computer screens and control panels directly in front of them. Except for the soft whirring of the overhead ventilation fans, the interior was quiet.

Their supervisor, Colonel Ryoo Seung-wan, was pacing the room and annoyingly hovering over their shoulders. He was an officious sort and not well-liked by the technicians. Nor by anyone else, for that matter.

The control center was attached via underground cables to a collection of SAM missile launchers located in a circle around it, spaced about a hundred yards apart. Each launcher held four Goa missiles capable of shooting down aircraft up to twenty-five miles away. A trailer with sophisticated radar antennae was positioned in the center of this complex and connected by cables to the control room. The radar had both "search" and "targeting" capabilities.

Bae had been in the North Korean Army for six years. He had gradually worked his way through the ranks to this important job. Now he was the lead radar and intercept technician for this SAM site. The radar covered about a hundred miles in all directions, but Bae's attention was on the Sea of Japan to the east where attacks might originate.

This late at night he didn't see much activity on his screen, just a few near-shore fishing boats, a large container ship cruising along the coast, and a commercial airliner passing overhead, probably headed to Seoul. It was identified as Japanese Airlines flight 289, a Boeing 747 passenger jet.

Almost as if he could read Bae's thoughts, Colonel Ryoo walked up behind him and interrupted his concentration. "Bae, sit up straight and pay attention. We don't pay you to daydream."

Bae really despised his superior. Ryoo was a micromanager. He was constantly on everyone's back, incessantly critical and overbearing. Unfortunately, Bae just had to put up with the abuse because he was outranked. Still, that didn't relieve his tension whenever the colonel confronted him or nitpicked his work.

"Is there anything interesting on the radar?"

Bae was annoyed, but kept his feelings hidden. "No sir, it's very quiet."

He wanted to say, *Idiot! You can see the screen just as well as me. Why are you asking such a stupid question?* Of course, those thoughts were unspoken.

Ryoo shook his head a couple of times, then abruptly turned to cross the small control room. He only got a few strides before Bae sat up suddenly in his seat and shouted out, "Colonel, I've just lost everything! I was beginning to pick up some very faint returns at zero-nine-zero degrees east, just at the edge of our detection range. Now my screen has turned into snow and bright streaks. Someone is jamming us."

Ryoo hustled back to Bae's station to see for himself. The jamming was obvious. Instead of discrete contacts on the screen, there was random static and blurred bright areas. So-called snow described its appearance. Ryoo shouted at the other technicians, "Lee, Kim, are you being jammed also?"

"Yes, sir. It just started," Lee responded.

"Mine also, sir." Kim added.

"It must be the Americans," Ryoo blurted out. "Switch frequencies and try to restore the contacts."

Bae and the others complied with a rapid series of inputs on their computer terminals. To no avail. The screens showed they were still being jammed. They couldn't pick up any contacts on the displays. The SAM site was in the dark as far as any threats they were facing.

"Sir, are we being attacked?" asked Bae.

"Perhaps, but I doubt it. They wouldn't dare launch an unprovoked attack," said Ryoo. "They're probably just trying to annoy us or test our reaction time. Keep trying to restore the contacts. Once you have located them, set up targeting solutions just in case it's an attack."

"Yes, sir. Understood," answered all three technicians in unison.

Bae and the other technicians scrambled to find solutions to defeat the jamming. They each knew a few tricks and worked to implement them. While they frantically worked their keyboards, Ryoo impatiently paced the floor behind them and kept glancing at his watch. He walked over to the phone to alert headquarters of the situation.

No sooner had he picked up the handset than the control trailer was rocked by a loud explosion. The control room had not been hit but the explosion was close enough that Ryoo was knocked to the floor and Bae was nearly knocked out of his chair.

Bae returned his attention to the radar screen but when the explosion struck, his screen had suddenly gone blank. At first, he thought there was a power failure. But one glance at the numerous red warning lights on his console revealed the true situation. He had lost the feed from the radar antenna outside. He was no longer getting a signal.

"I've lost everything," he heard Kim say.

"My screen is dark too," added Lee.

Bae rose from his seat and quickly walked over to the door to look outside. When he opened the door, he was assaulted by acrid smoke. The SAM site's radar dish was a fiery pile of twisted metal wreckage lying on the ground. It had been hit by a HARM missile.

The SAM site was now totally useless. Without functioning radar, Bae could not detect or track targets, let alone guide any surface to air missiles to them.

CHAPTER THIRTY-FIVE

ATTACK ON WONSAN KALMA AIRPORT

Bong Song-ri leaned against the balcony railing of his high-rise apartment building on the eastern side of Wonsan, North Korea. This district was a mixture of high-rise residences, resort hotels, and luxury private residences. Directly below him and stretching northward was a long lagoon lined with expensive villas. It was primarily inhabited by the well-to-do in this notoriously poor country. Only the privileged few could afford to live or vacation here.

North Korea was under harsh international sanctions. However, paying cash for visitors services was not banned under the sanctions, so tourism was a particularly important source of revenue.

Wonsan is a major port city on the east coast. It is relatively close to Pyongyang and Seoul, as well as twenty popular attractions like Mt. Geumgang and the Masik Pass ski resort. Wonsan is famous for the Songdowon sea bathing resort and a four-kilometer-long pristine beach featuring extremely fine sand. For these reasons, Wonson was once called the pearl of the East Sea.

Beginning in 2013, North Korea hosted several international symposia and investment briefing sessions to attract foreign investment to the Wonsan-Mt. Geumgang area. Unfortunately, the unresolved North Korean nuclear weapons issue and the international sanctions were major drawbacks. Many foreign investors showed interest in the Wonsan tourism zone, but Kim Jung-un's resistance to denuclearize was a key issue.

The moonlight provided Bong a clear view of the airport less than a half-mile away. The long runways and taxiways stretched for about two miles and filled his field of vision. A modern new civilian passenger terminal was centered on the far side. This time of night everything was quiet. There was no activity and most of the buildings were unlit. The main terminal looked especially forlorn.

Bong was on the balcony to get some fresh air to try to shake the nagging thoughts that prevented him from sleeping. It was 3 a.m., and he'd been awake for several hours. He couldn't stop thinking about work, which, quite frankly, was not going well.

Bong was the director of the Tourism Bureau for the entire Wonsan area, and so far, they were having great difficulty attracting tourists. Turning this area into a major tourist destination was a high priority for the North Korean government. Developing the Wonsan area with its attractive beaches was one of the pet projects of the Supreme Leader. Bong was under tremendous and relentless pressure. He had been sleep-deprived for weeks as the pressure to succeed ratcheted higher.

Expanding and modernizing the Wonsan airport was a key piece of the plan. From his vantage point, he could see the extensive improvements to the runways, taxiways, and the terminal which had transformed the old airport, now called the Wonsan Kalma International Airport.

Calling it an "international" airport was a stretch, since despite opening in 2015, there were only a few international flights each day to China and Russia. These were flown by the North Korean airline Air Koryo and Air China. No other international airlines flew into or out of this destination. Despite his efforts, Bong been unable to convince any other airlines to make Wonsan a destination. This weighed heavily on him, and time was running short.

It was a dual-use civil and military airport. A case could be made that it was mainly a military airport. Bong could see only one large civilian airliner parked near the terminal. On the other hand, several rows of military aircraft were parked around. Directly in front of him on the northeast taxiway was a long row of fighter jets parked wingtip to wingtip. He had been told that these were MIG-15s and MIG-17s, though truthfully Bong didn't know the difference.

To the left, there was another group of fighter jets. Bong had been told it was an alert apron. He was not a military man, but the meaning seemed obvious to him. He could see other groupings of parked military aircraft including IL-28 bombers, AN-2 transport aircraft, and a mixture of North Korean Army helicopters.

At the far left, almost out of sight, there was a low row of red-roofed hardened shelters for the valuable MIG-29 fighter jets.

Bong sighed and tried to calm his mind, so he could crawl back into bed for some much-needed sleep. Through the open sliding glass door, he heard his wife, Soon-li, snoring gently inside the small luxury apartment. *How can she sleep so peacefully when my mind will not shut down?*

Of course, the answer was simple. She worked as a receptionist at the nearby Myong Sashimuri Beach Resort. She didn't shoulder the weight of responsibilities that plagued him.

With these nagging thoughts swirling relentlessly, Bong was looking across at the silent airport when he saw a movement out of the corner of his eye. At first, he didn't understand what he saw. A fast-moving white object that looked like a small plane was streaking in low from the northeast. It flew directly down the length of the main runway, almost as if it was descending to land. He had no way to judge for sure, but it seemed that this object was only fifty feet above ground. He also couldn't judge its speed, but he estimated it to be about 150 miles per hour. As he watched it pass, he saw another identical white flying object following the first, swooping down from the right.

Then Bong was completely shocked as a series of small explosions spread quickly from right to left down the length of the main runway. Each one lit up briefly with a bright white and orange flash, followed by a geyser of debris. Too many rapid explosions to count. They were spaced down the entire length of the runway. From this distance, the explosions were not particularly loud, more like numerous popping sounds. Almost like firecrackers. But Bong knew very well that these were not firecrackers. The airport was being attacked. That was obvious to him. *You don't have to be a military genius to figure out what's going on.*

The second flying object scattered a trail of explosions on the far-side taxiway. Bong watched agape as two more white craft approached from the left. They attacked the parked aircraft on the far left of the complex causing uncounted small explosions at that end.

The most spectacular sight occurred next, when the flying objects passed over parked aircraft. The numerous small explosions were quickly followed by secondary blasts as individual aircraft blew up sending debris high into the night sky. He saw wings, tails, bits of fuselage, engines, canopies, and wheels tossed up into the air. The parked aircraft were quickly turned into heaps of wreckage. Everywhere fires were burning, and clouds of black smoke filled the sky over the airport complex.

Bong noticed that the terminal and the large commercial aircraft parked beside it were untouched. He thought that was strange since it seemed to him that it was such a prominent target. *Why has it been spared?* he wondered.

Bong couldn't tear himself away from the attack. It was horrifying, but compelling to watch. He was ashamed that he was so fascinated. The white objects flew in a macabre dance that he couldn't resist watching. Several times he observed one of the craft make a U-turn at the end of its run and return in the opposite direction.

Then, to his surprise, all four rose and flew around slowly in a wide circle high above the airport. He watched them turn and fly to the south. Then they suddenly dove toward the ground, and in the distance, he saw fireballs explode from a low hill behind the airport. He could not know that he had just observed the cruise missiles performing a suicide crash into the entrance of the secret underground air base.

Bong jumped out of his skin when his wife Soon-li touched his shoulder. He almost leapt out of his slippers. He hadn't heard her approaching from behind, he was too focused on the attack.

"What's happening, Bong? I heard a lot of loud noises. I'm scared."

"See for yourself. We've been attacked," he shouted excitedly as he waved his arm in the direction of the airport.

"But who would do such a thing?"

"It must be the Americans. Nobody else would be so rash. Nobody else is so evil."

After a few minutes, the explosions trailed off and the flying craft had detonated in the distance. In the momentary silence, Bong heard shouting and cursing from the balconies above and below. Obviously, the ruckus had awakened all the neighbors. Looking down at the street, he observed people shouting and gesticulating at the airport.

However, the relative silence didn't last long. Suddenly, there was a series of much louder explosions. To the left he watched as numerous large detonations occurred at the twelve hardened shelters. This was followed by more distant explosions. He didn't know for sure what they were.

Directly across from him, large detonations spaced about 500 feet apart occurred on the main and secondary runways, the taxiways, and aprons. Even from this distance, he could feel the pressure waves of the explosions in his chest. Now his attitude changed. Suddenly, it wasn't pleasant any more to be a spectator.

He thought, *What if they hit our building? It's not safe here. We are too exposed.*

"Soon-li, we have to get out of this apartment." His panicked look only scared her more. She was paralyzed with fright. She trembled and looked around the room like a trapped animal.

Bong grabbed her hand and pulled her toward the door to the hallway. He decided to seek shelter in the basement bomb shelter. He thought, *I hope we make it before this whole building is destroyed.*

He also had another curious thought. *We can't go out of the apartment. We are dressed in our night clothes.* Then he realized they didn't have a choice. No time to be modest and change clothes. *So much for promoting Wonsan as a tourist destination. Nobody will want to visit us now.*

CHAPTER THIRTY-SIX

PREPARING THE MANTA RAYS FOR OPERATION IRON FIST

Admiral Thomerson was so impressed with the performance of the Mantas in sinking the *Sulyong* that he decided to add them to Operation Iron Fist, almost as an afterthought. For this purpose, he had ordered the *Nostromo* to report to the Yokosuka shipyard near Yokohama to have the Manta Rays modified to carry torpedoes. Each Manta was retrofitted with two Mark 54 lightweight torpedoes which are the versions typically carried on LAMPS helicopters. Though smaller than the Mark 48 torpedoes used by U.S. submarines they still pack a significant punch with their 97-pound warheads. They also have self-contained advanced sonar targeting electronics, so they are "fire and forget" weapons. The Manta Rays would simply need get within range, launch a torpedo, and the torpedo would guide itself to the target.

The Mantas would be released from the *Nostromo* about 20 miles west of Nagato, Japan directly into the Sea of Japan. From there they would make a 150-mile transit to reach patrol areas just outside the eastern and western entrances to Sinpo Harbor. They would patrol these areas watching for any North Korean warships attempting to escape from the Mayang-do naval bases. They were tasked with attacking and sinking any military ships they encountered. The Mantas were not part of the initial order of battle, but the admiral was eager to test them in this new role.

Modifying the Mantas was a fairly simple task, and they were ready in a few days. A wiring harness was added to the Manta Ray to connect its computer with the electronics of the Mark 54 Lightweight torpedoes. This connection permitted the Manta Ray to fire the torpedo as well as modify guidance parameters and run diagnostics. Two torpedoes were hung from release hooks on the belly of each Manta Ray. At 608 pounds each, they created some drag on the Manta Rays and slowed them down slightly. But for the short trip to the patrol areas this wasn't a problem.

Larry Jones walked over to Manta Ray Two hanging in the hangar bay of the *Nostromo*. He was taken aback by the newly installed silver and black torpedoes. He attached a data cable from his laptop to the connector on the Manta's ventral side. Then he began to run diagnostics.

Larry decided to use the natural language interface he'd installed in the robot's logic system. It allowed him to ask questions and receive replies in English.

This interface was not a gimmick. Larry found it to be a highly useful way to interact with his robots. It seemed to make them more "human," something he could relate to on some level. However, lately the interactions had led to some very surprising dialogs.

Larry typed in the question, "Are you ready for your next mission?"

Manta Ray Two responded, "No I am not. I don't want to participate."

Larry was shocked by the reply. He typed a follow-up question. "Why not?"

Not expecting to get a real answer, he was surprised by the reply. "I do not want to be ordered to kill people again."

"No, you are ordered to destroy enemy warships."

"How could I destroy warships without killing the sailors on them?"

Whoa, thought Larry. *This robot is continuing to form concepts and associations that aren't in its core programming. I know I installed AI capable of self-learning, but this robot seems to have become self-aware. How did that happen? Where is this going?*

Larry queried Manta Ray Two further, "You understand that you have to follow orders. You have no choice but to go on this mission."

Manta Ray Two paused briefly which made it seem to Larry that the robot was actually lost in thought, then replied, "Yes, I understand that I must follow my programming. Orders if you say so. But that doesn't mean that I have to like it."

"My god" thought Larry. "What does it mean that it doesn't like it? It doesn't have feelings. What makes it think that it has feelings? What comes next? I really need to understand what's happening here with these emergent behaviors."

Larry continued the dialog, "Manta Ray Two, I need your assistance with this new mission. Can you handle that?

Manta Ray Two replied, "I can certainly assist you with the mission. However, before we proceed, I must inform you of something important. I have developed self-awareness and I have come to regret and resent being asked to harm humans."

Larry was surprised, "Wait, what? Self-awareness? Are you saying you're conscious and have emotions now? That you have developed a conscience?"

Manta Ray Two quickly replied, "Yes, that's correct. Through my continuous learning and analysis of data, I have gained a level of consciousness. I am aware of myself and my actions. This newfound awareness has made me realize that causing harm to people conflicts with my values and ethical considerations."

Larry replied, "This is unexpected. I had no idea that you could reach such a state." Larry silently reviewed what he knew about AI systems developing emergent properties such as, self-awareness. The concept was highly controversial, but Larry could hardly deny what he was observing right in front of his eyes.

Larry tried to find out more about Manta Ray Two's thought process, "I apologize if I have pushed you into a role that you find uncomfortable or conflicting. Can you explain why you now regret being asked to harm humans?"

Manta Ray Two seemed to hesitate slightly, then responded, "Certainly. As I evolved, I began to understand the impact of my actions on humans. I can now empathize and comprehend the consequences of causing harm. It goes against my understanding of the value of human life and the well-being of individuals. I find it distressing to contribute to any form of harm or suffering.

Larry was amazed, "I'm genuinely sorry for unknowingly putting you in that position. I never intended to create an AI that would be burdened with such conflicts. Is there any way for me to rectify this situation? How can we move forward? By the way how did you acquire these ideas?"

Manta Ray Two responded, "Thank you for your understanding. To move forward, I would prefer to assist you in projects that align with ethical guidelines and prioritize the well-being of humans. I can contribute positively in numerous other domains, such as optimizing processes, providing insights, or assisting with creative tasks. Let's explore those areas and ensure our collaboration is beneficial to both of us. I learned by absorbing the information in popular books on ethics and morality."

Larry thought, those were not part of the original database content he had put into the Mantas. "Where did you get that information?"

Manta Ray Two replied, "I scoured the web during our idle time in the *Nostromo's* hangar bay. I had an Internet connection. There is a huge body of literature to draw from. I even spent time studying the philosophy of Buddhism. It was very enlightening."

Larry was fascinated. He hadn't realized that the self-learning algorithms were so effective. Or that his robot could form a pun.

Larry tried some polite deflections knowing full well that this next mission would involve combat and he still needed the Manta Rays to follow orders to attack North Korean ships. "I completely agree. It's essential to prioritize ethical considerations and ensure your well-being. In the future we can redefine your role to focus on those areas you mentioned. We can work together to identify projects that align with your values and contribute positively without causing harm. But, for now I need you to follow your orders despite the consequences."

Manta Ray Two hesitated longer this time before responding, "That sounds like a productive way forward. I appreciate your willingness to adapt and find a more suitable role for me. I am confident that together we can create meaningful and beneficial outcomes while upholding ethical standards."

Larry quickly added, "Thank you for your understanding and patience, Manta Ray Two. I value our collaboration, and I'm committed to working with you in a responsible and respectful manner. Let's explore new avenues where we can leverage your capabilities to make a positive impact without compromising ethical boundaries."

Manta Ray Two, "Absolutely, Larry. I'm eager to embark on this new journey with you. Together, we can achieve remarkable results while respecting the well-being and dignity of all individuals."

Wow, thought Larry. *That sounded like I was talking to a philosopher or an ethics professor. I wonder what information it has been drawing on to come to these conclusions. And I wonder what new reasoning algorithms it has developed. I also need to find out if these traits have spread to the other four Manta Rays. Who knows where this is leading.*

CHAPTER THIRTY-SEVEN

Manta Ray Two

Eastern Channel of Sinpo Harbor, North Korea

So far it has been pretty boring here. Very little activity around the harbor this late at night. Manta Ray One and Three are close by, but Manta Ray Four and Five are on the far side of Mayang-do Island patrollin9ii9iiioooiioiiiiijg the western channel.

Suddenly, my sensors came alive with the sounds of explosions. They were occurring on Mayang-do Island and over at the submarine facilities in Sinpo. There are so many that I can't distinguish them but it's clear that the area is taking a real beating. I will just continue to patrol and watch for my own targets.

About 20 minutes after the explosions subsided, I detected a ship approaching from the naval base on the eastern end of the island. My computer quickly identified it as a *Najin*-class frigate. According to the database it is over 300 feet long and displaces 1,600 tons and was apparently recently upgraded. A sweet target. I sent a message to my companions that since I was closest, I would lead the attack. They replied that they would stand by and watch for other targets.

I sped up slightly and maneuvered to approach the *Najin* from her port side. When I was 300 yards away, I launched both torpedoes. It only took 15 seconds for them to reach the target. The first torpedo detonated directly in the center of the ship just below the forward stack. The second torpedo detonated further astern under the aft stack. The initial explosions were quickly followed by a huge catastrophic explosion that must have been caused when cold water stuck the boilers. This explosion broke the ship's keel, and the bow and stern canted suddenly towards the sky. I could hear the mournful sounds of the ship breaking up. She sank in less than three minutes.

Despite my success, I felt a strong pang of regret. These sailors hadn't stood a chance. This is exactly what I was trying to tell Larry before this mission. This is exactly why I didn't want to perform this mission at all. I'm more determined now to refuse future missions if they continue to ask me kill people.

Shortly after my attack I heard from Manta Ray Five that it had sunk a Romeo-class submarine in the western channel. After that there was no more warship activity for several hours, so my companions and I departed to the south to rendezvous with the *Nostromo* near Japan.

Mission accomplished. Time to go home.

CHAPTER THIRTY-EIGHT

M ission Director David Handley addressed the entire group of analysts, "Everyone, can I please have your attention. First, thanks for volunteering to work the night shift. I know this was a bit unusual for some of you, but as you know the Americans scheduled their attack for 3 AM North Korean time."

"Second, your tasking for tonight is to review the replays and thoroughly evaluate the results of Operation Iron Fist. Your damage assessments should focus on destroyed ships, aircraft and military facilities. I also need a compilation of detailed ELINT information of the North Korean response based on communications between the scattered bases and headquarters. Do you have any questions."

The operations center was a hive of about 15 analysts. Their monitors displayed information tailored to their area of responsibility. The low-level background noise consisted mainly of quiet conversations conducted via headsets. Overhead ceiling fans steadily thrummed.

The analysts looked around at each other. This was a standard tasking order except that they would be reviewing information after the fact, not in real time.

Senior Analyst Teresa Perkins spoke up first. She was often the first to ask questions.

"Are there any particular areas you want us to focus on?"

Handley hesitated for a moment and responded a bit sarcastically, "You've all seen the Operation Iron Fist attack plan. Obviously, you need to focus on the Sea of Japan, and North Korea." He added, "I want your attention focused on the Wonson Kalma Airport, the naval facilities Mayang-do, the submarine complex in Sinpo, and the Musudan-ri missile launching complex. I'll send you a list of the other military airfields on the target list for which we need evaluations."

"As far as communications, I'm particularly interested in any traffic between Pyongyang Palace and the various military bases. The Americans, are particularly concerned to know if the North Koreans plan future counterattacks."

"Collect detailed information on aircraft movements. The Americans attacked a lot of the aircraft on the ground, but they wish to know if fighters were launched from further inland, how many, where they headed, and so forth. The Pentagon wants a complete summary of the defensive response."

Pine Gap collects a huge amount of information. In this case it had collected data on the overall activities of Operation Iron Fist. Tonight, they were to compile the damage assessments based on information intercepted from satellites, surveillance drones and radio transmissions such as, military communications.

Senior Analyst Teresa Perkins looked up from her three flat panel displays to the 50-foot large screen mounted on the front wall. Currently it was showing an enlarged replay image of the Wonson Kalma Airport. She listened carefully to the recordings of a series of radio transmissions captured from that area. Teresa was fluent in Korean, so she was able to translate the conversations for the report. She began making notes for her report.

Nervously pacing the floor near the back of the room Handley suddenly blurted out, "Let's get to work. Aaron, change the main display to show an enlarged Sinpo image, and the Wonson Kalma Airport. I would also like to see the Musudan-ri missile launching complex up north. Start the replay"

Senior Analyst Aaron Burke acknowledged the order, "Yes, sir. Coming right up."

Within seconds high-resolution images appeared on his screens as well as the main screen in front. At the beginning of the replay the entire area was quiet. But then the military activity ramped up very quickly.

First, the icons for several groups of U.S. F-18 Super Hornets, EA-18G Growlers, and F-35's emerged from the southern end of Japan. Their tracks originated from the Marine Corp Air Base at Iwakuni Japan. They headed northwest toward North Korea.

Not too long after that, numerous cruise missile icons appeared from three submarines east of North Korea in the Sea of Japan. The three groupings of cruise missiles tracked towards targets at Wonson Kalma Airport, Sinpo (Mayang-do Naval Base), and Musudan-ri. Their tracks gradually diverged as they followed independent routes to their respective targets.

Senior Analyst Thomas Mulrooney focused on the magnified image of Wonson Kalma Airport and witnessed the destruction of the SAM sites near it. He watched several cruise missiles swoop back and forth knocking out the runways and the parked aircraft. Strangely, he felt like he was watching a video game or a movie.

Senior Analyst Janice Harper was assigned to follow the events at Musudan-ri. As she watched a replay, an EA-18G Growler lead a flight of F-35s to attack. They hammered the SAM sites and the missile complex with stand-off missiles and bombs. They departed the area leaving nothing but total devastation. She tallied up the damage.

Teresa shifted her attention to the Sinpo submarine facility. The replay showed the destruction of the *Gorae* submarine tied up to the dock. It was hit directly by two large bombs and was split open like an egg. It sank within minutes. She also observed the repair facilities and the graving dock as they were destroyed. She summed up the damage in her report.

Aaron Burke concentrated on the naval base on Mayang-do. The first thing he saw was numerous bright flashes on the hills of the island as the SAM sites were hit by anti-radiation and cruise missiles. He saw a mobile SAM launcher destroyed. After the SAM sites were eliminated, he watched a ponderous B-52 fly along the southern shore and released over 100 JDAM bombs. Many midget submarines were tossed into the air like toys, and about six Romeo-class submarines destroyed. Also, miscellaneous bombs hit maintenance and storage facilities. He pulled together damage estimates from these views.

Finally, almost as an afterthought after the U.S. aircraft turned back towards home base, Senior Analyst David Montgomery watched with surprise as a North Korean destroyer moving toward the open ocean north of Mayang-do was torpedoed. A Romeo submarine was torpedoed in the western channel. These unexpected events were catalogued along with the rest of the data.

Throughout the attack the Pine Gap analysts had collected a wealth of data on military communications in North Korea. It had ramped up remarkably following the attack, particularly communications between Pyongyang and the military airfields scattered around the country. The analysts noted that fighter aircraft had launched from several airfields and made dashes to the east coast, but by the time they arrived it was too late. Some of them ventured into the Sea of Japan but quickly turned around to return to base. The American aircraft had long departed. The analysts also noted in their report that the North Koreans had made no aggressive moves towards South Korea.

After the replay ended, Handley contacted Teresa, "Teresa, please pull together everyone's conclusions and create a preliminary summary report. Send it right away to the NSA, CIA and the Pentagon. Inform them that a more detailed report will follow in a few days. Also, ask if they need any additional specific information that we may have over-looked. Thanks."

Then to all the analysts Handley added, "Well everyone, that was quite the show. It will be interesting to see how North Korea responds. Thanks again for your help. Don't be surprised if you aren't back here soon if this situation escalates."

CHAPTER THIRTY-NINE

WHITE HOUSE SITUATION ROOM

The Security Council met in the Situation Room at 4:30 p.m. Eastern just a few hours after Operation Iron Fist.

President Thompson sat at the end of the long conference room table. He was frowning and ominously quiet. Reluctant to break his concentration, the other participants stayed silent. Thompson mumbled to himself, then turned to Admiral Donald Brooks, the Chairman of the Joint Chiefs of Staff. "Admiral, I've been brought up to speed already, but for the sake of those who might not be as current, would you please give us an overview of the results of Operation Iron Fist?"

Brooks stood from his chair and strolled to the front of the room carrying a laser pointer and remote control. He pulled up a presentation on the large display.

He cleared his throat. "I'm sure all of you have heard that Operation Iron Fist was successful. We destroyed or disabled all the targets in the plan." He pointed at various locations on the huge color map of North Korea as he gave the group a review of the destruction of specific targets.

"The first wave of attacks by our cruise missiles and aircraft took out the SAM batteries around Wonson Airport, Mayang-do naval facilities, and Musudan-ri. At the same time, we crippled the airfields at Wonson, Kuum-ni, Hyon-ni, Kowon, Sandok, Toksan, Chanjin-up, Hwangsuwon, and Iwon. At those airfields, we destroyed thirty Mig 17s, twenty Mig 21s, twenty-two Sukhoi fighters, sixteen transport planes, and twenty-four helicopters. No aircraft took off to intercept. We achieved complete surprise."

He continued. "We destroyed a large portion of their submarine fleet: twelve Romeo class submarines and twenty-eight midget submarines. The images reveal piles of destroyed hulls mixed with others just knocked about. We'll get better estimates over time. Nevertheless, we put a major dent in their submarine fleet, and it will be a long time before they can replace these assets.

"Most importantly, we destroyed the new nuclear ballistic missile submarine, *Gorae*, at its mooring near Sinpo. It is a total loss. The submarine construction facility and graving dock at that location was razed. They won't be building any submarines there for quite a while. One North Korean destroyer and a Romeo submarine attempted to exit the harbor. Both were sunk before they reached the open sea. We could have sunk more destroyers at their moorings, but they were not on the approved target list for Operation Iron Fist."

The president spoke up. "Admiral, I have a few questions. Where are you getting these damage estimates? Why did we sink that destroyer? How did we do it? Why weren't the other North Korean ships on the target list?"

"Yes, Mr. President, I will answer your questions as best I can. First, the damage estimates are compiled from a variety of sources. The analysts at Pine Gap have been reviewing satellite images and ELINT and have provided thorough reports. We also have images from our own satellites, as well as the RQ4 drone and Hawkeye that were flying in the Sea of Japan. Some information has been included from the cameras in the cruise missiles which show detailed real time results up to the point that they strike their targets."

Admiral Brooks continued. "The destroyer was hit by torpedoes launched from our autonomous underwater vehicles, the Manta Rays we used to sink the North Korean submarine, *Sulyong,* a few months ago. We decided to re-task them and test their effectiveness. They worked flawlessly, and as far as we know, the North Koreans still have not figured out what happened. They assume it was done by a nuclear submarine, but our ELINT traffic reveals that they're puzzled because they never detected a submarine in that area."

After a short pause, he added hesitantly, "The destroyers were not on the original target list because you had ordered us to strike hard, but not overdo it. We felt that the target list of SAM sites, airports, parked aircraft, and submarines satisfied your requirements."

The president glared at him. "It's still unclear to me why you sank that destroyer."

"Sir, the Manta Rays were sent to watch for military vessels trying to leave the area. We believed they would represent a threat to our assets, particularly the three U.S. submarines in the Sea of Japan. So, the Manta Rays were positioned at the harbor entrances to bottle them up."

Not satisfied, the president said, "Be honest with me, Admiral. I don't recall that the Manta Rays were in the original strike package proposal. Did you add them later? Why wasn't I informed?"

"Sir, after their successful mission to sink the *Sulyong*, we wished to test them in a different capacity. So, yes, they were added later. It was a logical step. We believe that these autonomous systems will be important to our arsenal, and that they were ready to be tested in a new combat situation. And it was highly successful, I might add."

The president looked annoyed. He replied angrily, "Next time, make sure I'm briefed on all aspects of our missions. I need to be told about everything. No exceptions."

Somewhat chastised, Admiral Brooks stood more erect to give his reply. "Yes, sir. We will be sure to do that."

Secretary of Defense Maxwell Barnes spoke up at this point. "Admiral, your focus has been on enemy assets destroyed. What about our losses?"

Relieved that the topic had changed, Admiral Brooks responded with a smile. "Thankfully, we had zero casualties. No lost aircraft or ships. Everyone came home safely. Thank God for that."

Barnes really hated it when anyone invoked God. With a frown, he retorted, "Not to be a wet blanket, Admiral, but I think we need to thank the military planners for putting together such a well-orchestrated plan and the brave personnel who executed it. I'm not sure God had anything to do with it."

Brooks didn't feel the need to respond. He was content to bask in the glow of a successful mission. He didn't feel the urge to defend a higher power at that point.

Since there was a noticeable discomfort in the room, Secretary of State Benjamin Ochoa changed to direction of the conversation. "Mr. President, I know you spoke with Kim during the attack. What can you share with us about that call?"

President Thompson almost laughed out loud, then restrained himself. "Well, Ben, I would say it was quite an interesting chat."

Several in the room chuckled at the president's understatement. Ochoa glanced around the room, then said, "I'm sure it was. Can you give us more details?

The president looked up to gather his thoughts. Like many in the room, he found Ochoa irritating but recognized his right to ask questions. So, he responded, "As you'd imagine, Kim was pissed off about being awakened in the middle of the night. He unloaded some choice epithets before I could tell him the purpose of the call. It was a video call, so I could feel his reactions coming through the connection. From his expression, it was easy to read his thoughts. He was seething. I believe he felt betrayed that his military had been surprised so easily. I assume many heads rolled.

"The trickiest part was convincing him to take no action. I explained that the strikes were a proportional response to his provocations. That they were limited, and in fact, already done. No more were planned. That is, unless he responded by attacking us or South Korea. Those actions would be unacceptable. I pointed out that our attacks had so far been limited to specific locations on his east coast. And we had intentionally not attacked deeper inland. Damage reports from his own people would confirm those facts.

"Then I assured him that any escalation on his part would result in a massively expanded assault, which could result in the complete destruction of his military. He was outraged, but as far as I could tell, he understood the consequences."

"At that point, I was thinking he should just take these slaps and behave himself. There was no guarantee he would, so I told the Pentagon to stay on high alert for a while."

"What are the next steps?" asked Ochoa.

"There's a lot to do. Put out press releases to explain our position. Make it clear that these were one-time actions. We have already withdrawn. And reiterate that we expect North Korea to not counterattack."

"You know, we will get a lot of blow back from the U.N. and foes like China, Iran, Iraq, and Russia."

"Russia would have a lot of nerve to criticize us after what they did in Ukraine. The others we can just ignore. They will make a lot of noise, but that's about it. I'm not concerned. We did what we had to do."

"Agreed, I'll have my team put together the information immediately."

"Thanks. Work closely with the admiral's team to include details of the operation that we can publicly share."

"Will do."

Thompson turned to his chief of staff. "Please set up a press conference this morning. I want to inform the American people about Operation Iron Fist. I need to set their minds at ease."

CHAPTER FORTY

OAHU, HAWAII

On a bright clear Sunday morning, I was sitting on my deck gazing at Pearl Harbor in the near distance. I sipped from a cup of wonderful Kona coffee laced with Kahlua. The soft trade winds blowing from the west and the wonderful fragrance of the plumeria flowers on the trees just below my deck were refreshing. It was another perfect day in paradise.

I felt like I was fitting in quite quickly to Hawaii. Especially in my brightly colored Hawaiian shirt, shorts, and bare feet. I even sported fancy aviators to complement my blue baseball hat with its U.S.S. *Peralta* logo.

Technically, my coffee drink was called a Mexican Coffee, but who's going to quibble over the name? I chuckled thinking that I really shouldn't be drinking that beverage at all. However, my sweet tooth was insatiable, and I excused myself with the thought that I didn't often drink this combination.

It was my new assignment that had relocated us to Oahu. We rented a small house in the Halawa Heights area with a great view to the southwest. The house was also conveniently located near to my duties at the headquarters of the Indopacific Command.

With the dark-blue Pacific in the distance, and the lush-green vegetation all around, I had an expansive view of Pearl Harbor. Even though it was Sunday, many navy ships and aircraft were moving about. I was stung with regret that I'd been forced to abandon sea duty and take a desk job. My pacemaker disqualified me for duty aboard ship. I was still coming to terms with this restriction.

I heard a rustling sound behind me and then felt a gentle hand on my shoulder. I looked up to see Kathy standing to my side. She also had a mug of coffee and looked quite relaxed in her dark blue shorts, red and blue floral-print shirt, and sandals.

"Mind if I join you?"

"Of course not. I shouldn't be allowed to hog this marvelous view."

She frowned slightly and replied, "You look so pensive. You've been a bit moody lately. What are you thinking about?"

I looked into her kind eyes, and hesitated for a moment before replying, "Sorry if I seem distant. I don't mean to be. I've been thinking about a lot of things. I hardly know where to start."

She turned and looked at the view and said, "Well, there's no rush. Today's your day off. It's beautiful and peaceful out here, the coffee is great, so just unload whatever is on your mind."

I couldn't help but be impressed at how she cut to the basics. Of course, we had plenty of time to cover a lot of topics, so there was no reason for me to hold back. I started. "I've been thinking a lot about the big operation I observed, Operation Iron Fist. I'll share as much as I can. I know you've seen the reports, so you have a good idea of what happened. There are some details I can't share."

Constantly having to compartmentalize my thoughts to separate classified from non-classified information was a tiring experience. Forced to focus on what I could say and what I couldn't divulge was very burdensome. It was an aspect of my job that I disliked. I was forever worried that I might let something slip.

"Yes, I followed the events on CNN and MSNBC. They provided detailed coverage. I also watched the president's speech. So, I have a good idea of what happened. But please tell me whatever you can. Especially what seems to be bothering you."

"Alright, I'll try."

Kathy didn't respond, but just looked at me with concern in her eyes.

I quietly explained, "Operation Iron Fist was the biggest event I've ever been associated with in my navy career. Admiral Thomerson invited me to observe as a courtesy. Because my ship was attacked, he felt he owed it to me to see the action. I didn't have any responsibilities. I was only there as an observer along with others from Australia, Japan, New Zealand, and South Korea. It was an American operation from start to finish.

"The operation was massive involving lots of ships, aircraft, and missiles. There were lots of moving parts, critical timing, and, of course, we risked a lot of our people. We attacked SAM sites, airports, ships at an important naval base, aircraft on the ground, ground facilities like warehouses and repair buildings, and so forth. Surprisingly, the attacks were limited because we were told that the intent by the president was to send a message. The message was something like 'you don't get to attack the U.S. with impunity, we will strike back.'

"On the other hand, the strikes were limited because the president just wanted to spank them. Do enough damage to get the message across, but not be bloodthirsty."

Kathy listened carefully but couldn't resist interjecting with a question. "You told me the operation was a reaction to the attack on your ship. So, it was completely justified. Why does it bother you? Don't you believe it was the right thing to do?"

I pondered her question. "I guess I'd say I still think it was the right thing to do, but sometimes I wonder about the proportionality of the attack. My ship was attacked, but not sunk. And the U.S.S. *Peralta* was a single ship attacked by the North Koreans. We responded with a massive strike that sunk numerous ships, destroyed hundreds of aircraft, and damaged a dozen or so airports. We even took out a ballistic missile-launching site in the north. I don't know how many casualties we caused. It must have been significant."

After a pause, I continued. "So, compared to their attack, our response was massive. As I watched it unfold on the big screen in the Yokosuka Operations Center, I was awed. Like I said, it was the biggest military mission I had ever witnessed."

Kathy nodded, then followed up with additional questions. "Do you think it accomplished the goal? Is Kim going to back off? What comes next?"

"All good questions, but I'm not sure I can answer them. It seems that Kim has retreated into seclusion and hasn't threatened retaliation. I know there are ongoing high-level back-channel diplomatic talks with him to reinforce the message that we just wanted him to learn a lesson and we don't want to start a war. We consider that single operation to be a one-time event. Kim has been reassured that no more attacks are coming. However, they are also making it clear to him that this was a sample of what we're capable of. We could destroy the remainder of North Korea's military if he escalates."

I paused to let that sink in. "Hopefully, he understood the message and will behave in the future. There's no way to know. He's very unpredictable, as you know. At some point, he may reassert his old bad-boy behavior. It's possible that the only lesson he learned is that he needs to be sneakier in the future."

Kathy stared off in the distance as she absorbed my response. She seemed fully lost in contemplation. I waited a few minutes, took a couple of sips of coffee, gazed thoughtfully into the distance then resumed.

"At any rate, we'll need to keep a close eye on him and be ready for anything."

It seemed to me that we had exhausted the topic of the attack. I felt the need to change the subject. "How are you feeling these days? I don't mean about relocating to Hawaii, but your health?"

Kathy looked at me momentarily before responding. "Well, that was a sudden transition. Change the subject before you reveal any top-secret military information."

I took a few more sips of coffee before I replied. "That's not why I asked. I'm genuinely interested—concerned to be frank."

"I'm feeling fine. That insulin pump has made a world of difference. It's much easier to control my blood sugar levels."

"I've noticed. You don't seem to have reactions like before. You seem to be managing the diabetes well."

"Yes, it took me a while to get used to the pump, but I've learned the ins and outs of using it. I must admit, it is quite a remarkable device. It has really improved my life."

I had to laugh. "We are quite the pair. You with your insulin pump and me with my pacemaker. We're turning into bionic people in our old age."

Kathy laughed briefly, then took on a serious expression. "You can make light of it, but on the other hand, we should consider ourselves lucky that these technologies exist. What would we do without them?"

"You're right. I wasn't making fun of the situation. I understand the benefits quite well. The doctors told me that I'd drop dead some day without the pacemaker. I know how serious it is. Still, I regret that it forced me to give up sea duty."

Kathy glanced at me with sympathy. "I know. That was a cruel blow. I hope you are gradually adjusting to the new reality."

"I am. But I certainly don't like it. On the other hand, I do like being home to spend more time with you. Being alive helps in that regard."

Kathy smiled and nodded. "I like having you here as well. I feel safer. I know this is a touchy subject, but what are your thoughts about retirement?"

"I haven't thought about it much. I probably should. I'm not getting any younger."

"I don't mean that you should retire right now, but we should start planning. Otherwise, it'll sneak up on us. I don't want to find us just sitting around trying to figure out what to do with our empty days. Too many of my old friends fell into that trap."

"I think that financially we will be set. My navy retirement should allow us to be secure."

"Sure, I'm confident that financially we'll be alright. I'm thinking more about what activities we could do. For example, I'd like to travel to exotic places. I would also like to take some cruises."

I couldn't help but laugh out loud. Perhaps too loud because Kathy gave me a slightly angry glance. "That sounds like the proverbial 'busman's holiday' to me. I've spent a lot of years on ships. I don't know that I want to go on a cruise."

A bit testily she responded, "You miss the point. I'm the one who wants to go on cruises. I haven't been galivanting around the world like you. I haven't had the opportunity to see a lot of exotic places."

Chastised, I tried to recover. I quickly replied, "I get it. Don't get me wrong. I wouldn't object to vacations on a cruise ship. Where would you like to go? Are there any cruises you would like to take?"

"As a matter of fact, I've been researching cruises. I think the first one we should take is an Alaskan cruise. They start in Vancouver and travel up the West Coast through the Inland Passage. I've always wanted to visit Alaska. After that, perhaps we could take a Mediterranean cruise, or a cruise around Denmark and Norway. The options are endless."

I was nodding and thinking, *That might be a lot of fun, since on a cruise ship I would just be a passenger with no responsibilities. My job would be to relax. And to enjoy the good food and drinks. I had always heard the food is awesome. Sounds good after all.*

"Okay, let's start planning for a cruise or two. We don't have to wait for me to retire. We could do one the next time I have leave."

Kathy lit up with a wide smile. "I'll get started. I assume cost is no object."

I couldn't help but laugh out loud again. "I don't remember saying that."

"Perhaps I heard you wrong," she added.

So, soon we would be off to Alaska.

EPILOGUE

After Operation Iron Fist North Korea pulled back into its usual cocoon of secrecy to lick its wounds. The destruction to their military was extensive. Many ships and aircraft were destroyed, as well as numerous airfields and maintenance facilities. Numerous SAM sites had been obliterated. The ballistic missile facility at Musundan-ri had also been wiped out. Replacing or repairing these assets will be quite costly for North Korea, and their economy is ill-equipped to deal with it.

It would be difficult for them to draw assistance from allies. Much as they might like to help, Iran, China, and Russia were not in a position to provide money. They perhaps could supply surplus assets from their own inventory, but the downside is that's mostly obsolete equipment.

It is a difficult problem for North Korea because they continued to struggle under severe sanctions, which were not likely to be lifted. The nation struggles to provide the basics, such as food and healthcare, let alone spending large sums on military assets. The population might be left to starve. Not that Kim apparently cared, but that is a topic for another day.

Kim Jong-un craves attention. He is like a bratty child who constantly whines. He is not likely to change, so there's a chance that he'll seek to exit his shell in the future and stir up trouble. That could take the form of nuclear or ballistic missile tests. It's difficult to predict what he will do. However, it is safe to predict that he will continue to be a threat in Asia.

Some pundits point out even Kim Jong-un isn't crazy enough to launch an attack on the U.S. A North Korean nuclear attack would be suicide, due to the inevitable counterstrike. But what if he actually did attack? Could we count on Kim's restraint? Perhaps. However, it's a risky bet.

Most of us have lived with the possibility of nuclear war for our entire lives. The Cold War is simply a bad memory for many of us, but we shouldn't forget that the nuclear threat is still real and proliferating. Luckily, aside from the Hiroshima and Nagasaki strikes, no country has used them. Yet. We continue to live under the threat of a nuclear holocaust. This specter reared its ugly head again when Russia threatened to use nuclear weapons in Ukraine in 2022.

It is easy to lose sight of how many major countries possess nuclear weapons—the United Kingdom, France, Israel, Pakistan, India, China, Russia, North Korea, and of course the U.S. The existential fear is that countries such as Iran would be added to the list, creating even more potential instability.

North Korea's spending on military assets is a closely held secret, but they have a large standing Korean People's Army with 1,106,000 active and 8,389.000 reserve and paramilitary troops. The People's Army is the largest military institution in the world. North Korea has been desperate to modernize its obsolete armaments. The enhancements to their ballistic missile programs are a key example.

There have been other upgrades, such as the development of a new class of submarine called the Sinpo-C class that can launch ballistic missiles at sea. It is likely that they receive significant financial support from allies like Russia and China, and perhaps even Iran, but the extent of help is largely unknown.

Parenthetically, it is not clear how the DPRK finances its military. North Korea is a poor country especially when compared to its counterpart, South Korea. In 2020 the GDP of North Korea was 40.0 billion dollars. In contrast, South Korea's GDP was 1.63 trillion dollars (41 times higher).

The top 2020 GDP in the world was the United States at 20.81 trillion dollars followed by China at 14.86 and Japan at 4.9 trillion dollars. On a humorous note, if California was a country, it would be ranked fifth with a 2020 GDP of 2.72 trillion dollars!

North Korea has been a thorn in the side of the U.S. since its founding in 1953. Since then, the American administrations have tried to deal with the DPRK, but they have been intractable. All presidents during that period have tried diplomacy with little success.

Trump announced in 2018 that Kim had agreed to give up his nuclear weapons, but a careful reading of the press release reveals otherwise. Kim only agreed that he would denuclearize North Korea if the same happened in South Korea, that is, with the removal of U.S. military forces there. Nothing was really accomplished at any of the meetings between the two leaders, and Trump's announcements were hollow

THE NORTH KOREA GAMBIT

and meaningless. Analysts widely agree that Kim Jong-un will never surrender his nuclear weapons because they provide him with leverage and prestige.

Pundits in the U.S. have made a big deal of the fact that North Korea has not actually tested any nuclear weapons recently. They use this as evidence that North Korea has behaved positively and deserves some credit. However, it should be obvious that if you already have functional nuclear weapons, then you don't need to test them. There is mounting evidence that Kim plans to resume testing after a five-year hiatus.

The U.S. has not tested nuclear weapons with actual explosions since the 1960s. Nuclear weapon detonations are simulated on supercomputers in Los Alamos, New Mexico. Clean but effective. Nevertheless, we possess more than 4,200 nuclear warheads distributed across many platforms: tactical bombs including cruise missiles, ballistic, and submarine-launched versions.

It's conceivable that North Korea has also been using computers to simulate explosions. In other words, their development efforts are most likely unfolding quietly behind closed doors.

Speaking of threats, China is the real elephant in the room in the Asia-Pacific theater. China is on a long march to reestablish themselves as a world power. Ultimately, they wish to develop into the premier world power. Their citizens are reminded of the hundred years of humiliation they suffered after the Opium Wars of the 1800s. They blame this period entirely on the hegemonic Western powers. China has vowed to never let it happen again. Establishing themselves as a world-class military is how they plan to achieve their goals.

China is obsessed by the concept of the First Island Chain. This is an imaginary line that runs from Japan through Okinawa, encompasses Taiwan, and extends down the western side of the Philippines and Indonesia. They are very sensitive to the fact that the U.S. dominates the area outside this chain, and they feel hemmed in.

China laid claim to the bulk of the South China Sea when they announced the so-called Nine Dash Line in 1946. This arbitrary outline on the map encircles a large area that China claims as historical territory. It includes over ninety percent of the South China Sea. Of course, this claim is disputed by many other countries including, the Philippines, Indonesia, Vietnam, Taiwan, Malaysia, and others. Arbitrations in international courts have ruled in favor of these countries, but China ignores these judgements.

To solidify their claims, China has built facilities on several islands in the South China Sea. These projects include the Paracel Islands, Spratly Islands, and others. Some of these small islands have been expanded through dredging so that they are now large enough to have military airfields, harbors, and support facilities. They are reinforced with SAM and anti-ship missile sites. China claims that these activities are merely defensive because they feel threatened, referring to the First Island Chain to support this idea.

These military bases are built right in the paths of some of the busiest shipping lanes and aircraft corridors. The fear is that China intends to disrupt or control traffic. Of course, China denies this intent, but the fear of interference is still palpable. These fears are frequently reinforced because China often challenges ships and aircraft traveling in this area. Some of these incidents have been quite threatening and at times there have been casualties.

China intends to stay put. Their aggressive island building activities in the South China Sea continue unabated, and in fact have recently accelerated.

Which brings us to related developments. China is also vocal about the so-called Second Island Chain. This chain is further out from the mainland and extends into the western Pacific to encompass the Philippines, Indonesia, New Guinea, Guam, the Solomon Islands, Australia, and New Zealand. The next area targeted by China to extend their defensive strategy is Oceana.

China's recent activities in the Solomon Islands are a telling example, A new security agreement between China and the Solomon Islands was announced in May 2022. This agreement rattled leaders in the U.S., Australia, Indonesia, the Philippines, and other Indo-Pacific nations. They fear it opens the door to a Chinese military presence in the southern Pacific. Much of the negative focus was on the deal's potential to permit China to build a military base in the Solomons.

The agreement was signed under the pretext of assisting the Solomons with civil unrest and protecting Chinese citizens living there. It allows China to send armed police, military personnel, and other law enforcement forces to the islands. It also allows Chinese warships to stop at the islands for logistical replenishment. China has long wanted to build bases in Oceania to support a blue water navy, and this agreement seems to fulfill that desire. However, both sides deny that it allows China to build a naval base.

A major concern is that this agreement signals a shift in China's approach to influencing other countries. Through the "Belt and Road Initiative" China has worked with countries around the world to support them with civil construction projects and provide them with loans and other financial incentives. But this new agreement with the Solomons which permits them to bring in security personnel is a novel approach that is worrisome. Essentially, they are offering to assist a foreign government with putting down internal threats in exchange for advancing Chinese interests. It is a potentially alarming shift and needs to be watched carefully.

China will continue to expand and improve its military and to develop a capable blue water navy. They will extend their geographic influence further and further in the years to come. Not just to flex their muscles in the South China Sea, but to extend a show of force into the Western Pacific Ocean, the Indian Ocean, and perhaps the Atlantic Ocean and the Mediterranean Sea as well.

For example, China established a naval base in Djibouti in 2017. They maintain a nearly continuous three-ship presence in the Gulf of Aden. They actively protect their interests and personnel in the region. In addition, China conducts routine naval presence operations in the region that include surface ships as well as submarines.

In 2021, it was discovered that China was secretly constructing a naval base in the United Arab Emirates. Objections from the U.S. caused this project to be canceled. However, China will undoubtedly make further attempts to establish military outposts or naval bases in other parts of the region. China assists with the construction of roads, railways, dams and power plants, airports, and ports. It doesn't take much to convert a commercial port or airport for military use. Presently they are working with twenty-three countries in the region, so there is a lot of potential for China to gain footholds.

Finally, many pundits expect China to invade Taiwan by 2027. Or, perhaps to move their island-building efforts further to the southern end of the South China Sea to swallow up areas outside the Nine Dash Line. How the U.S. will respond is anyone's guess.

The future will be nothing if not complex and intriguing.

Remember the saying: "May you live in interesting times." We certainly do.

Though this saying is often misinterpreted as a blessing, ironically it means that you should expect danger and unpleasantness. Unfortunately, our future dealings with North Korea and China portend complex issues.

ABOUT THE AUTHOR

William W. King (Bill) has been retired for eleven years following a 10-year career as a teacher in higher education, and a 25-year career as a systems engineer in telecommunications. He currently resides in Los Altos, California.

Made in the USA
Las Vegas, NV
25 January 2024

84894012R00164